Praise for *Talk Bookish to Me*

"A fun and sexy romp, with chemistry that gave me all the feels!"
—**Jennifer Probst**, *New York Times* **bestselling author of *Our Italian Summer***

"An engaging romp of a story about what happens when a romance writer uses her novel's checkpoints to win back her first love and her life becomes stranger and better than fiction. Thoroughly enjoyable."

—**Shelley Noble**, *New York Times* **bestselling author of *Imagine Summer***

"*Talk Bookish to Me* is your new favorite comfort read! More than a romance novel, it's an ode to the genre itself. With loveable characters, charming banter, and sizzling sexual tension, *Talk Bookish to Me* is an adorable escapist romp that's sure to put a smile on your face."

—**Kristin Rockaway, author of *She's Faking It***

"Chemistry that will captivate readers from the very first encounter!"
—**Sajni Patel, author of *The Trouble with Hating You***

"Add this book to your TBR list immediately!"
—**Sarah Smith, author of *Faker***

"It had me laughing, it had me shouting, it had me from the get-go."
—**Pernille Hughes, author of *Probably the Best Kiss in the World***

KATE BROMLEY

Talk Bookish to Me

GRAYDON
HOUSE

**GRAYDON
HOUSE®**

ISBN-13: 978-1-525-80643-8

Talk Bookish to Me

This edition published by arrangement with Harlequin Books S.A.

Graydon House
22 Adelaide St. West, 40th Floor
Toronto, Ontario M5H 4E3, Canada
www.GraydonHouseBooks.com
www.BookClubbish.com

Printed in U.S.A.

For my mom, as with everything else good in my life,
I couldn't have done this without you

Talk Bookish to Me

1

"Wait, was I supposed to bring a gift?"

I turn my gaze from the floor to the well-dressed man standing beside me. There are only two of us in the elevator, so he must be talking to me.

"I think it's a matter of personal preference," I answer. "I'm the maid of honor so I had to be excessive."

His eyebrows bob up as I adjust my grip on the Great-Dane-sized gift basket I'm carrying. The cellophane wrapping paper crinkles each time I move, echoing through the confined space just loudly enough to keep things weird. Because if everyone isn't uncomfortable for the entire ride, are you even really in an elevator?

I'm low-key ecstatic when the doors glide open ten seconds later. With my basket now on the cusp of breaking both my arms and my spirit, I beeline it out of there and stride into the rooftop lounge where my best friend is hosting her pre-wedding party, drinking in the scent of heat and champagne as I maneuver through the sea of guests.

Like most maids-of-honor, I flung myself down the Etsy rabbit hole headfirst and ordered an obscene amount of decorations for tonight's event. Burlap "Mr. & Mrs." banners dangle from floating shelves behind the bar as twinkle lights weave around the balcony railings like ivy. Lace-trimmed mason jars filled with pink roses sit on every candlelit cocktail table. Cristina and I worked with the tenacity of two matrimonial Spartans to get everything ready this morning, and it's clear that our blood, sweat and tears were very much worth it.

It's then that I spot Cristina mingling near the end of the bar. Beautiful, petite and come-hither curvy, I'd hate her if she weren't one of my favorite people ever. Her caramel hair spills down her back and her white high-low dress sets her apart from the crowd in just the right way—she's a princess in the forest and we're her adoring woodland animals. I'm her feisty chipmunk sidekick to my core.

I place my gift on a nearby receiving table and give a little wave when I catch her eye. She's waiting for me with a huge grin when I arrive at her side.

"Hey, lady!" she says, pulling me in for a hug. "Look at you, rolling in here looking all gorgeous."

We step apart and I stand up a bit taller. "Why, thank you. I feel pretty good."

It's also very possible that Cristina is just so used to me dazzling the world with yoga pants and sweaters every day that my transformation seems more dramatic than it is.

"Were you able to get any writing done this afternoon?" she asks, handing me a glass of champagne from off the mahogany bar top.

I get a twisting knot in my gut at the mention of my writing, or lack thereof. Having been dying a slow literary death for almost a year, I'm never without some stomach-turning sensation for long. The final deadline for my next romance novel is officially a month away and if I don't deliver a best-seller by then—

"Okay, you're making your freak-out face," Cristina interjects. "I'm sorry, I shouldn't have brought it up."

I inhale a shallow breath and force a smile. "It's fine. I'm good."

"Let's switch gears—are you sure it's not weird that I'm having a pre-wedding party? Was booking the salsa band too much since I'm having one at the wedding, too?"

Beyond grateful for the booming trumpet and bongos that are drowning out my own thoughts, I turn to the corner and find the ten-piece group playing with addictive abandon. Cristina's relatives, who are essentially non-trained professional salsa dancers, dominate the dance floor, and rightfully so. Cristina's brother, Edgar, once tried to teach me the basics but I'm fairly confident I looked like a plank of wood that was given the gift of limbs. Cristina recommended dance lessons. Edgar suggested a bottle of aguardiente and prayer.

"The band is amazing," I say as I swing back around, "and of course people have pre-wedding parties." I've actually never heard of a pre-wedding party. An engagement party, yes. A bachelorette party, absolutely. But what's going down tonight is basically a casual reception days before the mega-reception.

"Jason and I just have so many people coming in from out of town, plus we wanted the bridal party to get acquainted. We figured a little get-together would be fun."

"I'm all for it. Who doesn't want to pre-game for a wedding a week in advance?"

"I know I do," Cristina says, lifting her own champagne and taking a sip. "Everyone is here except Jason and some groomsmen. Can you believe that creep is late to his own party?"

"Should you really be calling your fiancé a creep?"

"He's my creep so it's okay."

"Valid point."

"Picture please! Will you girls get together?"

I look to my right and find a teenage boy with wildly curly hair pointing a camera at us. He's dressed in all black and looks so eager to take our photo that I can't help but find him endearing.

"Absolutely! Big smile, Kara." Cristina throws her arm around my waist and after we withstand an intense flash, the young man is gone before my eyes can readjust. "That was Jason's cousin, Rob. He wants to be a photographer, so I hired him for the night."

"That was thoughtful of you," I say, still recovering from my momentary blindness. "By the way, where is Jason?"

"He's at home. Two of his groomsmen are driving up and he wanted to wait for them since, apparently, grown men can't find their way to a party by themselves."

"Driving in Manhattan is intimidating. He probably didn't want them to get lost."

"Right, because neither of them has GPS? Jason should be here."

I'm honestly shocked that Jason isn't here. I love Cristina and Jason both to death but they're one of those couples that rarely go out socially without each other. Even when I invite Cristina over to my apartment for a wine night, she asks to bring Jason. I've always thought it was a bit much, but I guess it works for them.

"Okay, forget everyone else, let's toast." I clear my throat and hold up my champagne. "When we were both waitressing at McMahon's Pub in grad school, I had no idea it would lead to nine amazing years of friendship. Now I'd be lost without you. Here's to you having a magical night. I'm so glad I'm here to celebrate with you."

We smile and tap our glasses together, the ding of the crystal echoing my words.

I take a sip and the bubbly drink slips easily down my throat. Still savoring the sweetness, I ask, "So, who are these mystery groomsmen Jason's waiting for?"

"One is named Beau and I can't remember the other one. They're two guys he grew up with when his family lived in North Carolina."

"North Carolina? I thought Jason was from Texas."

"He spent most of his life in Texas, but he lived in North Carolina until he was ten. He somehow kept in contact with these two through the years."

"That's nice, him staying friends with them for so long."

"Yeah, it's adorable, but they still should have gotten their asses here on their own." Cristina is poised to elaborate when her gaze locks on something across the room. She tries and fails to look annoyed instead of excited.

"I'm guessing the groom has arrived," I say, glancing over my shoulder. My suspicions are confirmed as I see Jason making his way towards us, smiling at Cristina like a fifth grader saying "cheese" on picture day. He's tilting his head and everything.

"There she is! There's my incredibly forgiving future wife." Jason leans down and kisses Cristina before she can verbally obliterate him. He gives me a quick kiss on the cheek next and then shifts back to his fiancée's side, sneaking an arm around her waist and pulling her to his hip.

"So, I'm going to go ahead and disregard all the semi-violent text messages you've sent me over the past hour. Bearing that in mind, how's everything going?"

Cristina looks up at him, feigning disinterest. "It's going

great. Since you weren't here, I talked to several nice men. Turns out, pre-wedding parties are a great place to meet guys."

"I'm so happy for you."

"I appreciate that. Four contenders, specifically, really piqued my interest."

"Are they taller than me?" Jason asks. "Do they make a lot of money?"

"Obviously. They're way taller and all of them are independently wealthy."

"Nice. Kara, did you meet these freakishly tall and rich men?"

"I did and spoiler alert, I'm engaged now, too! Double wedding, here we come!"

Jason smiles and pulls Cristina in even closer, his gaze holding hers. "I guess this is where being late gets you. I'm sorry I wasn't here. Do you forgive me?"

"Don't I always?"

He leans down and gives her another picture-perfect kiss.

It's official. I'm dying alone. Just putting that out there.

"Now, where are these friends of yours? Oh! Let's set one of them up with Kara!" Cristina looks at me with a dangerous matchmaker gleam in her eyes.

"Actually, I already mentioned Kara, and one of my buddies said he went to college with her."

Went to college with me?

Jason looks towards the entrance and waves. "Hey, Ryan! Come over here!"

And then I go catatonic. I can't move. I stand stock-still, looking at Cristina like she sprouted a third arm out of her forehead and it's giving me the middle finger.

Someone walks past me and a soft breeze ghosts across my overheating skin. I stare in a state of utter disbelief as Ryan Thompson steps into view beside Jason.

"It's been a while, Sullivan," he says, his voice and light Southern drawl as steady and tempting as ever.

My champagne glass falls from my fingers and shatters against the floor.

"Kara?" Cristina's voice rings with concern as she nudges us away from the broken glass that's now littered around our feet. She grasps my elbow, but I don't feel it. She could back-hand me across the face with a polo mallet and I wouldn't feel it. My mind is spiraling, plummeting inwards as I come to grips with the realization that Ryan is standing two feet away from me.

Dressed in a navy suit, a crisp white button-down and brown dress shoes, he's come a long way from the sweat-shirts and jeans that were his unofficial uniform in college. His dirty-blond hair is on the shorter side, but a few wayward strands still fall across his forehead. Ten years ago, I would have reached up and brushed them aside without a thought. Now my hand curls into a tight, unforgiving fist at my side.

If we were another former couple, seeing each other for the first time in a decade might be a dreamy, serendipitous meet-cute—a Nancy Meyers movie in pre-production. We'd have a few drinks and spend hours reminiscing about old times before picking up right where we left off. It would be com-fortable and familiar as anything, like a sip of hot chocolate at Christmas with Nat King Cole crooning on vinyl in the background.

But we are not that kind of former couple, and I'm con-vinced that if Nat King Cole were here and knew my side of the story, he would grab Ryan by the scruff of his shirt and hold him steady as I roundhouse-kicked him in the throat.

It's a tough pill to swallow but Ryan looks good. Like, really good. His face is harder than it was when he was twenty-one and the stubble on his chin tells me he hasn't shaved in a few days, making him seem like he just rolled out of bed. And not rolled out of bed in a dirty way, but in a I-just-rolled-out-of-bed-and-yet-I-still-look-ruggedly-handsome-and-you-fully-want-to-make-out-with-me kind of way.

The bastard.

"Ryan," Cristina says, always the first to jump in, "Jason mentioned that you and Kara went to college together."

"We did." His eyes don't move from mine for even a second. "It's got to be what, ten years now?"

"Yeah, it's been a long, long time," I say quickly, turning to face Cristina. "I think I may have mentioned him before. Remember my *friend* from North Carolina?"

If someone were to look up "my friend from North Carolina" in the Dictionary of Kara, they would find the following: My friend from North Carolina (noun): 1. Ryan Thompson. 2. My college boyfriend. 3. My first real boyfriend ever. 4. My first love. 5. Taker of my virginity. 6. Guy who massacred my heart with a rusty sledgehammer and fed the remains to rabid, ravenous dogs.

Cristina is well versed in the Dictionary of Kara and recognition washes over her. "No way," she says, her voice dropping.

"Yes way," I answer happily, overcompensating.

Now it's Cristina's turn to panic. "Wow. Okay, wow, what a small world, huh?" She grabs Jason's hand in an iron grip, making him wince as she blasts an over-the-top smile. "Well, we should give you guys a chance to catch up. My *abuelita* just got here so Jason and I are going to say hello."

"Your *abuelita* died two years ago," I hiss.

"I know, it's a miracle. See you two later!" She drags her soon-to-be husband away before he can get a word out.

I watch them go, sailing away like the last lifeboat as I stand on deck with the string quartet, the cheerful Bach melody only further confirming that this ship is going down.

2

"So," Ryan says, drawing my attention back to him. "We meet again."

"We meet again," I answer.

He tilts his head, scrutinizing my expression. "I have to say, you don't look happy to see me, Sullivan."

I exhale out a bitter laugh. "Oh, no. I absolutely am. I'm downright joyful."

"Your demolished champagne flute tells a different story. Not to mention your monotone voice and the subtle, murderous glint in your eyes."

"Yeah, well, it was a slippery flute."

"Now, there's a line you don't hear every day."

His voice and words slip under my skin with sickening ease. I can already feel my patience wearing thin, a guitar string being tuned so tight that it snaps.

"Okay, fine. I'm shocked to see you and not in a good way. Is that what you wanted to hear?"

Ryan continues to study me with his unrelenting gaze. "It's not necessarily what I want to hear," he admits, "but I'd prefer that to polite lies. You never used to have a problem being honest with me."

"How we acted in the past isn't relevant to who we are now. You don't know anything about me anymore."

"Sure, I do," he says easily, too easily for my liking.

"Really, like what?"

"Well, for one thing, you still can't hide your emotions to save your life. Like right now, you probably think you're playing it cool but I'm definitely noticing an aggressive rage vein that's pulsing in the center of your neck."

I run my fingers across the front of my throat, then wish I hadn't. How can an open-roof deck suddenly feel suffocating? "You wish you were affecting me that much."

"I think it's pretty obvious I am. You seem five seconds away from hopping the guardrail and rappelling down the building."

"Trust me, after another five seconds with you, I won't need to rappel. I'll straight-up jump."

Ryan seems like he's about to grin, but stops himself. I gaze off to the side, spying a waitress making the rounds in the distance. My laser-focused eyes try to distinguish which appetizer she has on her tray, and I can tell from their shape that they're the mini empanadas. I try to will her closer via telekinesis but it doesn't work. A shame. I level a look back at Ryan with resigned defeat.

"Something else that hasn't changed about you," he goes on, "you're still melodramatic."

"Why are you so difficult? Why can't we just have a normal verbal exchange like other former acquaintances would have?" I feel someone's shoulder bump into my back and turn to see a group of Jason's work friends. I take a small step forward to give them more space.

"Hey, I'm perfectly composed," Ryan says. "You're the one who can't control your raging hate fire."

I squeeze my little black clutch with both hands as I glare into his irritatingly green eyes. "You always did bring out the worst in me."

"Aw, that's sweet of you to say. Have you been holding on to that little nugget for the past ten years or was it a spur-of-the-moment thought?"

"Sorry if the truth hurts."

"Yes, it does. Another lesson you taught me the last time we spoke."

I say nothing as I wait for Ryan to smirk or flash a sarcastic grin. Neither arrives and I'm a little rattled by their absence. Jason's colleague accidentally bumps into me again, making me move forward to keep my balance. I'm about to shift to the side to position myself more comfortably when Ryan's fingers suddenly brush my wrist.

"Switch with me," he says. He grips my hand and starts to pull me forward.

"It's okay. I'm fine." I adjust my stance to stand firmly in front of him but now there's only a foot of space between us. I'm also trying to pretend I'm not entirely aware that he's still touching my hand.

"Come on, let's just switch." He gives me another light pull and I decide to go with it, moving forward into his place while he takes my former spot. If Jason's work friend bumps into *him* next, he'll find a six-foot-two wall. Ryan doesn't seem to mind, though. He never did. He used to do the same thing in college. If we were ever at a crowded bar, he always positioned himself in such a way to block any overly boisterous party guests from bumping into me. It was sweet back then, and, unfortunately, it still is now.

"Look, let's both just take a break for a second," he says. "It's obvious neither of us is thrilled to see each other, but for Jason and Cristina's sake, I'm sure we can make it through one night in the same room."

"Fine," I agree, suspicious but willing.

"And if you're worried that I'm going to lose my mind and beg you to take me back like I did when I was a kid, rest assured, I've moved on."

I'm not sure if his words are meant to cut, but I still feel a sting.

"Glad to hear it," I say simply.

Ryan claps his hands together in front of him. "In other news, you look well."

"Thanks," I answer. As someone who uses all of their money to buy books instead of clothes, this little black dress was a splurge for me. It's off the shoulder, smooth as silk and the boning inside makes me appear much smaller than my usual size eight. That made the price tag easier to accept. I was paying for skinny fashion sorcery.

I even got my hair and makeup done. My deep brown hair, normally pin straight, is curled into soft waves, and my makeup looks alluring but tasteful. The whole beautification process was genuinely fun until I told the makeup artist that I didn't own foundation. The woman looked so offended, I half expected her to slap me across the face with a glove and challenge me to a duel.

"You also look...healthy," I eventually add. Ryan's eyes scrunch up at my choice of compliment, sparking me to go on. "And old. You look healthy and old."

"All right," he says, looking down at his impressive leather watch, "and our cease-fire lasted a whole ten seconds."

"I don't mean you look decrepit old, just *older*. I look older, too. I don't sleep enough and it's making me age prematurely. I have a sound machine, but I haven't started using it yet. Maybe that will help."

And I'm now discussing sleep strategies. Excellent.

"Anyways," I say, "I had no idea you were friends with Jason."

"Yeah, since we were kids. I assumed we'd all eventually fall out of touch, but the guy initiates group chat conversations like no one I've ever met."

"I think Jason is just one of those universally likable people. If Tom Hanks and Anna Kendrick ever had a love child, it would be him."

"That makes sense. He's more or less the human embodiment of a golden retriever."

I can't help but smile at Ryan's words and it's a familiar but bizarre sensation, like trying on an old favorite shirt that doesn't fit anymore.

"Cristina seems great," he says a second later.

"She really is. She's so nice and funny and unbelievably loyal." I don't even emphasize the word *loyal* but it still drops between us, heavy as a wrecking ball, shaking the ground and clattering glasses.

"There it is," Ryan says, sounding both expectant and disappointed. "I'm surprised you lasted this long, Sullivan."

"I'm not doing this," I reply, my heartbeat picking up speed. I refuse to play a game that neither of us can ever win. "Change the topic or I'm leaving."

Ryan's jaw is set in a hard line before he eventually makes himself relax. "Fine. Jason mentioned on the drive in that you live in the city now."

"I do," I answer. "I bought a co-op three years ago. I'm a full-on adult."

"I never really pictured you as the city type. I saw you as more of the sitting-on-a-porch-in-a-rocking-chair kind of girl."

"How flattering," I say. "Like a happy geriatric patient?"

A spark of amusement flashes in his eyes. "I didn't mean it like that."

"And in your vision of me is there an oxygen tank next to me on the porch or is it just me and my trusty service dog?"

He doesn't try to hide his smile this time and it shakes something loose in the pit of my stomach. I shove it back into place with violent force.

"All right, let's scratch the whole porch comment. I was clearly mistaken. You want another drink?"

"Sure. You going to poison it?"

"I'd hardly tell you if I was."

Ryan turns to the bar and I immediately yank up the top of my Spanx through the fabric of my dress. I'm all tucked in and standing normally when he faces me again, holding a beer for himself and handing me a fresh glass of champagne.

"You're a writer now, aren't you?" he asks.

I used to be.

"I am," I force myself to say. "Did Jason tell you?"

"No, I read your books. That's actually why I'm here. I was thinking with all of your success you would want to become my sugar momma."

I laugh. Too bad I also take a sip at the same exact moment. My drink goes down the wrong tube and I cough until it hurts. A drop of champagne spills out of my nose and it burns like hell.

"You all right?" Ryan asks.

"I'm fine." I hold the back of my index finger to the bottom of my nose and smile even though it's impossible to make this look good.

"Excuse me, can I get a picture of you guys?"

My finger is still plugging up my nostrils when I find good old Rob with his camera at the ready.

Really, Rob? I thought we were friends.

I lower my finger from my nose and sniffle a bit. "I don't think…"

"One picture won't kill us," Ryan says, wrapping his arm around my waist and drawing me to his side.

There's nothing suggestive about how we're posing, but having my hip pressed against his feels strangely intimate. I do my best to banish the thought away, facing Rob and giving him my best smile. It falters when Ryan leans down, bringing his mouth so close to my ear that I almost jump.

"This is kind of crazy," he says.

My stomach flutters, my body turning traitorous. Time slows down but I keep looking forward.

"What's crazy?"

"Me having you in my arms again. I never thought I would."

I look up at him the same moment Rob snaps the picture. The massive flash goes off, causing us both to squint in the aftermath.

"Thanks," Rob says before scampering off.

Ryan's hand falls from my hip as I instantly move away, situating myself across from him. "Okay, let's just maintain our distance, shall we?"

"Your body still reacts to me that strongly, huh?"

"If by reacting you mean physically recoiling, then yes, I had a very strong reaction."

Ryan looks close to laughing and for some reason, I feel the need to stop it from happening.

"And what are you up to now?" I ask. "What do you do?"

"I'm a structural engineer for a construction firm in Raleigh. It's more managerial than field work since I'm at the senior level, but I like it."

"That sounds nice. I always said you would be great at something like that."

"I remember," he says, his voice now carrying more severity than nostalgia. It's understandable. I'm sure seeing me again isn't easy for him either. As much as I choose to focus on all the wrong that happened between us, it's very possible that Ryan has spent the last ten years remembering all the right.

Maybe he's secretly happy to see me again. Maybe he missed me. Maybe he only came to New York so he could find me...

"Are you drunk, Sullivan?" he then asks, pulling me out of my head. "You look a little dazed."

I blink my eyes as I refocus. "No, I'm fine. It's just hot out here. Are you hot?" I fan myself with my hand, looking around to see if anyone else is doing the same. They're not.

"Am I hot? Is that a serious question or are you hitting on me?"

I stop fanning myself. "What? No, I'm not hitting on you."

"Are you sure?" There's a mischievous flash in Ryan's eyes and it makes him look so much like he did in college. I sincerely hope it goes away soon.

"I'm one hundred percent positive I'm not hitting on you. We're just talking."

"You seem jumpy for someone who's just talking."

"Yeah, well, you make me very uncomfortable."

Ryan gives me an understanding kind of smile as he takes a small step back, giving me space even though I'm sure he knows I'm not really uncomfortable. Just on edge. And confused. And slightly freaking out.

"Sorry," he says. "You used to like it when I would rile you up."

I swallow hard and say nothing.

"But clearly, those days are over."

"Yes," I agree. "Very much over."

Ryan nods and glances around before looking back at me. "All right, fun as this reunion has been, I better go check on Beau. He was taking shots the last time I checked and if I don't keep him in line now, I'll get stuck laying down bail money for him later."

"Funny, I would have guessed it would be the other way around."

"Sometimes it is, but I made the wise decision not to drink too much tonight. Wouldn't want one of us to lose our cool and cause a scene."

For a second I think he's talking about him and Beau, but based on the way he's watching me, I know he's referring to the two of us.

"It was good catching up with you, Sullivan. I guess I'll see you at the wedding. If I pass by your table with the other maiden aunts, I'll make sure to say hi."

"How gentlemanly. And if I pass your table where they seat the creepy toads who were invited out of obligation, I'll bring a scotch for you to cry into."

"Always so considerate. You have a good night."

And then it's over. Ryan turns and walks over to his friend, who is talking up two of Cristina's coworkers. I turn around to keep from staring when Cristina suddenly pops up in front of me.

"I cannot believe that Ryan is Jason's friend! This is insane! The two of you really seemed like you were hitting it off."

I shake my head and take another sip of champagne. "I can say with absolute certainty that we weren't. How do you know what we looked like anyways?"

"Um, because I was stalking you guys from across the room the entire time, obviously. Where did Ryan go? I lost him in the crowd."

"He's talking to your work friends," I say, nudging my head in their direction.

Cristina peers around me, tracking them with her eyes. "I knew I shouldn't have invited those two. They're more or less midrange prostitutes."

"Fantastic, then they should be perfect for him."

"Never mind them. New plan—what are you doing tomorrow night?"

"Tomorrow? Nothing, I think."

"Good. The four of us are going out to dinner. You, me, Jason and Ryan."

"What? Why?" I feel the floor tilting beneath me as the adrenaline of seeing Ryan evaporates in my chest.

"Why? Kara, your college ex-boyfriend just walked back into your life and is somehow the childhood friend of *my* fiancé. Did you honestly think I wouldn't force you guys together at every turn? Have we met?"

I can't think straight. I take a deep breath, but it doesn't help. Ryan is back and so are the ghosts of our relationship, twitching and howling as they claw to the surface after a ten-year sleep. I can feel the all-too-familiar stab of guilt starting to throb again, but I compartmentalize it and push it down. I always do when I remember what we did.

"No, I don't think this is a good idea at all," I say.

"Of course, it is. It's an awesome idea. I just watched your whole interaction and he legit stared into your eyes for ten minutes straight. Plus, Jason said he was completely shaken up when he found out you were going to be at the party."

"Well, he wasn't shaken up in front of me, that's for sure. He had all the calculated confidence of a serial killer."

"Okay, are we maybe overreaching now?"

"Maybe," I concede.

Cristina looks me over with a curious expression. "You

know, I don't think I've ever seen this combative side to you before. I have to admit, it's very interesting to witness."

"That's because I'm not combative," I say, taking a frustrated breath. "Something about Ryan always turned me into a raving lunatic."

"Fine, yes, I did sense some tension between you guys, but it was nothing definitive. I couldn't tell if you were going to tackle each other to the floor in a good way or a bad way."

"Definitely in a bad way."

"Agree to disagree. Anyways, he was probably being confrontational because he hasn't seen you in years and he needed time to adjust."

"I doubt it."

"Look, what happened between you guys when you were younger was tough, but you were kids. We're adults now and I promise tomorrow won't feel like a setup. I'm a financial planner for a living, Kara. Let me plan your life. I promise you will be happy with the results."

"There's so much more to it than you think." I sigh and look over the metal railing past her shoulder, seeing nothing but open air and city lights and still feeling trapped. In the midst of everything, I think of my dad, always finding him in the strangest moments. So many memories of him are faded after ten years, but not his disappointment in me. That still streaks through my mind with effortless clarity. And Ryan's presence amplifies it by a million. Why wouldn't it? I chose Ryan over him.

I have to get out of this dinner. It can't happen. I let out an artificial laugh that's meant to be subtle but winds up sounding disturbingly like the Joker's.

"You know what? I can't make it tomorrow. I have plans."

"You verbatim just told me you didn't have plans."

I choose not to respond.

"Kara, stop. There's nothing wrong with you hanging out with Ryan and there is zero pressure. With that being said, if you both happen to fall in love again and decide to get married and you and I have babies at the same time, that's fine, too."

My mouth feels dry. I look down at the champagne in my hand and wish it was water.

"I'm just kidding!" Cristina goes on. "In all seriousness, please don't be nervous about this. You and Ryan are important to Jason and me, so the two of you spending time together is inevitable. Better to get the weirdness out of the way now than to have an awkward time at the wedding when you should be having the time of your life."

Her eyes are soft and pleading and I know there's no path to victory here. I groan and slump my shoulders.

"You're the devil," I whine.

"And you're an angel," she answers with a sparkling smile. "I'll make reservations at Butter for eight o'clock. We're going to have an amazing time."

"I seriously doubt that."

I down my champagne in one determined gulp, wanting and needing to erase all traces of Ryan from my troubled mind.

3

It's just past nine in the morning as I sit on my softer-than-sin couch with my open laptop resting on my knees. Sunlight filters in through the sheer white curtains that cover my apartment's casement windows, warming my bare feet and giving life to small specks of dust that never seem to land.

I'm staring at my computer screen, my fingers still tingling with excitement.

I'm writing again. I've started my novel. The novel I've been struggling to write for the past year. The novel that's meant to be my glorious return to historical romance. The novel that is going to make or break me. I reread the words for a fourth time.

Charlotte Destonbury hated corsets. They hurt, they left marks on her skin and they took at least a half an hour a day to put them on and take them off.

Secluded in her sanctuary, the library of her family's York-

shire estate, Charlotte decided she'd had enough. She pulled at the shoulders of her emerald day gown until the muslin gathered around her lush waist—the waist that was always a drop too full to be considered delicate. She wasted no time reaching her hands behind her back, desperate to loosen the blasted strings. After enduring the deadly dull company of another suitor, forced on her by her father, she at least deserved to breathe properly.

Charlotte fell to her knees with a growl as she continued to do battle with the stays. Her mahogany hair escaped its pins, tumbling down her heart-shaped face and well past her shoulders. She had almost reached the top string when the library door suddenly creaked open. She froze as her startled gaze locked on the imposing figure now standing in the doorway.

Robert Westmond, the Earl of Stratton, stood transfixed by the untamed beauty all but rolling around on the library floor. She presented a tempting sight, wild and disheveled as she was. The top of her dress was already pulled down. It would be easy enough to join her there on the rug. His body begged him to do just that, but instead he merely stepped deeper into the library and closed the door behind him.

"Who are you and what are you doing in my house?" Charlotte's tone was as regal as a queen's despite her savage state.

"My name is Robert. I'm here to marry you." He watched with pleasure as shock and contempt flashed in the girl's exquisitely telling hazel eyes.

"Like hell you are," she seethed.

A feral smile crossed Robert's face. This was going to be enjoyable indeed...

It's a decent start—not perfect, but it's something. It's good enough that I won't edit it all away. I have characters, the beginning of a concept, tension. I can work with this. Relief and nerves shoot through me. Maybe I can pull this off.

The urge to write took me by surprise. I was still reeling

from seeing Ryan when I fell into bed this morning some-time after one. My body was drained but it felt like my brain was clipped with jumper cables, sparking with a sudden rush of outside energy. Sleep wasn't happening and after hours of tossing and turning, I wandered into the living room and ended up on the couch with my laptop.

Maybe I can write more now. It would be amazing to bang out another chapter. I'm about to dive back in when my cell phone rings beside me. I look down and see Samantha, my literary agent's name, flashing across the caller ID screen. I pick up the phone and accept the call with a tired smile. "Good morning, Sam."

"I just got the pages. I love them. Have you written more yet?"

I let out a mixture of a laugh and a sigh as I press the phone more firmly to my ear. "Not yet. I wish."

"Don't psych yourself out. I like the direction this is going in. It has *Delicate Dawn* vibes but with a much stronger female lead, which is exactly what the publisher is looking for."

I nod my head, remembering how easily my first novel came to me compared to the torture chamber experience this one has been. "I'm glad. I hope they'll like it."

"Now you just have to keep momentum. What was it that finally got you started?"

Sliding down a little in my seat, I rub my legs against the cotton cushions. "I'm not positive the two events are connected, but I ended up seeing my college ex-boyfriend last night."

"Well, well," Sam says playfully. "That's intriguing."

"Intriguing but potentially problematic for my mental health."

"Whatever. This is New York, Kara—we're all insane. When are you seeing him again?"

I take a deep breath and push my shoulders back, feeling my muscles stretch and release after hunching over my laptop for so long. "I'm actually having dinner with him and a couple of friends tonight."

"That's great! If this guy is what you need to get your book done, then you need to use every opportunity you have to see him again. Need I remind you of the very ominous deadline that's hanging over our heads?"

The tension in my shoulders is back with a vengeance and has brought friends.

"No reminder is necessary," I assure her.

"And if there isn't an opportunity, you need to make the opportunity. I'm talking you, him, your laptop, all of you locked in a room somewhere with no means of escape until the best novel of your life is sitting in my inbox."

My right eye starts to stress twitch and I quickly give it a rub. "It's kind of scary that I'm now at the point in my writing process where imprisoning my ex seems like the logical next step."

"I'm sorry, I don't mean to scare you. I just know you're banking on that on-acceptance check." My eye twitches again as Sam goes on, "I'm assuming there's no getting out of your Italy trip, right?"

I shake my head, slow and shameful and silent. My Italy trip. A long-awaited dream getaway that is steadily morphing into a money-draining terror. When I pulled the trigger on booking this vacation a couple months ago, I fully anticipated being done with my novel. My best work has always come as the shot clock winds down, and I've never missed a deadline. Ever. I actually thought paying for the trip in full on my credit card would be the last incentive I needed to get my act together. Oh, sweet summer child, how wrong I was.

After researching and planning and watching *Under the Tuscan Sun* for the hundredth time, I am now set to stay in Rome for six whole months. The apartment I'm renting is twenty minutes from Vatican City, and has an updated kitchen, two balconies and a claw-foot tub that all but guarantees a life of perfect happiness. I leave in just over a week, two days after Cristina's wedding.

The entire trip is also nonrefundable. And time is running out.

When I write a new novel, or am about to, I typically get half of my advance when I sign my publishing contract and the other half upon acceptance of the manuscript. I signed my new contract a year ago, using the first installment to cover my life, my mortgage and monthly bills, and leaving my on-acceptance check to pay for Italy. But here I am, with my manuscript nowhere near done while the interest on my credit card grows and grows, eating away at my sanity with gnawing jaws. Not to mention that the synopsis and first three chapters for my next book are due any day now.

My breathing turns heavy as panic starts to drip into my mind, slowly at first but then pouring in. I end up wheezing slightly into the phone.

"Kara? Try not to hyperventilate again. Where's your inhaler?"

"I'm all out of puffs."

"Why doesn't that surprise me? Listen, I know how fast you can write and I know you have this book inside you somewhere. You're one of the most talented authors I've worked with, but success has come relatively easy to you. Now it's time to fight for it. Only you can decide how bad you want this."

Sam's words seep through me, and a clash of emotions surges in my chest. I want to finish my book. I need to finish it—but the thought of seeking Ryan out to get it done feels highly twisted on so many toxic levels.

It means being physically near him, which will be a challenge in and of itself because a very real part of me wants to smash a bottle over his head. But then there's another part of me that's afraid I won't be able to shake off the weird, unbreakable pull that he's had on me since the day we met. The same pull I refused to acknowledge last night that left me feeling shaky and ashamed and like I was somehow betraying my dad all over again.

There must be a way I can see Ryan, get my book done, and make my way through this unscathed. Maybe I won't have to see him on a consistent basis. Maybe seeing him once was enough and I can ride the ripples of last night all the way to the end of my novel. If I can get enough writing done today, it would prove I only need to be around him once in a while. I can handle sporadic interactions with him if I have to. This can all just be an unfortunate work scenario I have to endure and I will not let him get in my head.

I adjust my position on the couch, sitting up straight as I grip the phone tighter. "I promise you," I say, my voice mirroring a determination I haven't heard or felt in a very long time, "I am going to get this novel done."

"Whatever it takes?" Sam asks.

"Whatever it takes."

"That's my girl! Give him hell, Kara."

The call goes dead and I drop the phone to my side. I rub the inside corners of my eyes before I look back at my laptop, hoping against hope that I get out of this alive.

Ten hours later, my optimism is steadily deteriorating as I fidget around in the back seat of my cab. I know I need to rally. I have to play nice with Ryan, or at least pretend to, for the sake of my book. I spent hours trying to write again this morning, much to no avail. I ended up watching a mind-numbing amount of TikToks, reorganizing my bookcase by color and accomplishing absolutely nothing else.

One of the cruelest parts of all of this is that having a muse is supposed to be a cathartic experience—freeing, even. I imagined myself on an Irish cliff, breathing deep and feeling invigorated, inspired and alive. All I feel now is angry, tired and bloated.

At least we're meeting at Butter, a Midtown restaurant worth salivating over. I fantasize about their hot rolls and the two types of butter that come with them on a startlingly regular basis.

Trying to hold on to my happy food thoughts, I twist some more in the cab as I adjust the waist of my dark jeans. I've paired them up with backless flats and a soft violet top because if I'm going to ride this double-date hot mess express, I'm at least going to be comfy while doing it.

The cab screeches to a stop a minute later and I use my arms to brace myself as I'm all but catapulted into the glass divider.

"Thanks," I mutter under my breath. The driver hears me but pretends he doesn't, only acknowledging my existence when I pay him the fare and step out.

Now standing outside the restaurant, I walk through the large glass doors and descend a flight of stairs to enter the dark yet inviting space. Butter has a clubby feel but still seems airy with the ceilings stretching two stories high. A massive backlit forest photo hangs over the main bar that's lined with wood paneling and metal railings, giving the scene a rustic industrial flair.

I look around the entrance lounge until I spot Cristina, Jason and Ryan standing in a second cozy bar area. Cristina sees me and waves, looking like the stunner she is in a maroon V-neck dress with Jason by her side, dapper and business casual in his typical hedge fund manager attire.

My eyes shift to Ryan next. I'd like to say I've gotten used to seeing him in everyday life, but it still feels like I've ventured through the looking glass. I'm half expecting a rabbit with a waistcoat and a pocket watch to scurry past as I make my way over to the bar.

"Hey, sorry I'm late."

Cristina gives me a big hug and I give Jason a kiss on the cheek. I hesitate as I turn to Ryan, not sure if I should go for a hug, a handshake or an epic stare-down. Taking the initiative, he grips my upper arm and kisses my cheek. It feels bad. And good. I should have gone with the stare-down.

"Have you guys been waiting long?" I ask, stepping back.

"Not at all. We've only been here five or ten minutes," Cristina answers. "I checked us in, so we should be set. You and Ryan relax and I'll tell them we're all here." She gives me a wink before promptly whisking Jason and her drink away towards the hostess.

Ryan exhales a quiet laugh. "Cristina's subtle."

"Super subtle. Let's hope she really is just checking in and not leaving us to have a romantic dinner alone."

"Would she do that?"

"Absolutely."

Ryan takes a sip of his beer and places the bottle down onto the bar. "Can I speak honestly, Sullivan?"

I find myself squaring my shoulders. "Sure."

"I'm sorry if I came off a little…abrasive last night. I know you and I have a lot of history, so for my part, I'm going to try to keep my distance and be civil when we're together."

I'm disappointed when I should be relieved. It's unsettling.

"That sounds like a good idea. I don't want to be the one bringing bad energy to Cristina's wedding week. Let's be civil."

"Civil it is. We'll give it the old college try." There's a trace of a smile on his face as I'm pretty sure we both mentally revisit a few choice things we tried together in college.

"Just out of curiosity," I ask, "what brought around this sudden change of heart?"

He picks up his beer and takes another sip. "I don't want to mess with anything Jason has going on this week, and my reason for annoying you seems trivial in comparison."

"And what reason is that?"

He pauses, seeming to reconsider something before saying, "That even after all this time, I'm still so mad at you."

I look away at his words, watching as a couple gets seated at a small table in the back of the dining room. They're holding hands and the man is laughing at something the woman said. I'm oddly irked by them.

"Fine," I say, turning back to face him. "And for the record, a big part of me is still mad at you, too."

"I guess we're even, then." He's staring at me with something more than just annoyance when I notice Cristina waving us over.

"Our table is ready." My voice is as biting as winter wind and I make no effort to stop my shoulder from bumping into his as I push past. I can sense him walking behind me a few seconds later as I follow Cristina, Jason and the hostess into the dining area.

We arrive at our rectangular booth and the happy couple sits next to each other, leaving me and Ryan to slide in side by side. Once settled into our seats, it doesn't take long for me to realize that sitting next to Ryan is going to be a problem. The booth is tight and his upper arm touches mine no matter how I position myself. Considering our somewhat hostile greeting, I don't think he's doing it intentionally, but maybe he is.

Maybe I want him to.

I bang my shoulder into the wall as my last thought jolts me into whipping away from Ryan's arm, shifting sharply in the booth to break the contact. Ryan doesn't look at me, but his back straightens as he keeps his eyes glued to the menu.

"Well," Cristina says, no doubt sensing our awkwardness. "I don't know about you guys, but Jason and I are starting with the gnocchi mac 'n' cheese. I would bathe in that stuff if I could work out the logistics."

Neither of us says anything and Cristina clears her throat as she goes on, "Okay then, how about we talk wedding business instead?" She reaches into the tote bag beside her and slams her thick wedding binder onto the table, rattling the cutlery and glasses.

"Yes," I agree, inching closer to the table. "I cross-checked the seating chart before I left, and all two hundred and eighty guests are accounted for."

Ryan lets out a slow whistle at the final head count. This wedding is no joke. I nearly fainted in relief when Cristina asked if it would be okay for her cousin to give the toast at the reception instead of me, since I usurped her by becoming maid of honor. The mere thought of speaking in front of that many people had me instantly scouring the internet for a doppelgänger to recite the speech in my stead. This is New York City, after all—I bet it could have been doable.

"Also, I'm picking up my dress from the tailor on Tuesday. It's only a couple of blocks away from the bridal salon, so if you need me to grab anything for you or any of the other bridesmaids, just let me know."

"Perfect." Cristina opens the binder and pulls out a pen. "The big day is almost here and it's imperative we all keep our focus."

Jason looks at me with a trace of fear and I take a big sip of my water. This is going to be a long night.

An hour later, our main courses are brought out and we have only just finished reviewing our nuptial responsibilities for the week. Cristina had no trouble laying down the law as Jason and Ryan jumped in every now and then with baiting comments. I just tried to enjoy the bread basket and not make any sudden movements.

"So, Ryan, tell us about how you and Kara met." Jason is smiling as he looks at us over his pork chop, blissfully unaware that his question just dropped onto the table like an unpinned grenade.

My fork stops in midair.

"I know you guys dated for a bit, but how did it all get started?"

My eyes dart to Cristina and she gets the message. She's a second away from changing the subject when Ryan quietly rests his fork down on his plate.

"We had a class together my junior year," he says.

"And you guys just started talking?"

"Sort of. I sat down next to her and pulled the romance novel she was reading out of her hands."

"Did you really?" Jason asks. "Well, that's one way to go about things. Did you always steal girls' books?"

"Not usually, no."

"So Kara was special, then."

I think Jason is trying to kill me.

Ryan doesn't answer and I'm ashamed to say that his silence scrapes at my pride.

"Or maybe it had nothing to do with me," I decide to say. "Maybe he was just an obnoxious guy who liked to bother innocent girls."

Ryan laughs to himself and sits back farther in the booth, pivoting to face me and boxing me in.

"That's funny, coming from the most uptight eighteen-year-old that ever lived."

"I was not uptight."

"You almost clawed my eyes out like a crazed possum when I didn't give the book back."

"That's because it was personal."

"It was personal because you were reading literary porn."

"It was a historical romance!"

"My mistake," he says calmly. "It was literary porn masquerading as historical romance."

"Stop calling it porn. That's not what it is."

"That's absolutely what it is. I scanned a few pages and I

went through a second round of puberty on the spot. My voice dropped a full octave."

"Oh, please. Romance novels are an art form and you have no idea what you're talking about."

"Whatever you need to tell yourself, Sullivan."

Ryan turns and picks up his fork with a grin as I glance over at Cristina. She's smirking back at me like the cat that got the cream.

Perfect.

The rest of dinner goes by without incident and before I know it, we're all outside and Cristina and Jason are hopping into a cab. I ask Cristina if Ryan and I should go with them, but she basically kicks me away with the heel of her foot and slams the door shut. The car screeches off and Ryan and I are left alone in front of the restaurant.

So much for this not feeling like a setup.

If Ryan feels uncomfortable, he doesn't show it. He stands confidently in front of me, the glow from the streetlights bouncing off the shoulders of his pale blue button-down as he slides his hands into his pockets.

"Where are you staying?" I decide to ask.

"The Shelburne Hotel. It's in Murray Hill, I think."

"Nice. That's actually right near my apartment." He nods his head and continues to look at me, waiting for something. I'm not sure what. "Okay, so I'm going to go."

"Do you want to share a cab?" he suddenly asks. "Or we could both get dropped off at my hotel if your place is that close."

"I'd rather not."

He rolls his eyes and shakes his head. "Why does everything have to be a fight with us? Let's just share a cab."

"Oh, well, when you ask so nicely."

I walk past him with a sarcastic smile and head for the curb. I'm scanning the street for available taxis when I sense him standing next to me. His arm touches mine and, this time, I know it's intentional.

"I'm sorry." His voice is so gentle that I consider it alarming. "I didn't mean to say it like that. Would you please share a cab with me, Kara?"

Fifteen minutes later, Ryan and I step out of the taxi in front of his hotel. I'd rather walk than have the driver take me the few extra blocks.

"Here we are," I say, glancing up at the maroon hotel awning. The nearby doorman keeps an eye on us, trying to gauge whether we're about to walk in or not. Ryan leans back on his heels and looks at the double glass doors.

"How far are we from your apartment?"

"Not far at all. About a ten-minute walk."

He stays quiet, his eyes still trained on the doors. I'm fully anticipating that we're about to go our separate ways when he blurts out, "You want to go for a drink?"

I don't try to hide my perplexed expression. "Why are you asking me to go for a drink? You just told me a couple of hours ago that you're mad at me and we should keep our distance."

"I know I did. I still think we should."

"Then I don't get it."

"Neither do I."

This is asking for trouble. I consider answering with a definitive no when I think back to my conversation with Sam. I swore to seize every opportunity I had with Ryan, spend time with him no matter what it takes—or how much it hurts.

"Fine," I say, doubting but not stopping myself. "Let's get a drink."

4

We end up walking five blocks to The Wharf, my favorite dive bar. Narrowly tucked in along 3rd Avenue, The Wharf is deceivingly huge. Once you navigate through the crowded bar area up front, there's a small flight of stairs in the back that leads to a covered patio filled with little dining tables. The patio only has two TVs, so the roaring sports fans tend to stay downstairs, leaving the upstairs relaxed but lively by extension.

But the hands down, best, take-your-breath-away part of the upstairs area is the old wooden shelving unit pushed along the far wall that is filled to the brim with board games. I'm talking Jenga, Connect 4, Scrabble, checkers, Battleship—they even have Dream Phone! (Dream Phone being the most thrilling and quasi-salacious electronic board game my ten-year-old self ever played, where Carlos in the neon 80's track-suit was, and always will be, my one true love.)

"This is awesome," Ryan says solemnly, looking up at the stacks of vintage games.

"I know." I have to respect his admiration for the game wall. I was the same way when I first beheld this magnificent sight. "Pick your poison."

"Dang," he says with a sigh. "If I knew I was going to be making a major life decision tonight I would have emotionally prepared myself." I scoot over so he can keep looking through the shelves until he eventually grabs the Jenga. "There are too many solid choices so I went with a safe bet."

"A fan favorite and always a good pick." I swipe the game out of his hands and lead us to one of the tables in the center of the room. We're stacking up the pieces when a waitress comes by a minute later. I order my usual Grey Goose bay breeze and he gets a beer on tap. The drinks come out fast and I'm ready to go for my first block as soon as they arrive.

"I should warn you," I say, "I'm a fairly well-known Jenga player in these parts, so you may want to manage your expectations of how this is going to go."

"Consider me warned." Ryan is fully focused on the game.

I go for my first block, a strategic side pull near the bottom. Ryan moves closer to the table as he considers his return move. He goes for a mid-level center block and three moves later, neither of us has uttered a single word. My face starts to feel warm so I take a sip of my drink. It doesn't help; if anything, it makes my cheeks rosier.

"On the plus side," I say, "I'm glad this excursion of ours isn't at all awkward."

"Absolutely," Ryan agrees, pulling out a side block and placing it on top of our tower. "Maybe other exes go for a drink and end up battling it out in a high-stakes board game in painful silence, but not us."

"Definitely not us. How embarrassing would that be?" I

purposely give him a creepy silent stare as I pull out my next Jenga piece. He sits back in his chair with a quiet laugh.

"It's nice to know you still joke your way through uncomfortable situations."

"I try my best."

"So, seeing as we're not a former couple who struggles to make conversation, why don't you tell me what you like to do when you're not writing?"

Polite conversation. *So good to see you again. Please save me from myself.*

"Well," I say, watching Ryan pull out his next block, "when I'm not writing, or trying to, I visit my family or go out with friends—one of my two friends, to be specific. And of course my reading game is as strong as ever."

"You always did live life on the edge."

"I'm a creature of habit," I say with a smile.

Ryan shakes his head, seeming amused as he surveys our tower, and I inwardly worry his engineering background will give him some sort of advantage. "Do you only read the type of books you write or do you read other kinds, too?"

I make my next move and easily stack my block on top. "Honestly, I'd like to say I venture out more into other genres, but ninety-nine percent of the time, I stick to romance."

"Don't you ever get bored?" he asks. "It has be repetitive after a certain point."

"I can see why you would think that, but to me, they're really not repetitive at all. There are so many subgenres of romance that if I ever do feel like things are getting a little stale, I just switch it up that way."

"What do you mean by subgenres?"

I'm happily surprised by Ryan's line of questioning and I immediately get a second wind. It's crazy how just talking about books gives me life.

"I mean that novels can be categorized even further within romance. There are subgenres but then there are also subgenres inside subgenres. So my main subgenre categories of interest would be historical, which we already discussed, and contemporary. Within the historical subgenre, I love a good Western/cowboy romance but I have also yet to meet a Highland/Scottish romance I wasn't down to read. In contemporary, I love a fun rom-com but I'm also always ready for a sexy military novel."

"So the romantically horny possibilities are actually endless."

I cough on my drink as I laugh a bit. "More or less."

"Interesting."

Then I pause, wondering if I should reveal this next bit. *Screw it.*

"I also take pictures of books."

Ryan pauses just as he's about to place a block on top of the tower. "You take pictures of books? As in, professionally?"

"No, not professionally—I take pictures of books around my apartment for my author page on Instagram."

"Got it," Ryan says, finishing off his move. "Pictures of the books you wrote?"

"Sometimes, if I'm hosting a giveaway or if I have a new book coming out. But I mainly do novels I'm reading or ones I've already read. I deleted all my private social media after we…"

"I'm aware," Ryan adds, filling in the short silence.

My breath catches a little but I go on, sliding out my next block. "So when I got my first book deal I started up my author page to try to get some sort of a following. Once I did, I noticed I only liked and followed pages that had pictures of books that were staged in these beautiful settings or that wrote reviews. I decided to give it a try and I liked it."

"That sounds fun-ish," Ryan says, seemingly trying to imagine what I'm describing. "So you're like a secret librarian photographer?"

"The proper term would be *bookstagrammer*," I say proudly. "And one of the best parts is that I've gotten a big enough following that once and a while publicists will send me a free early copy of a book from a publisher to promote on my page. Book mail is always the best mail."

"Sounds fancy."

"Very fancy." I lift my drink and take another sip. My straw is pushed against the bottom of the glass, leaving me with a big gulp of alcohol and none of the pineapple or cranberry juice. I close my eyes against the harsh taste before I put my glass back onto the table. "And what do you do for fun?"

"Secret's out," Ryan says, leaning forward and peering around our steadily growing tower. "When night falls, I also take anonymous pictures of my favorite books."

"You can try but it really is a highly competitive field."

"So I'm learning." He sits up straight, rolling a shoulder before carefully pulling out his next block. "Other than that, I go to the gym after work, I golf on the weekends, I'm in a fantasy football league…"

"Ugh," I interrupt, "I'm sorry to bust in, but I firmly believe that fantasy football is a plague on our society."

"And you're entitled to that opinion. *I* firmly believe it's the bedrock of our great nation."

"Okay." I chuckle. "You know, I'm sure fantasy football would be fine in moderation, but in my experience, that's never the case. How many leagues are you in during football season? Tell the truth."

"I may or may not be in three."

"My point exactly." I pull out my next block and the tower

starts to wobble. I don't feel comfortable breathing again until it steadies a couple seconds later.

"How do you know so much about fantasy football?" Ryan asks as I take a calming sip of my drink.

"My ex-boyfriend was in two leagues and he turned into an absolute freak of nature every Sunday."

Ryan stops his block mid-pull, his eyes revealing a trace of something I know he doesn't want me to see. Sensing my intrusion, he concentrates back on his block, gently placing it on top. "Were you guys together for a long time?"

A large group walks in then, more guys than girls, and I secretly hope they don't sit next to us. They're in good spirits but seem a little rowdy. Thankfully, they grab Operation and Trivial Pursuit and push a bunch of tables together in the corner, near one of the TVs. They end up making good background noise as I look back at Ryan.

"Mark and I went out for three years."

"Must have been serious," he says. "Why did you guys break up?"

"In the end, I think we both wanted more, but we were having problems for a long time before that. I felt like he was cold at times and he thought I had trust issues."

"Why would he think that?"

"Why do you think?" I ask poignantly.

A silence spreads between us, hidden and sticky, like one of those mousetraps you slide behind the fridge. Neither of us moves for fear of getting caught.

Ryan takes another swig of his drink. "Do you wish you guys could have made it work?" he asks a few seconds later.

"Sometimes. If I'm having a bad day, then I think, yeah, maybe I should have tried harder. Mark was nice and we could have had a happy life."

"And if you're having a good day?"

"On good days, I remind myself that there were major reasons why we were both willing to walk away."

Ryan nods and takes a slow sip of his beer.

"It's all right, though. What I learned from Mark is that when it comes to forever, you should end up with someone you're psyched to be with."

"Because if you're not psyched, then what are you?"

"Heading for breakup city, apparently."

Ryan smiles and it warms me up from head to toe. I wish it didn't.

"I don't know," he says. "I think there's something to be said for ending up with someone you're content with instead of someone you're obsessed with." His tone is friendly and easy, juxtaposing the weight of his words.

"But you can be in love with someone and not be obsessed with them," I counter.

"You think so?"

His gaze dares me to tell him he's wrong. I know he's thinking about us. How we were too consumed for our own good. How we turned everything up to a boil when we should have let it simmer.

"What about you?" I quickly ask. "Did you ever get close to settling down?"

Ryan watches me for a couple of seconds and is about to answer when my eyes are drawn to the patio doorway.

"Oh, my God," I whisper, sucking in a violent breath.

My gut feels like it's nose-diving into the floor. I drop my torso down and scrunch over the table, trying my best to hide behind our Jenga wall and the frame of Ryan's shoulders.

Mark is standing in the entrance of the patio. Mark, as in not-psyched-to-be-with-me, we-broke-up-three-months-ago Mark.

"What are you doing?" Ryan sounds confused and slightly

concerned as he gazes down at me, unaware that he is now my human shield.

"My ex is here."

"The one you just broke up with? Where?" He cranes his neck to search the room.

"Stop! Don't look," I seethe, digging my fingers into his knee under the table.

"Ouch! You don't have to stab me over it." He pivots a bit, pulling his leg free from my death claw. "What are you scared of? It didn't sound like you two ended on horrible terms."

"We didn't, but that doesn't mean that I want to see him right now."

"Okay, and when *would* you want to see him?"

"I don't know, but ideally I'd be holding a Pulitzer Prize certificate and wearing an evening gown."

A tired kind of smile appears on Ryan's face and after a moment of hesitation, his hand moves. I think he's reaching for his drink, but he's not. His hand slides down and pushes back the hair that's falling across my forehead. I don't move as his fingers graze my neck and linger near my ear.

"You know, Sullivan, no girl ever made me laugh as much as you do. That always bothered me."

His words shock me out of my somewhat panicked state. "Is that laughing at me or with me?"

"With you."

"Thanks. My agent always says I have a way with dialogue."

Now Ryan does move his hand to reach for his drink. "Are you done hiding? Are you going to go say hello?"

I peek around his shoulder to watch Mark and some woman sit down at a table across the room. They didn't even take a board game. The sacrilegious pair. "I can't go over. He's with someone."

"So what?" Ryan asks easily. "You're with someone. Tell him I'm your boyfriend."

I give him a flat glare. "I don't need you to be my pity date."

"I wouldn't be your pity date. We'd just be pretending. What's the harm in making him a little jealous?"

"I don't want to make Mark jealous and he's not like that anyways."

It's true. In all our years together, Mark was never jealous where I was concerned. But then, maybe I was suspicious enough for the both of us. Mark said it wasn't in his nature to act that way, but part of me always assumed that he just didn't care about me enough to get territorial.

I start to sit up and try to adjust to the very real possibility that I'm moments away from facing Mark and his new girlfriend. "Okay. I'll just go over there very briefly and say hi."

"If you don't want to say that I'm your boyfriend, you should at least tell him we're on a date. I dare you."

"I'm not going to lie. I'm no good at it and there's no point."

"I guess times really have changed. Quiet as you were, the Kara Sullivan I remember never backed down from a dare." Ryan finishes off his beer and places it softly onto the table, so as not to disrupt our game.

The college girl in me smiles at his cockiness while the woman in me gives him the stink eye. If he thinks a couple of smug comments will get me to do what he wants, then he's right, I have changed.

"Fine," I say with an air of certainty. "Since you're so desperate for people to think we're dating, I'll do it. Come over and introduce yourself when I wave. And if you sabotage any of the blocks while I'm away, I'll know and I'll put a curse on you."

Not waiting for a response, I get up and head in Mark's direction. He's sitting at a small table on the other side of the patio, facing me. The floor squeaks with every step I take, the worn-down boards begging me to turn and run.

Not going to happen.

I'm halfway there when he looks up and sees me, recognition and surprise washing over him. I arrive at his table a second later as he gets up out of his seat.

"Hi, Mark. Fancy meeting you here."

"Wow. Kara, hey." He offers me a warm smile as we then embark on one of the most awkward hugs of all time. Our arms can't figure out where to go and we end up looking like two nervous octopuses in a slap fight.

"How are you?" I ask as we step apart.

"I'm good. We were just stopping by for a quick drink after work."

Oh, were we?

Mark looks down and across the table and I figure I should take this chance to see who he's with, considering this person is now my arch-nemesis. My eyes follow his and find his dental assistant, Julie.

Dressed in navy slacks and a white sleeveless blouse, she looks pretty even after a full day of work. Her brown hair is pulled back in a delicate bun that I could never pull off and she doesn't have much makeup on, but with her clear skin and light green eyes, she doesn't really need it.

A pox on her.

Julie smiles and holds her hand up in greeting. Her cheeks turn red as we make eye contact and she almost seems ready to bolt. Mark gives her a sweet, reassuring smile and it doesn't take long for me to realize that this isn't just a work drink.

"Ah," I say softly, turning to Mark. "You guys are a couple now?"

He scratches behind his ear. "Yeah. It's very recent, though."

I nod my head, trying not to listen to the voice in my head

that's telling me there's no way this was recent. It must have been going on for months. Longer even. They work together. It would be beyond easy for them to slip away and I would never know. They probably had something going on all along.

"No, sure, I get it," I say. I keep my voice friendly even though a sliver inside me is falling to pieces. I even manage a smile for Julie.

"And you're here with?" Mark tries to look past me and I turn to see Ryan at our little table, watching our exchange with mild curiosity.

Then I remember I'm standing here because of a dare. Ryan's dare. The idea of making Mark jealous does suddenly feel more tempting, but as I notice Ryan's coolly overconfident gaze from across the room, I remember my original plan.

"I'm actually on a first date with that guy over there."

I step aside to reveal Ryan sitting in all his blue jeans and button-down glory. If you do have to run into an ex and his fresh-faced lady friend, it's helpful to be in the company of another ex who's taller and emits a small but distinguishable cowboy vibe.

"Oh," Mark says. "And how's that going?"

I look over my shoulder again and Ryan gives me a flirty chin raise. He really thinks he's helping me out. I turn back to Mark with a sigh.

"To be honest, not well. I knew him in college and he's been borderline stalking me ever since. I only agreed to go out with him in the hopes that it would tone down his fascination. It was either that or get a restraining order."

Mark's nervous gaze moves from me to Ryan. "Really? Are you sure you should be alone with him then?"

"It's fine. His passion for me is a little concerning but deep down, he's harmless. We'll have to get going soon anyways. He has digestion issues and if he doesn't get to a very secluded bathroom ten minutes after he eats, things get dicey real quick."

I turn to give Ryan a wave and he stands up a moment later. I swing back to Mark and Julie, who are exchanging a look.

"Here he comes," I say grimly. "We must be nearing the ten-minute mark."

Ryan is now walking over, closing the distance between us with his inherent swagger. I know he's thinking he somehow won. I can't help myself from saying one last thing to Mark and Julie.

"By the way, try not to stare at his glass eye. It doesn't fit right so it rolls around a bit and he's really insecure about it. He's getting fitted for a new one tomorrow."

Just then, Ryan arrives at my side and wraps his arm around my waist.

"Hey," he whispers close to my ear.

"Hello there," I answer with an angelic smile. "Let me introduce you to my friends. Ryan, this is Mark and Julie."

"It's nice to meet y'all." His typical slight accent rolls out nice and thick, like honey spilling over the edge of a spoon. He's clearly bringing out the big guns.

"Good to meet you, too." Mark is trying to look anywhere but at Ryan's eye, yet he can't seem to look anywhere else *except* Ryan's eye.

Silence stretches miles long until I jump in, taking Ryan's arm. "Okay, so we should head out. Why don't we just grab the bill and get going?"

"Sure," he answers, smiling easily at the uncomfortable couple in front of us. "Y'all have a good night."

There's no mistaking it. Mark is dead focused on Ryan's left eyeball. "Yeah, you, too," he says quietly.

I pull Ryan away and try to hide my victorious smile. We arrive back at our table and he draws back my chair.

"So I know you said your ex was nice, but he seemed strange, if you ask me."

I sit back down, distracting myself from laughing by looking for our waitress as he takes his seat across from me.

"He did seem a little off," I agree. "He was probably intimidated by you."

Ryan eats up my answer as he resumes the game and reaches for one of the last available blocks. "I'm happy I could help. Now, aren't you glad you went over?"

"I am glad," I answer truthfully. "I'm really, really glad."

Something in my voice makes him look at me longer than he should as he pulls out his block. The tower topples with a deafening crash, scattering all over the table and onto the floor, drawing the eyes and cheers of everyone around us.

I sit back in my chair with a satisfied smirk. "Jenga."

5

After leaving The Wharf, we head back in the direction of Ryan's hotel. We move down 41st Street at a leisurely pace, and I take a deep breath in as I catch the scent of hot falafels from a nearby cart.

"Do you like being back in New York?" I ask, looking straight ahead.

"I do. I always liked it here."

"That's probably because New Yorkers are so cool."

"Are you referring to yourself?"

"No, but it's nice to know that when you think of cool New York people you instinctively think of me."

Ryan looks over at me with an unreadable gaze. "You know, in some ways you're just as I remember you in college, but in other ways, you're completely different."

"How so?"

"You're more confident. You were so shy back then."

"I'm still shy," I assure him.

"You don't seem like it."

"I'm better at hiding it now."

Ryan stays quiet long enough that I look up and catch him staring. He gives me a small smile and turns forward.

"How's the writing going these days?" he asks. "You working on your next masterpiece?"

"My next masterpiece," I repeat, knowing I've only written one workable chapter in an entire year—and also knowing that I only wrote that one chapter because of him. "The novel I'm focusing on now is still in development."

"Exactly how many books have you written?"

"Seven in the past five years."

"A classic underachiever."

"Writing dominated my life for a long time," I say. "My first five novels were a historical romance series and my last two were contemporaries. The contemporaries didn't go over well."

"Why do you think that is? Did you not like writing them?"

"No, I did. It felt refreshing to try something new but I guess my readers weren't into it. It seems I'm better off in the past—in 19th-century England, to be specific."

"You always were an old soul." Ryan pauses before speaking again, a boyish grin appearing on his face. "What's it like when you write the dirty parts?"

"Really?" I ask. "How old are you?"

"I'm just curious about your creative process."

We move a little closer together as the sidewalk grows more crowded. Portable tables with vendors selling knockoff bags and NYC souvenirs line the pavement. "You can be honest," he goes on. "Do you laugh or do you get all serious? Do you dim the lights? Get a few candles going?"

"Don't belittle romance novels, okay? Romance is arguably the most popular and profitable genre of fiction in America. Everyone loves a love story."

"Love stories?" Ryan asks incredulously. "No offense, Sullivan, but I've read your books and *love* is not the first word that comes to mind when I think of the most memorable excerpts. If I had a dollar for every time you used the words *tender bud* to describe a freshly exposed nipple, I'd be a rich man."

"Oh, please. You're focusing on one aspect. And big deal, romance novels get racy at points. So what? Men used to have dirty magazines stashed away for years and the sky's the limit on what kind of circus-level porn people can watch on the internet now. That's exponentially worse than reading beautiful romantic stories about true love."

"Granted, and maybe romance novels wouldn't be so bad if everyone knew what was really going on in them. At least it's common knowledge that guys indulge in erotic—" he searches for the right word "—collections."

"Ha," I say.

"But you act so innocent reading those books. People would be stunned if they knew the truth. When I stole your book in college, I was scandalized."

"Were you? Were you scandalized, Ryan?"

"Yes, I was."

I give him a disapproving grin and turn to look forward. "How's your family?"

Ryan's sly smile slowly falls away. "They're fine. My sister, Sophie, is almost done with her doctorate in psychology, so she's trying to figure out where she'll start her practice."

"That's exciting. And how are your parents?"

"They're all right." He starts to walk faster as he glances across the street. "They're divorced now."

"Really?" I almost lose my footing and Ryan nods. "When did that happen?"

"About a month after we broke up."

Our casual tone is instantly torched. I only met his parents a few times, but they always seemed happy. Well-matched. From the way Ryan spoke, I knew his family was close. He talked about his parents and sister all the time.

"Why did they get divorced?" I ask, the tenor in my voice dropping.

"They told us they fell out of love." Ryan's eyes pan back to mine for less than a second, but they seem somehow dimmer. "It didn't really make sense at the time. They were high school sweethearts. People looked at them and thought they had it all. I thought they did. And then it was gone, like it was never there to begin with."

"Were you angry?" I ask as we stop at a crosswalk.

"I was real angry. I was young, I had just lost my girlfriend and then my family imploded for what seemed like no good reason. I didn't buy their excuse."

I shift my weight from one foot to another. "Was it an excuse? You don't think falling out of love is a valid reason for people to separate?"

"I'm sure it is, but my parents split up because my dad was having an affair for the last two years of their marriage."

Well, damn.

The light turns green and we cross the street, moving along with the flow of traffic.

"How did you find out about your dad?" I soon ask.

"He told me the truth a few weeks later. He thought I would understand."

"And did you?"

"No." Ryan puts his hand in the arch of my back, ushering me forward to walk a step in front of him as the sidewalk becomes thick with foot traffic.

I don't know what to say so I don't say anything.

"No matter how I tried to shape it, it felt like my dad chose himself and this other woman over our family. We were expendable to him—just afterthoughts."

"Did he stay with her?" I ask softly over my shoulder. "The other woman?"

"Margot. Yeah, they're married now." I slow down until Ryan and I are walking beside each other again, and he goes on, "The day he told me the truth, I asked him why he couldn't have just stayed with my mom. They didn't hate each other. They didn't fight. They could have gone on as they were. He told me you shouldn't make a life with someone just because you could."

I breathe out a quiet sigh. "How did your mom take it?"

"She tried to put on a brave face but most times she just crumbled. She leaned on my sister and me for support for a long time, especially in the beginning. Now that so much time has passed, I think she regrets how much she depended on us."

I nod my head, unsure of where to go from here. "How's your mom now?"

"She's better. She was on antidepressants for a few years but she's not anymore."

Ryan and I step aside as a woman passes with a stroller before we start walking again. "Anyways, she's been dating this guy, Joel, for a few months. He seems nice enough and she looks happy."

"That's good," I say hesitantly. "The beginning of a relationship is always exciting."

Ryan forces a smile and it's hard for me to return it.

"Why didn't you tell me when it happened?" I ask a few seconds later. "I would have been there for you."

He lets out an ironic, gray kind of laugh. "I did try to tell you. You remember the day you finally answered one of my phone calls?"

I slow down my pace until I stop walking altogether. Ryan does the same and turns around to face me like it takes all the energy in the world. The months after our breakup still seem cloudy but I remember that day. It's branded deep inside my memory and never healed right. Ryan called me every day for a month after we split up, sometimes more than once, and I never answered. But that day, I did.

"That was the day of my dad's funeral," I tell him.

His eyes go blank as he stares back at me. "What are you talking about?"

"He passed away three days earlier and when you called, the funeral had just ended."

Ryan is immobile, at a loss and maybe a little in denial. I should have eased into it more. The thing is, there will never be a right way to talk about my dad being gone. It still makes me sick and it comes out awkward, and ten years later, I have yet to process it.

"What happened?" he asks.

I take a breath but it doesn't help. "He was hit by an elderly driver."

"He was in a car accident?"

I can feel myself trying to hide away inside myself, burrowing down to a safe space where I don't have to hear my own story. That place doesn't exist. "No. He was hit while he was crossing the street."

Surprise, confusion, anger, contemplation. Those are the phases people usually go through when they learn about my father's passing.

Surprise that his death wasn't something typical, like a heart attack or an illness. Confusion when they internally ask themselves, "Did she just say her father was mowed down by a ninety-one-year-old driver who didn't see the red light?" Anger when I say no, the driver didn't go to jail. All the DA required was for him to surrender his license. And contemplation when they say to themselves, "I guess it *was* an accident. The man was extremely remorseful and it was his first offense." Followed by the inevitable, "I'll never let my parents drive past their eighty-fifth birthday."

"Why didn't you tell me?" Ryan asks, pulling me back to the present.

"I couldn't."

"Why not?" he demands. When I talk about my dad, people are always sympathetic. *Poor Kara*, they think. Ryan is the opposite. His manner is almost accusatory.

"The night before it happened, my dad and I had a fight. It ended badly." I'm hoping to leave it at that but I can see Ryan is expecting more. I try to speak again but my voice catches. Guilt takes altering forms with me. Sometimes it's a stab, other times a dizzy spell. Right now, it feels like a slow squeeze around my throat—nothing fatal, but enough pressure to remind me that it's there and it's never leaving.

I roll my neck a bit and add, "I just couldn't talk to you. I needed to suffer and, on some level, I think I wanted you to suffer, too. That's why I said what I did the last time we spoke."

Ryan levels a look back at me that hits like a punch to the gut. "What were you and your dad fighting about?"

I should make something up. I should spew out the first generic excuse I can think of. But I can't, so I don't.

"We were fighting about you and me. I told him I wanted to go back to you."

Ryan's immobile until he shakes his head. "This is ridiculous," he says, his tone clipped and frustrated. "You should have told me. I could have helped you."

"I didn't want your help," I fire back. "Listen, let's not talk about this anymore. It's over now so there's no point dwelling on it."

"Are you serious? You can't tell me that and expect me to be okay with it."

"Can we just not talk about it anymore?" Then, quietly, "Please?"

I can tell he's fired up, but he forces himself to nod, his jaw tight and his eyes dark. We continue walking at a strained speed in total silence. Three blocks seem to last forever until we're back in front of his hotel.

Out of nowhere, I have the urge to ask him something.

"You've told me more than once that you read my books. Did you like them?" I don't know why it's important for me to know, but it is.

"I did like your books," Ryan says after a pause. "They're not my style but they were great."

I accept his answer with a small smile. Seconds tick by until I say, "Well, apart from a few minor bumps, I think this was a fairly civil evening."

"Right. Hardly any bloodshed."

I'm not quite sure how to take that comment. I don't have time to dwell on it before he steps forward and gives me a brief hug. I'm soon stepping back, a little startled as I stand across from him.

A second later, I go from startled to panicked when he reaches forward and takes hold of my hand, slowly entwining his fingers through mine.

This isn't right. People who can only tolerate each other aren't supposed to hold hands. This is all wrong. Completely wrong. *Then why aren't I pulling away?*

"What are you doing?" I ask, my voice shaky.

"I don't know how to act around you," he says, looking down at our hands before moving his gaze back up to mine. "After we broke up, I used to imagine that I'd get you to fall back in love with me so I could leave you. I used to think about that a lot."

My breath turns shallow. I try to pull my hand away but he won't let go.

"You're acting like I ended things for no reason."

"I know why you ended things," he says. "Forget what I said. I'm not setting you up for some evil plot. I'm just trying to figure this out. I thought I hated you."

"I thought I hated you, too."

Ryan loosens his hold on my hand while also pulling me closer. "You know what I like the most about reading your books? I like how when I read them, I hear your voice in my head. I like knowing that I can hear you when no one else can."

I don't move as his eyes shift from uncertain to clear. He leans in, going so slowly and giving me plenty of time to stop him. I don't. Our foreheads touch and his breath is warm against my face. I feel it everywhere.

I inch upwards, brushing my nose against his as my free hand trails up the middle of his shirt. A button rubs against the flat of my hand, feeling cold and out of place against my skin. Our lips touch but only barely, that half second before a kiss when you decide to fall over the edge or step back to safety. I'm ready to fall, fall, fall when Ryan drops my hand and moves away.

"I'm sorry," he sputters. His breathing is accelerated but he's quick to control it. "We shouldn't have done that."

I nod, opting to not voice a response.

"I should go. I'm sorry." He doesn't hesitate before turning around and walking away, not bothering to wait for the doorman as he swings the door open himself. He disappears into the lobby, and my hand, the one he just held, falls lifelessly to my side.

I'm in a haze as I walk home. I can't believe how weak I was. After I swore to treat this like a work interaction, I almost let him kiss me. I almost kissed him. I'm beyond disappointed in myself as I try to figure out where I went wrong. I'm still a disgruntled mess when I get to my apartment. I lock the door behind me and unbutton my jeans, breathing comfortably for the first time in hours.

My laptop is sitting on my desk, parallel to the door. I can feel a flurry of words racing through my head, looking for a way out. I cross the room in several determined strides and flip it open. The screen illuminates the space around me as I pull my chair back and sit down. My latest document appears and I begin typing at a furious pace.

"And where is young George dashing off to so eagerly?"

Charlotte suppressed a gasp as Robert stepped beside her on the stone patio. He had been a guest at Greenspeak Park for a week now at the invitation of her father, Lord Destonbury. She should be used to his presence at this point, but something about Robert always kept her feeling out of step.

Turning away to watch her brother scurry into the gardens, Charlotte smoothed out the nonexistent wrinkles from her lilac morning dress. "George is hunting for a yellow primrose. Or pirates. Whichever he comes across first." Robert chuckled gently beside her as she went on, "I like to come up with little tasks to distract him."

"What does a nine-year-old boy need distracting from?"

"From thinking of our mother, mainly." Charlotte instantly regretted her words. She never shared her grief. Not with anyone.

"I'm sorry," Robert soon said, a serious tone lining his velvety, deep voice. "George is very lucky to have you. I lost my mother at a young age as well and I would have loved to have had an older sister or brother to look up to."

Charlotte found herself puzzled by Robert. Since the day they met, she made it clear that she would never agree to a match between them. And still, here he was, opening up to her about his family as if they were the oldest of friends.

"George told me you took him out riding yesterday," she quickly said.

"I did. I was happy for the company. Why? Is he not permitted to ride?"

"No, I was glad to see some color in his cheeks. I often worry about him."

"Does your father share your concern?"

"My father worries for nothing but himself and his own amusements. Which is why he's determined to have me married and gone from the estate as soon as possible."

Robert assumed as much. He had only ventured to Greenspeak last week to discuss a property line with Lord Destonbury when the man insisted Robert seek out his daughter, who he mentioned was of the perfect age to be married.

"Is that why you're so opposed to me?" he then asked. "To spite your father?"

"I need to stay at Greenspeak for George. I will not leave him here alone."

Robert looked at Charlotte with a hidden smile. So that's why she wanted no part of him. She was protecting her brother. He wasn't surprised. He was in awe of her. His little lioness.

At that same moment, Charlotte stole a glance up at Robert. She couldn't deny she felt a certain attraction to him. How could she not? Gazing off into the distance, he looked impeccable but completely masculine in his blue tailcoat, brown buckskin breeches and Hessian boots. She forced herself to turn away as a flicker of heat began to spread through her chest and stomach and beyond.

Inexperienced as she was, Charlotte could sense what was beginning, and she had no doubt that wanting a man like Robert Westmond would cost her far more than she was willing to pay...

I pull my fingers away from the keyboard, dizzy and a little out of breath. I'd like to think it was solely due to the excitement of making headway with my story, but I know it's not just that. My night with Ryan is still buzzing around me. There's no mistaking it now. I've linked him to this novel, and I won't be able to have one without the other. As if my writing process wasn't painful enough.

And with the way things left off tonight, I'm sure he's going to do whatever he can to stay away from me. But it's also becoming increasingly obvious that if I'm going to finish this book by my deadline, I can't afford to stay away from him. It's going to be a battle only one of us can win, and that person has to be me.

6

The next morning, I'm dressed in stretchy pants, a long knotted T-shirt and running shoes when I exit my Tudor City apartment building. Nestled between 40th and 41st Street, the towering prewar building has vintage steel windows and romantic stone architecture. The interior gives off a distinct English manor house feel, so much so that when I look out the hallway windows, I sometimes expect to see rolling countryside instead of the United Nations or Long Island City.

I spot my friend Maggie standing outside the Tudor City Greens, a small gated park that's parallel to the building's entrance. There aren't many cars on the road as I cross the street, but that's usually the case. The uncommon quietness of the block is part of the reason why I fell in love with Tudor City and used the signing advance from my biggest book deal as the down payment for my one-bedroom co-op.

Maggie's eyes are closed with her face tipped towards the sun when I reach her side.

"Hey, hey!" I call out.

Maggie and I met five years ago at the New York Sports Club. We both joined the gym on a whim and quit after a month (we weren't allowed to drop out earlier due to contractual reasons). We hit it off right away when we both got the giggles during a yoga class. It's amazing how fast a bond can form when twenty people are giving you death glares in tandem from eco-friendly mats.

"Morning," she says, giving me a hug.

Her curly black hair is pulled back in a high ponytail with a pair of sunglasses resting in the unruly waves. Wearing a pair of skinny jeans with a stylish but effortless white V-neck and strappy sandals, she looks casual while exuding feminine confidence. I want to dress like her when I grow up.

"So I'm thinking I need to find the most substantial meal this island has to offer. Are you ready to join me on this endeavor?"

"Ready and willing," I answer.

"Phenomenal." Maggie locks her arm through mine and starts walking, pulling me along in the process. "How about The Smith? Their Sunday brunch is always on point."

"I'm all about it."

"The Smith it is. And if we walk fast enough, we won't feel like gluttonous monsters when we split the s'more in a jar for dessert."

"We shouldn't feel that way regardless. God didn't put us on this earth to not eat s'mores."

"Amen," Maggie agrees. "And after we eat, I need to stop at Old Navy—my last stain-free blouse got assaulted with finger paint at the nursery school last week. I don't know how this keeps happening to me when I'm not even the art teacher."

"The struggle is real."

"It's very real. Marjorie nearly threw my ukulele at me yesterday when I stopped for a water break. People have no idea what a volatile field music therapy can be."

I didn't even know music therapists existed until I met Maggie. When I went to her apartment for the first time and found it flooded with instruments, I was taken aback. When she spent the following half hour playing the piano, the guitar, the violin and a dash of percussion, I almost hit the floor.

I've always been jealous of musicians. They play and get lost in their music, escaping to an untouchable place that I want to go to, but can't. That's probably why music therapy is so transformative for so many people—it's a little taste of magic.

"I love Marjorie," I say, remembering her from the time I shadowed Maggie at work. "But I thought you said the nursing home lost funding for music?"

"They did, but they got another grant, so we're back in business. I'm in the school Monday, Wednesday, Friday and the nursing home Tuesday and Thursday."

"You have the best job ever," I tell her. "You're like a musical saint walking amongst us."

"Oh, yes. I'm the Fraulein Maria of Midtown. The second my austere but compelling Austrian naval commander appears, I'll be all set."

"Meh, forget that. Then you'd have to be the stepmother to seven children, and the student loans for that crew would be insane."

"True. I'm still working on my own."

"Aren't we all?"

"Let's pivot from the student loan talk. It's too depressing. How was the big pre-wedding extravaganza?"

Cristina and Maggie walk that fine line between acquaintances and friends, with me as their common denominator. They're close enough that Maggie is invited to the wedding but not close enough to have been at the party.

"As a matter of fact, it was a little unreal. My ex-boyfriend was there."

"Mark?" she almost shouts. "What was he doing there?"

"No, not him, but I saw him, too. I'm talking about my ex from college."

"Wait, hold on." Maggie pulls me closer to her side as we make our way past pedestrian traffic on 2nd Avenue. "Start over. How did this happen?"

"Turns out Ryan, my college ex, is Jason's friend from when they were kids. So not only is he here for the week, but he's going to be a groomsman in the wedding."

"Well, this all sounds very fairy-tale-esque to me. College sweethearts reunited. Did you make out at midnight?"

"That's a hard no. We didn't end things on good terms back in the day and it didn't seem like a whole lot changed, until last night."

I turn to Maggie for her response when she's suddenly looking down, frantically digging through her bag.

"One second," she mutters. "My phone is vibrating."

Pulling said phone out, she swipes her fingers across the touchscreen. She stands eerily still before yelling, "Yes!"

"What is it?" I ask.

"I won the *Oklahoma!* digital ticket lottery!" she sings. Maggie tends to break out into song more often than not. She's all but jumping up and down as she cradles her phone to her chest like a baby.

"That's awesome," I say, feeding off her excitement. "I didn't even know *Oklahoma!* was on Broadway."

"It only came on recently, but this version is edgy and fresh, and the cast is incredible."

"Can't fight that 'Surrey with the Fringe on Top.'"

"No, you cannot," she agrees, happily tossing her phone back into her bag. "I have two hours to claim my tickets online so when we get to the restaurant, our table needs to become mission control for a couple of minutes."

"Fine by me."

Maggie links her arm through mine once again, glowing from her musical theater victory. The funny thing is, she's actually won discounted show tickets a bunch of times, but you'd never know it from her reactions. To her, each reduced-price ticket is the new best day of her life. She's addicted to Broadway musicals. She calls it her hobby but it's beyond that. Musicals are to her what romance novels are to me—necessary.

"Okay," she says, winding herself down, "now that I've had my good news, I want to hear more about yours. You were talking about Ryan. Go on. How'd he look?"

My smile inadvertently changes to a scowl. "Ryan was always good-looking."

"And he couldn't have been a bad person if you used to date him. You're one of the pickiest people I know. How long were you guys together?"

Maggie and I cross the street at the corner of 48th and 2nd, now only a few blocks away from our destination.

"We were together for two years, the last bit being long-distance."

"Were you guys really close?"

He was everything. All of it. He was all I thought about on the inside and everything I saw on the outside. I took my first love experience and ran with it hard and fast until my lungs burned and my legs fell out from under me.

That's my first thought.

"We were close," I decide to say. Maggie looks as though she heard my initial response. "He was funny and sweet and he was the first guy to ever really notice me, to see me like that."

"To see you like what?"

"I don't know," I answer. "Like something so special he could hardly believe it."

"Did you love him?" she asks.

It takes me a second to respond. "Yes. Too much. More than I should have."

"Well then," she demands, "what happened?"

"It was a tough situation. It was the culmination of a lot of things."

"Such as?"

I fight off my initial urge to detach. It's strange—after all this time the pain is still there. It's silent and weakened but still alive. Still breathing.

"After Ryan graduated, he got an internship back in North Carolina and he threw himself into his work. I had just started my junior year and we thought we could handle being apart. In the beginning it was okay, but as time went by I heard from him less and less. He wanted to turn the internship into a job, and it seemed like there wasn't room for anything else. Including me. We would go days at a time without talking."

"That's no fun," Maggie says. "Was that it then? The distance?"

"No." I pause, hearing the familiar hiss of a memory as it slithers its way back through my consciousness.

"There was this girl in the internship program with him. Madison. They got close. She would always post pictures of them working late or hanging out on the weekends. Ryan kept saying they were just friends, but thinking of him with her all the time chipped away at me and I couldn't stop it. She was beautiful. So beautiful that it turned me ugly."

"Did you say something to him about it?"

"Yes. He would just tell me that they were friends and I had nothing to worry about, but it still felt like he was emotionally cheating. He confided in her. He liked spending time with her. And all the while, I was hundreds of miles away, poring over their every post on social media like a deviant and feeling smaller than I ever knew I could."

"Did anything happen between them?" Maggie asks.

I don't answer right away. Instead I look down, noticing the jagged cracks in the weathered concrete.

"When things started to get really strained between us, I flew down to Raleigh to surprise him. I had asked him what he had planned for the weekend and he said he was staying home. I got to his apartment around nine o'clock that night and when I knocked on the door, he didn't answer. I called him ten times and got sent straight to voice mail."

We're in front of the restaurant now but neither of us goes inside. Maggie passes her bag from one shoulder to the other. "What happened next?" she asks.

"I sat outside his apartment until two in the morning before checking into some scary, seedy motel. I think I slept for a total of twenty minutes."

"Oh, boy."

"Yeah. When I went back to his apartment the next morning, he was hungover and in his clothes from the night before. He was shocked to see me but excited, too. He picked me up and gave me a big hug. I think he was still drunk since he didn't notice I was about to cry. I asked him what he did last night and he said he stayed in and watched TV."

Maggie nods and I go on.

"I lost it. I told him I knew he was lying and when I tried to leave, he said everyone from work went out and got wasted, and he ended up passing out at Madison's. Obviously, I flipped. He swore nothing happened, but he had just lied right to my face. And in the midst of everything, I asked him, if he were single, would he be dating Madison? He wouldn't give me a straight answer and that was it for me. I was miserable all the time and he was clearly at the point that he couldn't be honest with me. I told him we were over."

"How'd he take it?" Maggie asks hesitantly.

"Not good. He begged me not to end things and said he would do whatever I asked. He'd said he'd quit his internship and move to New York. I knew I was hurting him, but we couldn't go on the way we were. You shouldn't have to force a relationship to work when you're twenty and twenty-two."

"Very true," Maggie says. "So that was it? That was the last time you spoke to each other?"

"After the breakup he called me a lot. I never answered but every day I could feel myself getting closer to picking up. One night, he called when I was at my parents' house. I told them I was thinking of giving Ryan a second chance and they got so mad. They knew what happened when I went to visit him, and they thought we were done for good."

"Didn't you think that, too?"

"I did, but I also missed him so much. I thought I'd feel better after we broke up, but I felt more depressed than ever. My grades tanked, I barely hung out with my friends… I was in a bad place and my parents—my dad especially—resented Ryan because of it. We got into a big fight after he called. He told me I was acting like a zombie and that being with Ryan was draining me. He said love wasn't supposed to be like that and he raised me to know better. I ran out of the house."

"Oh, no," Maggie says, guessing where I'm going with this.

"Yeah. The accident happened the next day."

Sometimes I wish my dad had been a worse father. That he didn't coach my softball team from first to eighth grade. That he didn't go on every little-kid ride on our trip to Disney and act like he was having the time of his life. That he didn't make a little chef's hat for me to wear when I'd visit him at his pizzeria two blocks from our house. If he didn't do those things, him being gone wouldn't feel like a giant hole cut out in every memory I have or will ever have. But he did. And I'll never stop missing him.

"I was numb after that. I had spent my last moments with my dad fighting over a boyfriend who barely called me and who had sleepovers with other girls. I stormed out like a selfish spoiled brat and after a lifetime of having an amazing relationship, my father left this world being disappointed in me. The guilt was suffocating, and I became filled with so much hate. Hate for me, hate for Ryan, hate for our entire relationship. I blamed us and I hated us."

"Damn." Maggie sighs. "Did you tell Ryan when it happened?"

"No. The day of Dad's funeral, he called just as it ended. I picked up and he said he needed to talk to me. I was out of my mind and hearing his voice sent me off the deep end. I told him I was done listening to his problems and that I couldn't believe I wasted as much time with him as I did. I said I had never been happier than I was that last month without him. I told him every time he called, I laughed at how pathetic he was."

"Me oh my. And his response was?"

"That he had been dating Madison for months behind my back and that he was only calling me out of pity. He'd said he didn't want me to show up crying at his doorstep like I did the month before."

Maggie flashes a pained expression. "You guys were an intense pair."

"Yeah. And then last night, he told me he was calling that day because he just found out his parents were getting divorced."

"Of course they were," Maggie says, almost laughing. "Because this breakup wasn't tragic enough. Do you think he really was seeing that Madison chick while you were together?"

"I don't know. I did until last night."

"What was it like at the party? Was he still pissed? Did he seem different?"

"We were both bitter—with good reason, I guess."

"Do you think—" she hesitates before going on "—do you think you would have forgiven him back then if it turned out he made up the Madison stuff?"

"I'm not sure. With everything that happened, it just felt like we were too far gone. And after my dad, I didn't think I deserved love anymore."

"Does that mean you think you deserve it now? Because you do."

I don't answer, partly because I don't want to and partly because I can't. Thankfully, Maggie accepts my silence.

"Man," she says a few seconds later, "full disclosure, after hearing all that, there's no way I'm not getting my own s'more in a jar. Let's do this thing."

I let out a chuckle as the tension breaks, breathing easier as we finally enter the restaurant. We're early enough to be seated right away without a reservation and we follow the friendly hostess to a table near the retractable window wall in front. The ambiance is warm and bright with pristine white tiles and reclaimed wood accents.

We settle into our seats and accept our menus, but I've already made up my mind. I'm going with scrambled eggs, whole wheat toast and, apparently, my very own s'more.

Maggie seems as prepared as I am as she sets her menu in her lap. "So, where do you two go from here? What were you talking about before when you mentioned last night?"

A warning bell rings out in my head, wordlessly shaming me as I remember the kiss that didn't happen.

"It was dumb. Ryan and I had a moment and we almost kissed, but thankfully we didn't."

"Excuse me?" Maggie asks. "Why wasn't that the first thing that came out of your mouth?"

"Because it doesn't matter. Nothing happened and I'm glad it didn't because Ryan and I are over."

Maggie gives me an unsatisfied huff as she sits back in her seat. "I reject that statement. The way you just told me that story, which, by the way, makes me want to go home and sing "Drivers License" in full voice while wrapped in a blanket, one hundred percent proves how *not* over you and Ryan are."

"Yes, we are," I insist. "Sam says I should use him to finish my novel. She thinks he's my muse."

"And is he?"

Knowing the truth but not wanting to say it, I look away to glance around the restaurant. It's beginning to fill up now. It seems like no one can resist the siren song of brunch on a sunny Sunday in Manhattan.

I turn back to Maggie with a sluggish breath. "Both times I've seen Ryan, I've gone on a writing bender. I don't know why but he just gets something going in me."

"You mean like your raging teenage hormones?"

"Yes, thank you. That's very helpful."

"Well, I'd like to formally cast my vote and say that I'm with Sam. If Ryan is your inspiration, then you need to go with it. It's about time you mixed a little business with pleasure."

A nervous kind of nausea sweeps through my abdomen at Maggie's suggestion. I snatch the folded napkin in front of me from off the table and drape it across my lap. "Okay, I'm done talking about me. What's going on with you? How's Grandma Noreen?"

Maggie smiles, as she does when I mention her grand-mother. "She's amazing. I just saw her yesterday."

Grandma Noreen is Maggie's mother in everything but name. The matriarch of the family through and through, Grandma Noreen raised Maggie and her younger sister, Hannah, since they were kids. Maggie goes up to visit her in her small town in Connecticut every week and talks to her on the phone twice a day without fail. Noreen just turned ninety-three but looks decades younger. Maggie swears it's because she uses a ton of moisturizers and sleeps under a heated electric blanket year-round.

"Hannah seems to be settling in, so that's good, and it's a relief to know that Grandma is getting consistent social interaction. It helps keep her sharp."

I was selfishly so relieved when Maggie's sister moved in with Grandma Noreen last month. After a bad fall last year, I could tell that her living alone was weighing on Maggie, so much so that I half expected her to move up there herself. Needless to say, Hannah received one of my famous gift baskets upon move-in day.

"I'm starving," Maggie then says. "I strategically wore these pants so I could binge-eat to my full potential."

I look under the table to take note of her clothes. "You're wearing jeans. No one can eat to their full potential in jeans."

"These are not jeans, they're jeggings. Fancy jeggings, but jeggings nonetheless. And I am completely ready to put these bad boys to good use."

"I applaud your commitment."

Maggie smiles and begins to scan the space for our waitress or waiter when she suddenly sits up at full attention. I follow her eyes and turn my head to see two guys now standing beside our table.

"Hi, Kyle!" Maggie says, her singsong voice as soft as a bell.

"Maggie. It's good to see you again." Kyle is tall, dark and very handsome.

I give my friend a speculative glance as she touches her hair, finding it still kept up perfectly. "You, too. We're just having a quick bite. Kara, this is Kyle."

"Nice to meet you," I say, shaking his offered hand.

Kyle then pats his friend on the shoulder. "And this is Adam."

I sit up with a bit more enthusiasm myself as I take in a man with brown hair, friendly brown eyes and one dimple. He isn't as tall as I'd like, but I can get past that.

Hello, Adam.

"Nice to meet you," I say.

"Likewise." He extends his hand and I reach out to grasp it. He has a nice grip, confident and warm.

Kyle leans down to whisper in Maggie's ear, effectively making Adam and me the third and fourth wheels.

"So, do you live around here?" he asks.

"I do," I answer. "I'm in Tudor City on 41st Street."

"Oh, nice. That's near the water, right? I love that block."

A smile spreads across my face. "Me, too."

I'm gearing up to keep our conversation going when Kyle pats Adam on the shoulder once again. We say goodbye and Maggie and I watch the boys walk away until they're out of view.

"And who, pray tell, was that?" I ask, turning to Maggie.

She shrugs with a smirk. "I met Kyle last week at my cousin's birthday."

"I daresay he is very handsome. Got a good feeling about this one?"

"I don't want to get ahead of myself but it's fair to assume that he's my future husband and the father of my unborn children."

"Fantastic. Does he know that yet?"

"No, but he will after we go out for happy hour this week."

"Because half-priced drinks are notoriously conducive to enduring love."

"That's what I always say."

I shake my head with a grin as our waitress appears and introduces herself. We tell her what we'd like and are told that select cocktails are included with our brunch special.

"Excellent!" Maggie beams. "My friend and I will each get a Bellini. We're actually here celebrating our engagements."

I almost choke on my water at Maggie's words. The waitress congratulates us and walks off to get our drinks.

"Are you high?" I ask through a laugh.

"What? I honestly think marriage proposals are on the horizon for us. Kyle and Ryan are very lucky men."

"I wouldn't count on it," I say.

"Oh, well. Gotta fake it till you make it."

7

"So I send you a freak-out text, and you show up thirty minutes later with *pandebono* and coffee? I've made my decision. I'm marrying you instead of Jason."

"We're going to be a beautiful couple."

I step inside as Cristina pushes her door back farther, dressed in a faded NYU T-shirt, soft lounging pants and fuzzy slippers. We plop down onto her couch moments later and I edge my sneakers off before curling my feet into the blue velvet cushions.

Cristina and Jason's NoHo apartment is a beautiful loft with exposed brick and visible ductwork along the ceiling. Plush rugs and contemporary artwork make the space feel homey even with the industrial atmosphere. The place would be perfect except Cristina swears a stowaway mouse lives in the radiators. She hasn't spotted her tiny, non-rent-paying roommate yet, but those guys can be unavoidable in an old building like this.

"Now, what's with all the 'send help' messages?" I ask, leaning forward to rip open the bakery bag that's separating us from our cheesy bread goodness. "Did Jason's work people still not RSVP? Did the florist finally send over the center-piece sample?"

I glance around the apartment but see no trace of the human-sized purple orchid centerpieces that are going to grace all forty tables at the reception.

"No, no centerpieces as of yet," Cristina says. "I have to talk to you about something else."

Her voice sounds calm but I also catch the uncertainty. I sit back, giving her my full attention. "What's wrong? Is everything okay with Jason?"

"No. I mean, yes, he's fine. I'm just a little stressed at the moment and I need you to help center me."

"Okay, but remember you're less than a week away from your wedding. Stress is normal."

"This is not normal. Guess who's moving in with us for the next six days—what could be considered the most important six days of our lives."

"I don't know," I answer after hesitating. "Jason's mom?"

"Oh, god, don't even joke about that! Jason's mom is en-camped at the Four Seasons and would happily remain there for the rest of her natural life. No, I'm referring to your boy toy, Ryan."

I hate to say it, but the mere mention of Ryan's name is enough to make my whole body tense. "Ryan is moving in with you? Why?"

"Oh, this is a great story," Cristina says, laughing without the slightest trace of humor. "Ryan is staying with us because he was kicked out of his hotel. Apparently, he brought his dog with him, because of course people do that when they're at-tending out-of-town weddings, and the dog trashed the room while we were at Butter last night."

"Are you serious?" I ask. "He left his dog in the hotel alone?"

"No, Jason's other genius groomsman, Beau, was supposed to watch him but decided to go meet up with one of my friends from work. A guest made a noise complaint so the manager went in, and you can imagine what happened from there."

"And now Ryan and his dog are moving in with you?"

"That is correct. Beau is loaded, so he got his own room at a different hotel that doesn't allow dogs, and Ryan is staying here. Jason thinks it won't be a big deal and feels bad because any hotel Ryan books now will be ridiculously expensive. I offered to pay for it myself but eventually caved because some lunatic started a rumor that you're supposed to compromise in relationships."

I'm about to come up with a comforting response when Cristina's apartment door swings open, banging against the wall. We crane our necks to look behind the couch and in walks Jason, followed by Ryan, followed by one slightly overweight bulldog.

Cristina turns back to me and takes a deep breath in through her nose. "I'm going to have a panic attack."

"No, you're not," I say quickly and quietly, getting up from the couch. "Hey, guys!" I cross the room with a friendly smile, and it almost falters when Ryan openly grimaces at me. I consider vampire hissing back at him in response, but then figure one of us should act like an adult. I do my best to ignore him as I squat down in front of his canine better half, who's now pulling excitedly against his leash, trying to get to me.

Ryan's dog has bristly white fur with wide caramel patches, and I instantly want to pick him up and cuddle him even though he has to be north of fifty pounds. I scratch all over his head and neck, triggering him to stomp his foot in rapid succession against the floor and to bring his face very close to mine. His big, dark eyes tell me that if I stop petting him, he might die. Melodramatic and possibly eats too much. This dog gets me.

I stand up to reach Ryan's eye-level, asking, "What's his name?"

"Duke," he answers, like he'd rather not tell me.

"Hey, Kara!" Jason is now wrapping his arm around my shoulder as he turns us around. Cristina glares at him from the couch and he nudges his chin in her direction, leaning in close to me. "Have you talked her off the ledge yet?"

"You need to tread lightly, my friend," she snaps back at him. "I'm still not sure if I'm speaking to you. Kindly leave the room."

"Guess not." Jason pats the side of my arm and makes his way into the kitchen as Cristina turns back around in a huff, facing away. I'm drinking in the whole sorry scene with regret when a twisted idea comes to mind. An idea that can possibly save Cristina and my career in one fell swoop if I'm unhinged enough to do it. My eyes shift to Ryan, who is now retreating into Jason's office as my inner confidence meets with riotous doubt and fear. Then I stop thinking altogether.

"Everyone," I call out. "I have a thought. How about Ryan and Duke stay at my place until the wedding?"

A general silence falls over the room.

"Do you mean it?" Cristina asks, almost whispering.

"No," Ryan answers quickly. "No, it's all right. I wouldn't want to intrude."

"It wouldn't be any trouble," I assure him.

"Duke is a handful. I couldn't put that on you."

"I love dogs and my building is pet-friendly."

Ryan stares daggers at me in a subtle kind of way and I smile sweetly back at him. He looks to Jason for help, who turns to me after some obvious internal debate.

"That's nice of you, Kara, but don't worry about it. Ryan and I are going to buy an inflatable bed to set up in the office for him and Duke."

Cristina whips around on the couch to find Jason. "Say one more word and I will cut you." She jerks back around to me.

"Honestly, that would be the biggest help ever. We would have loved for Ryan to stay with us but we have so much on our plate with the wedding. Now you guys can really catch up and everyone wins."

Everyone then turns to Ryan, who is solely focused on me. "Can I talk to you for a second?"

I nod and follow him as he steps to the windows on the far side of the room.

"Why are you doing this?" he asks once we're out of earshot.

"I'm just trying to help Cristina. In case you haven't noticed, you've escorted her right to the brink of a nervous breakdown."

One look at Cristina's hopeful eyes proves that I'm right. "We wouldn't have been any trouble," he says half-heartedly, knowing it isn't true.

"This coming from the man who was just evicted from his hotel." That earns me a flat glare. "What are you afraid of? Are you worried I'll kill you in your sleep and empty your bank account?"

"I wouldn't put it past you."

"Well, you can rest easy because I have more important things to do. I have a deadline coming up and I'm going to be working around the clock."

Ryan glances across the room to where Duke is making himself at home on the couch. Cristina is now following his path with a Dustbuster, vacuuming up any of his fur that clings to the fabric.

"So you really want to do this then?" he asks, turning back. "You don't think the two of us sharing a space will be at all dangerous?"

"Dangerous for me or *you*?"

Ryan doesn't answer right away. I know he's trying to think of an alternative plan, but nothing comes to mind. This is happening.

"I guess we'll find out, Sullivan," he says. "You want me, you got me."

There's something final about his words that make me a little drunk with power. It's like I'm possessed when I say, "Just like old times."

Ryan's eyes sear into mine. Apparently, my sass wasn't appreciated.

Too bad.

I flash a quick smile and step around him to find Jason and Cristina.

"All right, so I'm on my way to Queens right now to have dinner with my mom and Jen, but I'll be back in the city by eight. Ryan," I say, turning to him, "you can head over around then. Cristina will give you my address and phone number."

"Terrific," he says unenthusiastically.

I give him a merry wave and head for the door. I'm halfway there when Cristina jumps in front of me.

"You are my hero," she says in a hushed tone. "I worship the ground you walk on and you have my unwavering loyalty forever."

Jason comes to stand beside her. "I think what she means to say is 'thank you.' And on a side note, if Ryan steps out of line, just give me a call. I'll set him straight."

"Thanks for the offer but I can handle him." I look over my shoulder, feeling like I'm having a slight out-of-body experience and trying not to smirk. "See you later, Ryan."

It takes twenty minutes on the Long Island Railroad to get from Penn Station to the Little Neck stop in my childhood neighborhood. From there, I walk six blocks past Laundromats, pizzerias, bagel shops—all the staples of Queens society.

I'm then at the house where I grew up—a brick three-bedroom with a small front yard. I walk up the cement stoop steps and automatically check the mailbox beside the door.

There's a fair amount of mail, the first of the pile being addressed to Tim Sullivan. My airways tighten a bit but I don't mind. I like that he still gets mail.

As I go through the squeaky screen door and walk into the living room, I imagine my dad sitting in his recliner. My private tradition. He'd look away from the Yankees game on the TV to find me in the doorway. He'd smile and stand up, giving me a hug and telling me I've been away for too long, even though I come to dinner every weekend.

I run my hand along the top of the recliner now but the leather is cold. Untouched and unused. I take my hand away before the feeling can linger, moving through to the dining room and into the kitchen to find my mom and my sister, Jen, sitting at the oval oak table.

For as long as I can remember, my mom was always a pretty mom. She had a great figure, she ate what she liked, she had a piña colada every Friday and dessert was something we enjoyed as a family. These days, she's a different kind of pretty.

Once my dad died, she became fixated on fitness. She walks over five miles a day, is on a first-name basis with every employee at her local gym and our family desserts are a distant memory. I can't even utter *ice cream* without having anxiety that I'd set off some kind of *Goonies*-esque booby trap. Not that working out and eating only healthy food is a bad way of life—obviously it's not—but I'm more of a fan of everything in moderation.

Stepping deeper into the kitchen, I pass her weekly weight and BMI chart that's pinned to the fridge with a popsicle stick magnet I made in kindergarten. Her stats are impressive and she meets her every fitness goal with gusto.

"Hello, family," I say, giving Mom a kiss on the cheek. She stands up and gives me a hug that makes me gasp. She's clearly taken her free-weights routine up a notch.

"Hey, honey. You're right on time." I glance at the clock

above the stove, relieved to find that it's 5:30 p.m. on the dot. Mom gets prickly if she has to eat past 6:00 p.m. I look to the counter next and find the meal that she prepares every Sunday. Baked salmon, mashed cauliflower, and salad made from the organic greens and tomatoes she now grows in the backyard.

"What, no cheese fries?" I joke. She rolls her eyes and I hold up the mail. "I picked these up on my way in. There's a couple in there for Dad."

"Oh." She takes the letters and her smile fades for the briefest of seconds before she plasters it back on. "Okay, thank you. I'll just sort through these later." She puts the mail into a drawer and closes it. Jen and I pretend not to notice when her hand stays on the handle for longer than necessary.

I then turn to kiss my pale and pregnant older sister. If someone didn't know that Jen was having a baby, they would never notice her tiny bump. I choose not to think about the nagging fact that my expecting sister and I could share the same jeans.

"Where's Denny?" I ask her. Denny is Jen's husband of four years.

"He couldn't get out of work. He'll make it next time."

Denny runs the radiology department at Long Island Jewish Medical Center. Even though he has nothing to do with obstetrics, it still means delivery room VIP treatment for Jen when the baby comes. *Would you like a hot-stone massage after your next contraction? Yes, please!*

"How are you feeling?" I ask.

She answers with an unhappy "Humph," as I sit down in the empty chair beside her. "I throw up every two hours, have migraines every three hours and I sweat so much when I sleep that it looks like I swam night laps in the ocean."

"You mean like a beautiful mermaid?" I try.

"Like a beautiful mermaid's angry, constipated stepsister."

"That's a really vivid description."

"I can get more vivid if you have the stomach for it."

"I don't."

Mom sits down at the table with a sigh. "Don't be gross, Jen."

"I'm not being gross."

"Yes, you are. And, Kara, don't forget to take home the grilled chicken I made for you. Yours has the blue lid, mine's in the red container. I made it just the way you like it with extra lemon."

"Thank you! As if I'd ever forget my weekly grilled chicken haul."

Jen turns a little green. "If you two keep discussing poultry, I'm going to start dry-heaving."

"And moving right along," I interject. "Mom, do you still have that silver serving tray Aunt Grace gave you?"

"I think so. Why?"

"I'm late for an Instagram post and I need to shoot a book by tonight. Also, do you have any flowers? Flowers would look great with this cover art, but if you don't, I can use your antique tea set instead. I'll stage it on the front room windowsill, or I can use your bed if you have your fluffy white comforter out."

"I'm beginning to think you only bought me that comforter for your own selfish reasons."

"Your assertion is both highly offensive and partly true."

My mom grins and shakes her head. "Okay, you know I fully support your booksta-pictures but—"

"It's bookstagram," Jen says. "Bookstagram. You should know that since it's one of the keys to Kara's livelihood."

"Whatever it's called," my mom groans. "You should be focusing on your own book. The longer you wait, the more difficult it's going to be. You don't want to take too long and then get stuck in a funk."

Too late.

"I know, Mom, and for the record, I did start my next novel." *Thank goodness.* "It's in the very early stages, though, so I'm still figuring it out."

"That's exciting! Do you have pages for me to read?"

My mom can be my toughest critic but she's also my biggest fan. Even though reading on the computer hurts her eyes, she still read my first manuscript after every edit I went through, which ended up being about ninety-seven drafts. I never would have worked so hard to get published if she wasn't there encouraging and pushing me along the way.

"It's not quite ready yet, but hopefully soon."

"Tell us about Cristina's party," Jen says, rubbing a hand over her stomach. "I need to live through you so I can forget my own miserable existence."

"I had a good time. The party was nice and I wore this new off-the-shoulder dress."

"I thought you were going to wear the dress I got you?"

My mom looks at me expectantly and I adjust my seat, crossing a leg over my knee as I close myself off a little. She's always been addicted to buying Jen and me clothes. Problem is, she and I have had very different styles since I became a preteen and fell madly, deeply in love with a vintage sweater my aunt bought as a gift. It felt like I was donning a socially appropriate wearable quilt and there was no turning back for me after that.

"I did try on the dress you bought but you know I don't do sleeveless."

"You would feel amazing wearing whatever you wanted if you carried it off with confidence," she says easily. "Living like I do, I feel empowered every day. We should make a vision board together!"

Here we go.

Ever since my mom became a fitness fanatic, she's been continually trying to recruit Jen and me. I've tried to humor her. I part walked, part jogged a 5K with her last year and we've gone to the gym together plenty of times—I opt to use her guest pass but she would prefer that I sign up for a lifetime commitment in blood. I don't begrudge her for loving to exercise, but I know she begrudges me for not feeling the same.

All my life, I was never overweight but I was also never underweight. Where other girls were toned and trim, I was softer and curvy. When my friends went to dance class, I played tennis and softball. I came out of the womb with my upper thighs touching and they've refused to be parted ever since.

I'm generally happy with my body, but my upper arms are my no-go zones. Short sleeved/off-the-shoulder shirts and dresses are my jam and I've done very well for myself as-is.

"Thank you for the suggestion, but the sleeveless life just isn't for me. I'm all for making a vision board, though."

"Me, too," Jen chimes in. "First things I'm putting on my board are a Target shopping spree and an English country house. Or at the very least, I want to manifest a world where I can eat grilled cheeses and watch period dramas all day long."

"Same," I agree. "Those are actually sensational choices."

"You girls are missing the point," my mom says. "How is Kara going to find someone if she's not her happiest and most confident self?"

My eyes shift to the floor as I try to remind myself that she means well. That she's somehow blind to the fact that her pep talks feel more like sharp digs I'm never able to dodge.

"I'm perfectly happy, Mom. And I don't think I'm destined for a nunnery just because I don't love my arms." My answer sounds rehearsed because it is. We've had this conversation a billion times.

"All I'm saying is that if you invest time and energy into healthy self-care, it will do wonders for your self-esteem."

"But what makes you feel good about yourself isn't necessarily the same for me," I argue. "You may not believe it, but every time I read a new book while wearing pajamas, I physically get a runner's high."

"That's not possible."

"I know my truth."

My mom sits back with a sigh. "I realize that this is probably a sensitive topic, but I still don't understand why you and Mark broke up. He had a great job and he was nice."

Of course, it's easier to rank a man's profession before his personality when you're not the one marrying him.

"Yes, Mark was nice, but he and I weren't right for each other."

"And why was that, Kara? Because he didn't ride in on horseback and ravish you like one of the characters in your novels?"

"Mark and I didn't work out because we didn't have the chemistry needed to sustain a lifelong relationship, on top of our other issues." I then add, "Plus he always flossed in front of me and it made me want to vomit."

"He was a dentist! There's nothing wrong with him practicing sensible dental hygiene."

"Okay, enough." My voice is even but firm. "Mark and I are not getting back together and I'm very satisfied with both my physical and mental health, so you need to relax and let me live." I then turn to Jen, not giving my mom a chance to respond. "Now, where was I?"

"The party," she says, popping a saltine in her mouth from a travel-sized box she's hiding in her lap.

"Yes, the party." I'm about to elaborate when my phone vibrates in my sweater pocket. I pick it up and see a text message from an unknown number. "One second." I type in my security code and the message pops open on the screen.

Just giving you a heads-up, I snore louder than Duke.

My stomach flips. I know I told Cristina to give Ryan my number but him texting me right now feels too strange to be real. I grip my phone with both hands and type, Not surprising. Guess I'll have to break out that new sound machine after all.

Blinking dots pop up right away. At least he's not one of those guys who take five hours to text back.

I also do chanting meditation at 5:00 a.m. with a substantial gong solo, performed live by me. Would you like to participate?

I smile to myself and look up to find Mom and Jen watching me. "Sorry," I say. "It's Cristina with wedding stuff." I glance down and quickly type, I'll take a rain check. Thanks, though.

My phone buzzes.

Let's get down to business, Sullivan. Are you luring me to your apartment so you can seduce me or what?

I laugh then and it doesn't go unnoticed by Mom and Jen. Thankfully, they return to their own discussion and I text back, lowering my phone underneath the table like a guilty teenager.

Absolutely. I type, emboldened by our easy back-and-forth. Here's a preview—I'll be wearing back-to-back sweat suits as I ignore you completely and work on my book all day. Good luck resisting that sultry dance.

Wow. How about some warning before things get X-rated?

You're an idiot. I'll talk to you later.

The blinking dots pop up one more time.

See you at home.

Dear God, what have I done?

I place my phone down onto the table in front of me, feeling nervous and excited. I'm reminding myself that this is purely work-related when I notice my mom and sister staring right at me.

"Hi," I say innocently.

"Who was that?" Mom asks. "And don't bother saying it was Cristina."

How to play this…

"That was a guy I met last night."

Mom looks at Jen before turning back to me. "Well, that's good. Are you interested in him?"

I pause before answering. "I am possibly interested in him." I don't mention that I'm referring to Ryan. My mom met him plenty of times in college and always liked him, but after being privy to all the details of our breakup, I don't know how she'd react to him now.

"And what does he do? What does he look like?"

"He's an engineer and looks-wise…he's tall. He has sandy-blond hair and a strong jawline. His eyes are green with little specks of brown along the edge."

"Ooh la la," Jen says. "That's a lot of detail for a first encounter."

I inch my chair closer to the table. "Yeah, well, he's Jason's friend so we talked for a while."

"Are you going to see him again?" My mom is trying to sound disinterested while verbally circling me like a shark.

"As a matter of fact, we're meeting up tonight."

"Wonderful! I want to hear all about it tomorrow. Now, you girls head into the dining room and I'll grab the dinner." Mom gets up and Jen and I leave the table, walking into the dining room side by side.

"You know, horrible as it is being pregnant, it really is an incredible experience. You need to get moving if you're going to have babies someday."

"I have time," I say, stretching my shoulders. "I was a late bloomer so my egg quality is way younger than it should be."

"You can't actually know that that's true."

"I absolutely can. I didn't get my period until I was sixteen so when I'm thirty-four, my eggs are still going to be in their late twenties."

"Did you really get it that late?"

"Yeah, I did. So even if you think I'm a spinster, my eggs are still sparkling young debutantes."

"Fine," Jen chuckles, "but even with your younger-than-average eggs, you still have to keep it rolling in the love department. At least you met a new guy."

I fail to mention just how not new Ryan is as we sit down at the dining room table.

"I sure did," I say instead. "Wish me luck."

Things to do before Ryan gets here:

1. *Tidy everything.*
2. *Dust everything.*
3. *Vacuum everything.*
4. *Buy healthy food to strategically place in the front of the refrigerator.*
5. *Move romance novels with mega-dirty titles out of the living room bookcase and into the bedroom bookcase.*
6. *Turn around romance novels on bookcases that have groping illustrations on the spine.*
7. *Put my published books on display.*
8. *Do laundry.*
9. *Hide granny panties (aka hide ninety-eight percent of all my panties).*

Having managed to check off every item on the list I wrote out after the mad dash back to my apartment, I toss the piece of paper into the waste bin beside my desk. Ryan is officially in the building, on his way up at this very moment. All that's left to do is get this freak show of an experience on the road.

As if on cue, there's a loud knock on my door.

Here goes nothing.

I take a deep breath as I cross the room. Another echoing knock sounds out before I clutch the doorknob and swing the door open.

Ryan is standing there in jeans and a gray T-shirt, a travel bag on one shoulder and holding Duke's leash in his right hand. Duke looks up at me like he's moving in permanently. All that's missing is a vintage, dog-sized luggage set.

"No backing out now, Sullivan." Ryan readjusts the travel bag on his arm as my eyes are drawn from Duke to him.

"Wouldn't dream of it. Come on in."

"I think Duke needs some time to get acclimated first." He squats down to give the dog a thorough petting. "All right, buddy, we may have been kidnapped and forced here against our will, but I'm sure we can survive for a few days."

"Nice. And here I was thinking I did a good deed for everyone involved."

"I told you she was self-righteous, didn't I?" he says to Duke. "Don't worry. We'll persevere."

"You know what? How about the dog stays and you go become a subway dweller? You'd probably thrive in one of those underground communities."

"You think so?" Ryan asks, standing up with a smile.

"I'm fairly positive. You seem normal on the outside, but below the surface I bet there's a charismatic cult leader just waiting to burst free."

"I appreciate your train of thought but I think I'll tough it out in here for now. We wouldn't want to disappoint you."

I imagine punching Ryan right in the face. "Okay, well, you have five seconds. Come in or don't. I'll survive either way."

"This is going to be a long few days, Duke." Ryan walks into the apartment with his portly but adorable dog trotting along in his wake and I shut the door behind them. He's passing my bike that's dangling low from a bamboo rack, which also doubles as my entryway table, when he suddenly stops short.

"No way," he says. "You still bike?"

"Of course," I answer. He dings the bike bell and I feel a certain level of motherly pride. Not to be creepy, but I couldn't love my bike any more than if she had actually come from my own body. A turquoise three-speed, she has café-style handlebars and a silver rear rack that matches the heavy-duty front wire basket. She's smooth and whimsical with endless character and I will never give her up. Her name is Calliope—Callie for short.

"How often do you take her out?" he asks.

"A couple times a week. Mainly to the grocery store or my friend's apartment. On nice days I go to Central Park."

He grips one of the handlebars, shaking his head to himself and smiling in earnest. "This is you in bike form. It's awesome." He walks through after that and I'm a little surprised by his reaction.

I've loved biking ever since I was young and that love stayed with me all through college. I'd even fixed up an old seven-speed that I got cheap online and gave it to Ryan as a birthday present when we first started dating. I always figured he went out riding with me to appease me, but maybe he enjoyed it more than I thought.

Following him and Duke into the living room, I have to say that a bulldog makes the space seem even cozier. I wonder if Ryan would let me borrow him for a few of my posts. Books and dogs are an irresistible Insta combo.

"I like the name Duke," I soon tell him.

"Thanks. I couldn't change it now even if I wanted to. I spent too much money on monograming."

Inadvertently, my mind travels back to the romance novel Ryan stole from me the first day we met. "You didn't name him after *The Devilish Duke*, did you?"

Ryan places his bag down beside the couch and glances around the room before turning back to face me.

"Not really. Fond as that memory is, my sister was with me when I adopted this guy and she helped me name him. She goes to Duke University."

"Oh, cool." For the record, I'm super-psyched I made it blatantly clear that I remember the title of the book that started our relationship. I would hate for Ryan to think that I moved on or anything.

Anxious to change the subject, I walk deeper into the room and ask, "How long was the drive up from North Carolina?"

"It was a little over nine hours."

"That's rough. I can barely make it to Long Island without feeling sick."

"Well, if you still drive like you did in college, I'm not surprised. I think at top speed you only ever went thirty miles an hour."

"I'm a defensive driver."

"You're an old-lady hunchback driver."

"Let's not throw stones, okay? You're the grown man who drives everywhere because you're afraid to get on an airplane."

"You and I both know I experienced a trauma," Ryan says solemnly.

"You had some turbulence on a flight to Denver as a child. I'm not sure that can be considered a trauma."

"When you're seven years old, dramatic turbulence feels like you're plummeting directly into the pits of hell. I would have thought you'd be a little more sensitive."

"I *am* sensitive, but it's kind of extreme that one bad flight made you anti-plane for the rest of your life."

"I'm a man of the open road, Sullivan. I'm set in my ways and I'm not changing for anything."

"Whatever you say," I mutter.

Ryan strolls over to the living room bookcase, where he begins perusing the titles. Thank goodness I moved the worst of the novels into my room. I currently have every mild to moderate book that I own on display in the bookcase he's now inspecting.

"How do you choose which books to read?" he asks.

Still looking at his back, I interlock my fingers in front of me. "I don't know. I see what catches my eye at a bookstore or I'll buy something that's getting posted about a lot."

"That's a wide net. Is there anything special you look for in books besides the consistent sweet, sweet lovin'?"

"You actually want to talk about books right now? Do you have four or five hours to spare?"

He glances over at me with a chuckle. "I think I can handle it."

"Okay," I say. "Well, when it comes to what I look for in each specific book, I guess it's easiest to break it down by tropes—tropes being plot devices or themes. Examples of different tropes in romance would be friends-to-lovers, enemies-to-lovers, fake relationships, second-chance romance, forced proximity, mistaken identity..."

"So there's a lot," Ryan interjects, sensing I am prepared to go on forever.

"Yes, a lot. Most of which are very fun and intriguing."

"But if there's only a certain number of themes, aren't books with the same trope carbon copies of each other?"

"Not at all, because each book approaches the trope in a different way. The characters are different, the location is different…" I try to think of how to phrase this in a way that Ryan would connect with.

"All right, so you asking me if books with the same trope are carbon copies of each other would be equivalent to me asking you if every baseball game you watch is the same. I mean, they're all just playing baseball, following the same rules and always ending the same with one team winning. It must be boring."

"Which would be an absolutely blasphemous statement."

"Exactly. In baseball, they're going through the same motions with the same end-goal in mind, but you're still happy to follow multiple teams and watch them play because every game is different and exciting. The same is true with romances. Each love story is its own unique experience."

"All right," Ryan says, rubbing his hand across the stubble on his cheek, "I'm not even trying to stroke your ego here, but you should know that what you just said was wildly insightful."

A wave of pride flushes through me as I feel myself going a little red. And that right there is the bookish runner's high I was trying to explain to my mom.

Like I said, I know my truth.

"Thank you, but I'm sure other people must have used that metaphor before."

"As they should. I have a much better understanding now."

"I'm glad I could help you walk in the light."

"So which one of these tropes is your favorite?" Ryan asks.

"Oh, man." I suddenly feel like I have to pick which of my nonexistent children I love the most. "I like so many of them. But if I had to pick, my top three would maybe be best friend's sibling…"

"Say what now? That counts as a category?"

"Not a category. A trope."

"Well, that's an extremely specific *trope*."

"Most of them are. You know what, scratch that, best friend's sibling has been moving down my list lately. Okay, official top three…forbidden love, forced proximity and enemies-to-lovers."

"And I'm assuming enemies-to-lovers is…"

"What it sounds like—people who hate each other but then fall in love."

"So exactly what it sounds like," Ryan says, the room turning oddly quiet. "Nice. I'd read that."

I'm sort of unsure if there's an implication there or if I'm overthinking it. "Right. Okay, enough of the literary discussions for now." I cross the space between us to gingerly usher him away from the bookcase.

"It's not my fault. Being around all these books is making me embrace my intellectual side."

"That must be a foreign experience for you." I then pivot to watch Duke sniff and snort on each of the brass legs of my white coffee table.

"Wow," Ryan says behind me. "Success has really changed you, Sullivan. Remember when you used to be nice to me all the time?"

"Yeah, when I was teenager. I made fun of you then, too, but I kept it internalized because you were cute."

"And I'm not now?"

I twist around to face him, my head tilting as I take in his appearance. Ryan isn't cute. He is painfully good-looking.

"You're okay," I answer.

"All right, as much as I love the direction this conversation is now going in, I need to fill up Duke's water bowl and set up his bed." Ryan then moves across the room and squats down in front of his bag, unzipping and digging through it.

He pulls out a large water bowl, a huge plush blanket and a pillow in the shape of a bone that says, "You had me at woof."

I move to stand in front of my kitchenette. "The sink is right over here. Feel free to use the fridge or stove as much as you want. It's not exactly *Chopped* quality but it gets the job done."

"That's okay, I got it." Without another word, Ryan about-faces and disappears into the bathroom, which is just outside my bedroom. Confused, I follow his trail until I'm standing in the doorway, watching as he fills up Duke's water bowl in the sink.

"What are you doing?" I ask.

"Getting Duke some water."

"I can see that, but why are you filling it up in here instead of in the kitchen?"

"Because this is where Duke sleeps."

I try to absorb that last bit of intel but it doesn't quite get through. "Pardon?"

"Duke likes to sleep in the bathroom."

Ryan finishes filling up the bowl and sets it down by my feet. Before I know it, I'm jostled aside by Duke as he nudges past me to get to his water. All but shoved out of the room by the thirsty bulldog, I shift to stand just outside the door frame. Ryan carefully folds up the thick fleece blanket until it turns into a bed that looks so soft, I wouldn't mind giving it a go myself. Once he's done, he stands up and leans back against the sink.

"Why does he sleep in the bathroom?" I ask.

"I'm not sure. Since the day I got him, that's just where he goes to sleep."

"So he's going to be in the bathroom every night?"

"Most likely, yes. Is that a problem?"

"It's not a problem," I say, "but what if I have to use the toilet while he's lounging around or whatever?"

Ryan shrugs. "Just make sure to watch your step. Duke won't bother you."

"So your dog will just sit in there, watching me?"

"Duke," he clarifies. "His name is Duke so please address him as such. He's a human being, Kara."

"My mistake, so *Duke*, the human dog, will be in there and staring at me?"

"It's possible but I wouldn't worry about it." Ryan pushes off the sink to stand up straight. "Honestly, Duke wouldn't wake up if a marching band came through to do their business after a hotter-than-normal curry dinner. You have nothing to fear."

"Phenomenal."

Well, it looks like a midnight trip to the bathroom with a heavy-breathing animal waiting for me in the dark is in my immediate future.

I head back into the living room and sit down on the couch. Duke follows and launches himself onto the cushions beside me, water trickling down from his mouth. I try to avoid eye contact, but he stares at me until I give in and start petting his beautiful coat. Ryan walks into the room and claps his hands together.

"Well, Duke's room is all set up."

"Great," I say, getting up and turning around to face the couch. "This is where you'll be sleeping. Lots of my friends have crashed on this little beauty and then asked to stay forever so you should be good."

"My partner in crime seems to approve." Duke sprawls out over my vacated spot, making himself even more comfortable. And then he farts. Loudly.

"Ugh!" I laugh as I cover my nose.

Ryan winces and turns his head away from the overpowering smell. "Come on, man, we talked about this!" He waves his hand to create some airflow but it's pointless; the stench is way too powerful.

"I have some air freshener," I offer through my hands, which are still serving as my gas mask.

"That's all right. It'll pass after an hour or two."

"Oh, wonderful." I reach over to the coffee table to pick up the blankets and pillows I have waiting. "These are for you. Sorry I don't have a pullout couch, but I don't have many overnight guests."

"Oh, no?" Something about Ryan's tone makes me think that he's wondering about my overnight guests of the male variety. Good. He smiles when I don't answer and goes on to say, "The couch is great."

"Cool." We look at each other and a lengthy silence ensues. I foist the blankets towards him. "So here you go."

"Hey, do you mind if I take a quick shower before I turn in? The guy in the elevator with us was hacking up a lung and I'd hate to give you swine flu on my first night."

"Sure," I answer, crossing my arms. "You know, you really are as odd as I remember."

"I'm usually not. I think you bring it out in me."

"I get that a lot."

"And speaking of me being odd, I have one more small request."

"Oh, boy," I say, "let's have it."

"Would you mind if I lowered the thermostat at night? I have trouble sleeping unless my room is super cold. Duke doesn't do well in the heat either."

"Okay," I answer, walking over and checking the thermostat beside my bedroom door. "It's already set to sixty-eight."

"Yeah, I'm thinking more like sixty-two."

My eyes go wide. "Damn, Elsa. That's really cold. How do you live in North Carolina?"

"It's not easy." Ryan chuckles. "I have central air but my electric bill is out of control. When it's hot at night I just feel like the whole room is stuffy and I toss and turn and I'm in a bad mood the next day... It's just no good all around."

"Can't have that, then," I say, adjusting the temperature. "Into the arctic we go."

"Are you sure it's not a problem?"

"Very sure. Sweatshirts and sweaters are my second skin anyways."

"Nice," Ryan says, soft and with a smile. A warm quiet fills the room despite the descending temperature until he goes on, "So, about the shower?"

My mind floods with imaginative visuals. Ryan naked in my bathroom. Ryan naked in my shower. Ryan naked and wrapped in one of my towels.

I whirl around and walk back to the kitchenette. "Yeah, go ahead." I make myself look busy by opening the refrigerator. The additional cool air has a calming effect.

Once the bathroom door closes, I turn to make sure Ryan is out of sight. Seeing he's gone, I slam the refrigerator shut and power-walk over to the mirror that's hanging above my couch. I take in my flushed reflection and tuck my hair behind my ears.

I then turn once again to survey the room. Everything is as it should be and Duke is now sitting on my reading chair like it's his throne.

"Are you enjoying New York so far?" I ask him.

He gives me a brief glance that tells me he would prefer it if I didn't disrupt his reverie. Not wanting to push my luck by petting him while he's in his Zen state, I opt to sit on the couch, grabbing the remote and turning on the TV.

I'm ten minutes deep into my favorite Bravo reality show when I notice the shower water is no longer running. I immediately try to settle into a casual seated pose and focus on the screen—but that proves difficult when Ryan walks out of the bathroom wearing nothing but a deep gray towel.

His hair is pushed back and off his face, dripping small droplets of water onto his shoulders and his cut chest. He's fit but not overly so, looking athletic but not like one of those guys who goes to the gym at an extreme level and has bulging muscles.

He's a guy you just know will have an amazing dad-bod someday. Like, when he takes his kids to the beach, moms will look at him and think…maybe he trained for the Olympics at some point in his younger life. I mean, he probably didn't get *into* the Olympics, but still, maybe he participated in the qualifying rounds.

"Sorry, I left my bag out here," Ryan says.

"I'll get it." I push up off the couch and grab the bag, which is a couple feet away. A second later, I'm standing directly across from Ryan's half-naked body.

This is totally fine. Completely normal.

I reach out to pass the bag over, and as I do, his hand brushes against mine.

In one of my books, I could milk a hand graze for at least a page, but in reality, I'm not sure if the contact holds any weight at all.

"Thanks," Ryan says with a smile before walking back into the bathroom. He shuts the door and I cover my face with both of my hands.

Pull yourself together! This is business!

I take a breath and am the picture of composure when Ryan walks back into the living room a couple minutes later, wearing navy basketball shorts and a white short-sleeved undershirt. He looks…gross. I'm choosing to believe he looks gross.

"Are you hungry? We can order something if you want."

"No, thanks," he says. "I'm pretty tired so I think I'll just crash."

"Sounds like a good idea." I walk past him as he heads for the couch and turn back around to face him once I'm standing in my bedroom doorway. "So, does Duke go into the bathroom now or will he meander in later?"

"He'll stay with me for a bit, then head in when he's ready to sleep."

"Got it. Can I ask why you brought him with you to New York? Wouldn't it have been easier to get a dog-sitter and leave him home?"

"That *would* have been way more convenient, but Duke has a ton of separation anxiety. I went on an overnight business trip once and he went nuts even though my mom was staying with him at my place. He wouldn't sleep and he peed all over the floor, which he never does."

"Oh, no," I say, my heart aching. "That's awful."

"Yeah, he was a rescue, so we know he came from a bad situation. He's much better now, but sometimes his past comes back to haunt him."

My gaze falls to the ground as I think to myself that I know the feeling. When I look back up, Ryan is watching me with understanding eyes. I shift around by the door and take a quick breath as I put on a smile.

"Okay, good night, then."

Ryan smiles awkwardly back at me and raises a hand to scratch his shoulder. "This is all kind of surreal, isn't it?"

"Just a bit," I answer.

"Listen, I know I was giving you a hard time, but thank you for letting us stay."

"It's fine. I like the company."

"Me, too. Hotels actually creep me out."

"Really?"

"Yeah. They're impersonal and sterile. I'd always pick sleeping on a friend's couch if given the choice."

"So we're friends now?" I ask.

"I'd like to be. I think I would have tried to stay friends with you even after everything if you would have let me."

I feel a slow drag in my gut at Ryan's words. Maybe we could have stayed friends after our split, but I don't see how. A no-contact policy was the only way I could get over him. To let Ryan into my life at all back then would have been to let him fill it completely and I couldn't do that. Not again.

"Friends," I murmur. "I think I'd like that, too." I take a step back and grip my bedroom doorknob. "Good night."

"Good night, Sullivan."

I close the door and a strange sensation takes hold in me. I feel defenseless but somehow still in total control. Exhausted but wide-awake. My laptop catches my eye in the middle of the mattress and without hesitating, I move to the bed and sit cross-legged. I flip open the computer and enter the password. My manuscript appears on the screen and I immediately start typing.

Charlotte and Robert walked side by side through the stuffy portrait gallery, dutifully following Charlotte's father as he blathered on about his illustrious family. He was a tall but sweaty sort of man—slippery as an eel and as good-humored as a tree stump.

Robert could tell that not all the paintings were original to the gallery. Faded marks on the wall were visible behind smaller artwork where large-scale paintings once hung. He wondered if Lord Destonbury was quietly selling off his family heirlooms to keep his creditors at bay. The ton knew Phillip to be a gambling man, but the extent of his debt was unknown.

"Excuse me for a moment," Lord Destonbury said, exiting the gallery and leaving Charlotte and Robert very much alone.

Charlotte turned to Robert, not appearing the least bit surprised. "Clearly, my father isn't the most effective chaperone."

"Chaperoned or not, you have nothing to fear from me."

Charlotte looked at Robert with an assessing eye. "Nor you from me." She turned and continued along the gallery, Robert following her with a grin. They had only walked a few feet when she turned on her heels to face him once more.

"Forgive me for being so direct, Lord Stratton, but I don't understand why you're still here. You seem a decent sort of man. I'm sure you have friends. No doubt there are women in London who would be all too glad for your company. I told you I won't marry you, so why do you remain?"

Robert closed the distance between them. He did not touch her, though his eyes revealed just how badly he wanted to. Restraint had never been difficult for him. Until now. Charlotte gulped but held her ground. It affected him more powerfully than he cared to admit.

"I remain here because I care for you," he said after a moment. "Do you think you could ever care for me?"

"I...don't know. But even if I did, it wouldn't change my mind."

"How about we make a bargain? I will refrain from making you an official offer of marriage until I depart in a month. If you do not love me by then, I will go and never return." Robert reached out his hand, waiting for Charlotte to accept the wager.

A moment later, she confidently placed her hand in his. "Done. Shall I send a servant to help you pack at once or must we really wait until the end of your stay?"

"I'll take my chances," Robert said with a smirk. "Though, for an agreement such as ours, a handshake seems rather formal. Let's seal it with a kiss, instead."

Charlotte had no time to react as Robert swooped down and expertly pressed his lips to hers, eliciting a surprised squeak as he slipped a hand to her waist to pull her in close. She was stiff and nervous to start but soon relaxed under the gentle insistence of Robert's warm mouth. The kiss was slow—soft and drugging— and she was set adrift within it. She was sure this was how Robert intended it. Even with him holding back she could still feel his want for her, the hint that there was so much more waiting for her when she was ready. She swore to pull away but ended up leaning into him farther when he was the one who drew back, but only just barely.

"Much better," he whispered, his nose brushing along hers. "I'm looking forward to the next couple of weeks, Charlotte. Let the games begin."

9

I'm drawn out of sleep by the sweet smell of pancakes. Breathing the aroma in, I roll off my stomach and onto my back, rubbing my eyes with the cuffs of my thick woolly sweater that hangs well past my wrists. If I didn't have it on, I probably would have gotten frostbite last night. Ryan legitimately sleeps in an ice cave.

The clock beside my bed reads 7:18 a.m. If pancakes really are happening and it's not just my bottomless pit of an appetite dreaming it up, then that means Ryan is now a morning person. Yet another reason why any relationship between us would be doomed for failure.

I drag myself out of bed and head stealthily into the bathroom, sneaking by without Ryan seeing me. Thankfully, Duke has vacated the premises, so we can forgo any power struggle. I turn on the faucet and throw a few handfuls of water onto my face until I'm fully awake.

Once dried, I give myself a once-over in the mirror and I

can feel my skin beginning to thaw. Ryan must have put the thermostat back to normal. I take off my sweater to reveal a sleek heather-gray pajama shirt with matching pants that Jen got me for Christmas last year.

I quickly brush my hair and teeth and I stride out into the living room before I can rethink it.

"Pancakes?" I ask in my hoarse morning voice. I'm about to say more but am quickly overpowered by the smell of something burning. As in full-fledged burning.

I look to Ryan, dressed in khaki shorts and a navy T-shirt, as he pivots around in front of the stove, completely frazzled. Holding a spatula in one hand, he waves the other back and forth over a smoking frying pan. "I may have burnt the bacon," he says.

"I can see that. It was nice of you to try, though." I cross the room to push the windows open behind my desk, hoping to help air out the space.

"I'm usually a good breakfast cook but I think I got too ambitious in going for the pancake-bacon combo on an unfamiliar stove."

I step closer towards the kitchenette and Ryan cautiously feels the handle of the frying pan. Not finding it scorching, he picks it up and dumps the charred bacon into the garbage. "Your fridge was very well stocked. I'm usually proud of myself if I have milk from the same year in mine."

"I went shopping before you got here." I raise my hands over my head in a stretch and Ryan turns around to busy himself with something at the counter.

"Don't feel obligated to buy a lot of stuff on my account. I can reimburse you for the groceries if you want."

"No, it's fine," I say. "Besides, if you make breakfast every day, I should be the one reimbursing you."

"Honestly, I don't usually cook a hot meal for myself every

morning." He moves back to the stove as he scoops the last pancake off the pan and onto a plate. "I may be showing off for you a bit."

My heart skips a beat and I wish it wouldn't.

"How are you even up this early?"

"Believe it or not, some of us have boring, real jobs and it's not easy to break those schedules." He looks through my kitchen cabinets and stops when he finds the maple syrup.

I sit down at my small bistro dining table that only seats two, situated a few feet from the kitchenette. "You're just jealous because my job is cooler than yours."

"You're probably right." A moment later, he places a plate in front of me with a pleased look on his face. He leans over my shoulder, bracing his weight on the back of my chair. I twist my head to look up at him. "Are you impressed?" he asks.

I take a startled breath when I realize just how close he is. "Quite impressed."

"Good."

My cheeks warm as he walks back over to the stove, and I'm glad he doesn't see it. I cut into my pancakes soon after as he sets his plate across from me and sits down at the table.

"When did you adopt Duke?" I ask before I take my first bite.

Ryan smiles a proud pup-dad smile as he sips his coffee. "I got him last April, and Big Boy will be four next month."

"What made you decide to adopt him?"

"It was my sister's idea. Sophie's obsessed with dogs. She has two of her own and she fosters a bunch for a rescue shelter in her area. She thought a dog would be good for me."

"Why's that?" I ask.

Side note, these pancakes are delicious. I have to exercise serious discipline not to scarf them down and instead take ladylike bites.

"She was always giving me grief about how much I worked or how much I went out. She thought a dog would give me a sense of balance."

"I see. So your sister performed a dog intervention."

"I guess she did. Anyways, I went to the shelter and it was love at first sight." He then begins to prepare his pancakes, but not in the traditional way. Rather, he cuts the pancakes into pieces and pushes them all to one side of the plate. He then proceeds to pour a pool of syrup onto the other side and dips each piece in before every bite. A wistful look crosses my face as I watch the strangely meticulous process. I forgot he ate his pancakes like that.

"That's really sweet," I eventually say, focusing back on our Duke discussion. "And do you like having a dog?"

"I love it. We play out in the backyard before work every morning and a dog-walker comes by midday. There are usually two scenarios when I get home from work. One, he's waiting for me by the door. Two, he's in my bed, drooling all over my pillow while eating a treat."

"I can picture that." I chuckle.

"Yeah, he's the best. When I drive home from work, it's nice to know he'll be there. He won't get sick of me or leave."

I start to smile but then stop as his words sink in. I look up and he looks down, taking a bite and giving the impression that he made some kind of mistake. With his seemingly boundless confidence, could Ryan have abandonment issues? Did I play a part in that? Did his parents? I'm trying to figure out what to say next when he quickly brightens back up and goes on, "He's just awesome. If having a dog is a preview for what kids will be like, I'm ready for it."

"Really?" I ask, choking on my food a bit. "You'd like to have kids soon?"

"I do. I want to be a youngish dad and after everything

that happened with my parents, having a family of my own
has become an important goal for me."

I guess I shouldn't be surprised, but I am.

"What about you?" he asks. "Do you see yourself having
kids?"

I take a break from eating, resting the edge of my fork
against the plate. "I guess I've always imagined myself as being
a mom. I don't know if it's going to happen soon but it's definitely something I want. I've just been so focused on my writing for the past few years that family thoughts have been more
a back-burner item for me than a pressing issue."

"That makes sense. I'm sure you'll be a great mom when
the time comes."

We both smile and manage to fill the next few minutes
with small talk until Ryan gets up from the table and cleans
his plate.

"So, I have some groomsman business I need to do today.
We're picking up our suits, grabbing some food, and then
Jason has it in his head that we should all buy matching shoes."

"Crocs or sneakers?"

"Neither, unfortunately. Would you be able to watch Duke
for a few hours? If it's too much, I can come back in between
errands to walk him and feed him."

"No, it's okay. I can manage."

"Are you sure?"

"Fully sure."

"That would be amazing." He walks over to his bag beside
the couch and pulls out a piece of paper. "I leave this behind
for anyone watching Duke. It's his walk schedule, his food
schedule and the exact amounts for all his food. Also, if you
want to go out without him at all, there's a suggested playlist
that always gets him to fall asleep. I'll text you a link so you
can download it. If you leave while he's sleeping, everything's

fine. If you leave while he's awake, he'll bark for hours and pee on every available surface."

"Play the playlist, don't leave when he's awake, got it."

Ryan walks back to the table, handing me the paper, and I quickly read it over. "There's a surprising amount of Celine Dion on here."

"He has a thing for powerful Canadian songbirds. There's a lid for every pot."

"It appears so."

"Well, I should head out. Jason said the lady at the suit place is trying to overcharge us, so I need to help smooth things over."

"And how do you plan to do that?" I ask, lowering the list to the table.

"I'm going to dazzle her with my wit and masculine good looks, obviously."

I sneer as I push my fork forward with the tip of my index finger. "Do you have a Plan B?"

He grabs his wallet and cell phone from the couch and slides them into his back pockets as he crosses the room to the entryway. "Why would I need a Plan B?"

"No reason," I say nonchalantly.

Ryan pauses. He leans back against the door with his arms set across his chest. "Do you doubt my wit and masculine good looks, Sullivan?"

I shrug as I continue to adjust my cutlery.

"Because I can recall quite a few times when you very much enjoyed my manly charms."

"I think you saying the words *manly charms* probably means you don't have any."

"I'm offended. Here I thought I was so smooth back in my heyday."

"Unfortunately not. Even in my favorite memories of you, you were only partly charming."

A playful grin crosses his face. "That's fair. In my favorite memories of you, you were only partly clothed, so I guess we're even."

My insides stir in a toasty way as a few of those memories come to mind. "Okay, move it along, freak. Let's quit while we're ahead."

"Yes, ma'am." He's reaching for the door when he suddenly turns and picks up a small paper bag that I didn't notice on the entryway table/bike rack. "I almost forgot," he says, walking back over and handing it to me, "I got this for you when I took Duke for a walk this morning. I remembered they were your favorite."

I take the bag, noticing the logo of a bakery a few blocks away printed on the front. I reach inside and pull out a delectable cinnamon scone that's somehow still warm. I can't stop the smile that spreads across my face. When we were at school, Ryan would surprise me with cinnamon scones at least once a week after he found out how much I loved them. The act itself was considerate, but what I loved most about them was that they meant he was thinking of me when I wasn't there.

The memories leave me feeling slightly off kilter as I place the scone onto the table. "Thank you," I say, trying to sound less affected than I am. "They're still my favorite."

"I'm glad," he replies.

"By the way, I can't believe they let you in with Duke. I've been there a bunch of times and they never allow pets inside."

"Come on, Sullivan. There's not a person alive who can resist that face."

I follow his gaze and look over at Duke. He's sitting on the floor a few feet away, vigorously scratching behind his ear as he stumbles over a bit onto his side. Ryan's right. Duke is too adorable to be real.

"All right," he then says, "I'll leave you to enjoy that. Shoot me a text if you have any questions."

"Will do."

"I'll see you tonight. Good luck." Ryan gives me a good-bye salute as he exits, and Duke follows his path to sit by the door, already waiting for him to come back.

"Duke," I groan as I drop my head down on the table. "What the hell am I doing?"

An hour later, Duke and I arrive at Maggie's studio apartment in the Theater District. Teaming with rehearsal spaces and theatrical agencies, this is the neighborhood where Maggie can potentially bump into musical cast members in their down time. She claims she lives in the area for the competitive rent, but I think the selfie she took last week with half of the ensemble of *Hamilton* in a local tapas restaurant speaks for itself.

"Whoa, whoa. What is this?" Maggie's eyes bulge as Duke charges easily into the space.

"This is Ryan's dog."

"Come again?"

"His name is Duke and he and Ryan are staying with me for the next few days."

"We don't talk for one day and this is what happens? Wait, did you ride over here?"

"No, though I did try. Duke was pumped to get in the basket but there's no way it was strong enough to hold him. My life flashed before my eyes after going ten feet."

Maggie shuts the door behind us as I give her the abbreviated version of the last twenty-four hours. I've just finished and am leaning down to unhook Duke's leash when he begins to pant at an alarming rate.

"Is he okay?" Maggie asks.

I squat in front of him, petting his neck and back in sooth-ing strokes as I try to calm him down. "Maybe he's not used to going up four flights of stairs after a long walk. I know he goes outside a fair bit, but I don't know how far he usually goes." Duke is still huffing and puffing as I nervously pet him faster. "It's okay," I coo. "Let's just relax. Everything's all right."

"He looks like he's having a heart attack. Do dogs have heart attacks?"

"Just get him some water before he passes out."

Maggie scurries into the kitchen and starts swinging open cabinets. "I swear, Kara, if that animal drops dead in my apart-ment I will never forgive you."

"He'll be fine. He's just not the most athletic guy in the world."

Maggie sets a large bowl of water onto the floor and I keep petting Duke as he drinks it down. His breathing evens out and a minute later, he sets off on the prowl. I follow his path until he settles into the bathroom, sprawling out and looking spent. Confident that he's now okay, I cross the room to plop down at a bar stool beside Maggie's tiny kitchen island as she falls back onto her couch.

"Well," she says, "you two certainly know how to make an entrance. Is life always this eventful over in the love nest?"

I pause before answering. "It's okay, I guess."

"I refuse to believe that you came all the way over here with no good stories. You're not that cruel."

"I just feel strange talking about this."

"If you're worried about being strange, you're about five minutes and one obese bulldog too late."

"Fair enough. I think…" I take a deep breath and let it all rip. "I think I might still have feelings for Ryan and I don't want to and I need you to help me make it stop." The words spill out of my mouth like a quick-flowing stream and Maggie stares back at me, completely deadpan.

We're several seconds into utter silence when she says, "If this is happening, I need coffee." She hops up and grabs her purse and keys from off the coffee table. "Will Duke be okay if we run out for a few minutes or do you think he'll ransack the place?"

I get up to check on him and find him already asleep on Maggie's bathroom tiles. Celine wasn't even necessary.

"We can go but we have to be quick. There aren't any choking hazards around here, are there?" I quickly look around to double-check, but Maggie is surprisingly minimalistic besides her multiple instruments. Knowing Duke will be safe, I set an alarm on my phone for twenty minutes. "Okay, let's go."

A few blocks later, Maggie and I are sitting across from each other in Frisson Espresso, Maggie's favorite coffee house, on 46th Street. The charming shop is on the smaller side, but the white walls and colorful art make it feel chic and cozy rather than crowded and claustrophobic.

Two baristas man the lone espresso machine, creating individualized coffee that doubles as art. My mocha latte has a tulip foam design that is so intricate, it seems wrong to drink. It's too late to know if Maggie's iced coffee had a foam design since she's essentially inhaling it.

We snag seats in the corner and even though the table next to ours is nearly on top of us, we're comfortable. I take my first sip as Maggie finally comes up for air and places her coffee onto the table.

"Okay, I am now properly caffeinated. Speak."

I suddenly wish I was drinking wine instead of a latte. "Well, like I said, I think I may still have feelings for Ryan and I need you to help me make those feeling go away as quickly as possible."

"Yeah," Maggie says, seeming unmoved. "I'm going to go ahead and not participate in any of that."

"Why not? You have to help me. This is bad."

"Why is it bad?"

"It's bad because our past has way too much baggage, plus I'm not even sure if he's interested in me or he's just using me for my couch."

"Are we back at this again? Of course he's interested in you, Kara. How did he act this morning?" She picks up her coffee and twists it around, swirling the ice inside the cup.

I sit back in my chair. "He was fine."

"But what was he like?"

"He was normal." Then quietly, "He made pancakes."

Deep silence ensues.

"I'm sorry, I must have misheard you. Can you repeat that one more time?"

I pick at the edge of my cup with the tip of my finger. "I said he made pancakes."

Maggie slams her drink down onto the table. "Come on, Kara! Everyone knows that pancakes are the international breakfast food of love. You guys are absolutely getting back together, so I don't want to hear any more complaints. You're losing your mind and you're taking me with you."

"It's not that simple," I try to explain.

"Ugh, fine. So you guys have a tortured, soap opera past. So what?"

"It's not just that. How can I be with Ryan when he and I were the reason for what happened with my dad?"

"What are you talking about?" Maggie voice is peppered with confusion. "You and Ryan didn't cause anything with your dad. That was just bad timing."

I shake my head. I shouldn't have brought that part up. That's just for me.

"Never mind that bit. I just don't think Ryan sees me that way."

"Yes, he does see you that way, and I know for a fact that you can get him back with minimal effort. People will wait in line at the DMV for a substantially longer time than it will take for you to rekindle this romance."

I take a big sip of my coffee, tulip or no tulip.

"Straight men want women, Kara. It's as simple as that. It doesn't matter if it's their wife, a girlfriend, an ex-girlfriend or the friendly but eccentric band geek from their senior year music composition class."

"That last description feels very specific to you."

"It was. Kurt Wyatt and I went on to have many a tryst in the instrument storage closet. I still think about those days fondly." She gazes off into the distance for a bit until I clear my throat and she focuses on our conversation. "So yes, all I'm saying is that if a guy sees a woman and he's attracted to her, then he wants her. And if he's single, he'll go after her if she even slightly alludes to the fact that she wants him, too."

"But I don't want Ryan just to want me."

"Then what do you want?"

I take a second to think about it. "I don't know. I want more than that."

"You want more, meaning you want him to love you again."

I don't correct her. I don't tell her no. I should. I need to.

"You do," she affirms. "You want him to love you again."

"I didn't say that."

"You don't have to. What is it about him that's so special anyways? I've never seen you this wound up over a guy before."

"I don't know." I find myself glancing around the café, feeling like I shouldn't be talking about this and, more importantly, that I shouldn't be having these feelings at all. "He's just different. He's nice and he's absurdly great with Duke. He's weird but in a quirky, interesting way. He thinks I'm funny, so I let my guard down with him. I consider myself a happily boring person, but to him, I'm exciting. I just like seeing myself the way he sees me, I guess."

I stop there as Maggie looks over at me as if two huge cartoon hearts are bulging out of her eye sockets.

"You are going to marry him," she says. "You're going to marry him or you're going to have mind-blowing, bodice-ripping, otherworldly sex with him and I'm entirely okay with either option."

My cheeks streak red and the skin on my neck starts to itch. "This whole conversation is ridiculous and I'm pretty sure it's giving me hives. Falling back into something with Ryan is the last thing I should be doing right now."

"No, it's not," Maggie argues. "You like this guy and you deserve to feel wanted and I'm going to help you. Making a man fall in love with you is the same as making him want you, just with a couple of extra steps. And it will be even easier for you because Ryan already loved you once so all we have to do is make him love you again. It's like renewing a library book. You love library books."

"I do love library books, but what about the fact that I'm going to Italy in less than a week? Isn't it selfish for me to pursue this when I'm about to leave?"

"It is in no way selfish. Just because there isn't a picture-perfect future cemented in place doesn't mean that you shouldn't go after what you want."

Her argument is sound. But then again, she's saying what an ashamed part of me wants to hear.

"First things first. You have to make Ryan want you, but

that shouldn't be a problem since you guys have already been together. By the way, what was this troublemaker like in bed?"

I push my chair back to distance myself from the table. "Yeah, I changed my mind, I'm not doing this."

"Will you relax? I'm not telling you to throw him to the floor and bang him into oblivion—though I do think that's a good option. What I mean is, you have to get him thinking about you in that kind of light again. Plant the seeds, so to speak."

"And how do you suggest I plant the seeds?"

"Are you seriously asking me that? You're bestselling romance novelist Kara Sullivan! You should be a lust-game master. How do the people get together in your novels? Do you use any sort of formula?"

"I don't think of it like a formula, but I guess there are certain steps I take to get my characters together."

"Good. Let's start there." Maggie looks over to the woman at the next table, who is working on her laptop with an open notebook beside it. "Hi, I'm sorry but can we borrow a piece of paper and a pen?"

The woman hesitates for a second and looks from Maggie to me. I give her a smile, hoping we're not creeping her out.

"Sure," the woman hesitantly says, tearing a piece of paper out of her book and handing it over with a pen from her bag.

"Thank you so much." Maggie takes the paper and pen and immediately gets to work. She writes *Seducing the Cowboy* on the top of the sheet and underlines it.

"Hey, that would be a good title for a book. You think you could use it someday?"

"I'm going to go ahead and guess that there's a lot of books with that title."

"Figures. It's catchy."

I squirm in my seat, growing more uncomfortable by the second. Maggie holds her pen at the ready.

"Okay, so what's step one?"

I take a breath and at the end of a few minutes, Maggie has written out all the basic steps my characters typically go through to find love, in her own words. The list states:

1. *They meet.*
2. *They have issues—internal and external.*
3. *They have goals.*
4. *One or both need the other to achieve said goals.*
5. *They clash (smooch).*
6. *They're drawn together (hard-core smooch).*
7. *They clash again (smooch and over-the-shirt stuff).*
8. *They're really, really drawn together (smooch and under-the-shirt stuff).*
9. *They give in (full enchilada).*
10. *It all falls apart.*
11. *I hate you.*
12. *I love you.*
13. *Happily-ever-after and babies.*

"Now," Maggie says, reviewing the list and drawing another column, "let's add some romance-novel-specific actions that you and Ryan can accomplish."

"This makes no sense. Fiction isn't applicable to real life."

"Let's just see. Give me the actions."

I sigh and rub my hands on my thighs as I think. Five minutes later, Maggie's second self-worded list is complete, now in bullet points.

• *Throw the flag—challenge the heroes, get under their skin.*
• *Touchy-feely time—create physical contact (i.e. trip, fall, horse-*

back activities won't work here). Once they're close, chemis-
try takes over.

- *Anger hookup—argue, get in each other's faces and then get*
  frisky to ease the tension.
- *Oh, hey, other handsome stranger—make him jealous.*
- *Cheers! Heroine and hero get drunk.*
- *Secrets, secrets are so fun—have one or both reveal something*
  deeply personal. Now it's them against the world.

"This looks promising," Maggie says when she's written her last point. "And one more thing…" She lifts the pen once more, putting a *1* next to the first column, a *2* next to the second column and then a *3* next to something she scribbles at the bottom of the page. She hands me the paper a moment later and I skip to the end.

3. Ciao! Finish that book and off to Italy.

"You're welcome," she says.

My cell phone timer then starts to ring, reminding me it's time to get back to Duke.

"We better go," I say, folding up the paper and sliding it into my bag.

"Off we march into battle." Maggie finishes the last of her coffee and gets up to toss the cup into the trash beside the door. I'm sliding my chair back and standing up as well when the woman sitting beside us gives me a little wave, trying to get my attention.

"I'm sorry," she says, "but I couldn't help overhearing pieces of your conversation. Did your friend say that you're Kara Sullivan?"

I'm caught off guard but quickly respond with a small smile. "Yeah, that's me."

The woman seems flustered by my response but smiles back.

"Oh, my gosh! I have to tell you, I've read all of your books and they really are just wonderful."

I'm flattered by this lovely lady with exceptional taste in literature. "Thank you so much. I'm glad you enjoyed them. It was nice meeting you."

"Oh, you too!" she says. I'm poised to leave when she leans forward again in her chair. "I'm sorry, but I have to ask you... Do you—do you just lead such a romantic life?"

I look down at my hopeful reader as Maggie walks out the door. I say the first thing that comes to my mind.

"I'm working on it."

Maggie and I are standing in the doorway outside her bathroom, looking down lovingly at the still-passed-out Duke. His tongue is dangling out of his mouth and his feet shimmy a little with each passing snore.

"Why does he sleep in the bathroom?" Maggie asks.

"Don't know. Ryan says he has since he got him."

"Sounds like you have a couple of winners on your hands."

"Ah yes," I agree, leaning down to attach Duke's leash to his collar and petting him awake. "They're two princes, all right."

He wakes up with a big stretch and I gently lead him across the room.

"So just to recap," Maggie says, sneaking in front of me to hold open her apartment door, "don't be you tonight. Tonight, you are one of your sexy, brave characters who fears nothing and gets exactly what she wants."

"I am fully prepared to consider that suggestion."

"Not quite the commitment I'm looking for, but I guess I'll take it. I want to hear all about it tomorrow."

"And so you shall," I say as Duke and I walk out into the hallway. He's more than hesitant when we reach the top of the stairwell but eventually starts to descend after a little coaxing.

"Now remember," Maggie calls out as Duke and I finish the first flight of stairs, "try not to stress too much, and when in doubt, think romance novel!" Her door slams shut a second later and her advice rings out in my ears.

Think romance novel. Think romance novel...

My inner mantra is soon interrupted when the shrill sound of dog barks echoes through the stairwell from somewhere below. Duke takes off in a fury down the stairs and I'm propelled forward by his sheer weight and momentum. It takes all the balance I possess to keep my footing as I slide down the steps on the heels of my feet.

"Duke! Stay!" I beg.

He drags me faster as we hit the main floor and go barreling through the foyer. I turn sideways, tensing myself for impact as I slam into the entrance door, thinking it's an absolute miracle that it didn't shatter. Duke goes up on his back paws, jumping against the glass and barking nonstop at the small but noisy Chihuahua standing on the other side.

I close my eyes and grab my shoulder as intense pain shoots up and down my arm.

Well, I can't say that any of my romance novel heroines have rocked an arm splint in the midst of their scandalous seductions, but I suppose there's a first time for everything.

10

Charlotte's breath ripped from her chest as she ran out onto the deserted balcony facing the eastern edge of the estate. She looked skyward as she struggled to calm herself, concentrating on filling her lungs with the crisp night air. She assumed she was alone, but she should have known Robert would follow her out into the darkness.

"Are you all right?" he asked as he moved to her side.

Still gazing up into an endless pool of stars, Charlotte steadied her voice. It wouldn't do for him to know that she was crying. "I'm fine. Just tired."

Robert moved closer still, trailing his fingers against hers. Charlotte sighed at the soft contact.

"George said you and your father had an argument."

"We do that quite often." Charlotte moved her fingers back against his. She knew it was wrong, but she didn't care. She couldn't stop. "I thought George had gone up to bed. I'll go speak to him."

She began to walk away but Robert took hold of her wrist and pulled her back. As he looked down at her tearstained cheeks, something primal curled up and snapped inside him. He would have loved to beat Phillip Destonbury to a bloody pulp, but the look in Charlotte's eye stopped him. She needed him and he would not leave her. Not for the world.

"What did your father say to you?" he asked.

She slowly met his eyes, wanting so much to be wrapped in the comfort she knew he would give. "He said I'm becoming a useless shrew just like my mother. He said I'm spoiled and willful and if I don't do everything in my power to convince you to marry me, he will make me live to regret it."

Robert's free hand balled into a fist. If he heard much more, he didn't doubt that he would throw Charlotte over his shoulder and take her away from this place forever, consequences be damned. "Tell me what I can do to help you. Tell me how to make this right and I will."

"I want to forget things for a while," she whispered, her voice breaking. "Can I do that? Just for one night?"

She didn't wait for an answer. Charlotte turned to Robert and wrapped her arms around his neck, pulling him down to crash her lips to his. Robert was surprised but more than willing as his arms instantly locked around her waist. She had finally come to him on her own and he had no intention of letting her go.

The kiss escalated as the two finally crossed some kind of invisible line. Charlotte opened her mouth to him, demanding more and kissing him with an innocent abandon that nearly brought Robert to his knees. He answered her passion with a growl and fitted her even more tightly against him.

Time slid away until Charlotte pulled back, gasping for air. The look in Robert's eyes sent delicious shivers through every inch of her.

"Come to my room tonight," he pleaded, bending forward

*to kiss the side of her throat. "Once the house is asleep, I'll
send my valet to bring you to me. Say yes. Be mine, even if
only for tonight."*

*Charlotte tilted her head back, giving Robert full access to
the sensitive skin along her neck. "Yes," she whispered. "Yours,
tonight…"*

I stop typing with a naughty smirk. Things are about to get
real in Greenspeak Park! My oven timer sounds a second
later, forcing me away from my characters, who are completely
ready to go for the gold.

To be continued.

I close my laptop and rush from my desk to the kitchenette.

I ignore the persistent ache in my shoulder as I put the finishing touches on my fettuccini alfredo, pushing through the
pain and stirring another handful of cheese into the thicken-
ing sauce. Once I'm satisfied, I turn off the burner and cover
the pot with a glass lid. The clock on the stove reads 6:34.
Ryan said he'd be back around this time.

I untie the bib apron that I still have from when I was a
barista at a bookshop in college and toss it onto the counter,
revealing a pale blue T-shirt with a gray sweater and navy yoga
pants. I originally wore jeans, but they felt too fancy and I'm
attempting to come off as cute yet casual while also giving
off the impression that maybe I do yoga.

Deciding to partake in some liquid courage, I take a half-
full bottle of Riesling out of the fridge and pour myself a glass
before I head into the living room. It's not like I *need* liquid
courage, though. All I'm doing is cooking a meal for an attractive man who I have tons of emotional ties to while trying to
live out a romance novel outline in the hopes of finishing my
book and sparking a physical relationship that could possibly

lead to something more, but probably not because I would be dishonoring my father and going straight to hell.

Yeah, I take a big ol' sip of my wine.

I'm sitting down on the couch next to Duke when I hear the lock turning in the door over the Van Morrison I have playing. I take another sip of wine and roll my neck.

It's go time.

"Hey," Ryan says as he enters the apartment. He's holding a large black garment bag in one hand and smaller bag with a shoebox inside in the other. Duke flings himself off the couch to jump and claw at Ryan's legs, his butt shaking in excitement in a painfully adorable way.

Ryan hooks the bags on the hanging coatrack that's mounted beside my bike and leans down to give Duke a good scratching. "Hey, buddy. What's going on?" He stands back up after a few seconds and looks over at me with a smile. "Hi."

"Hey. How'd everything go?"

"It was good," he says. "Wedding attire is hereby done and for the record, I did get the lady to lower the price, so if you wanted to submit your apology to me in writing, I'll give you some time to do that." I roll my eyes and Ryan goes on, "How were things around here?"

"Everything went fine. Me and Duke hung out and I got some writing done."

"That sounds nice. I'm a little jealous."

"Yeah, we're quite the dynamic duo. I don't want to rub it in your face, but he straight-up told me he likes me better than you."

"I bet. Well, despite his turncoat love for you, I'm glad you guys had a good day."

"Thank you. You want some wine?" I get up from the couch and walk over to the kitchen area before he answers.

Ryan meets me there, seeming unsure as he watches me

pour him a glass of Riesling. It's probably not his drink of choice but he'll have to make do since I don't like beer. I wish I did. I always wanted to be a cool, beer-drinking girl, but the scent of the stuff is just so off-putting. If I had to imagine what a bottle of fermented armpit juice would smell like after sitting out in the Nevada sun for a month and a half, my guess would be beer.

"I've never had white wine before," Ryan says.

"Well, as a connoisseur, I promise you this bottle is quite lovely."

"It's strange to think that you barely drank in college. You went from zero to wasted in two drinks flat."

"I'm still a bit of a lightweight but I have gained some experience since then."

"Oh, really?" Ryan asks. "I might need you to prove that to me."

Prove my experience? With him? Um, okay!

"So how was your day?" I ask unsteadily as I finish pouring his glass.

Ryan twists around to lean back against the kitchenette counter as he picks up his wine. "You already asked me that."

Crap.

"Did I?"

"Yes, but I'd be glad to go again. My day was good. It was weird not being at work, though. It felt like I was skipping class."

"Don't you ever take a day off just for fun?"

"Not really. Why would I?"

For some reason, Ryan's words give me pause. Is he so set in his routine that taking a day off doesn't even cross his mind? Or does he have nothing or no one worth slowing down for? Whatever the case, I don't want to press him. Rather, I turn to the stove and pull the lid off the pot of fettuccini.

"You hungry?" I ask.

Two minutes later, we're settled at the dining table with our food hot and plated in front of us. I'm about to dig in when Ryan lifts his glass.

"I'd like to make a toast," he says. "Thank you for making this amazing meal, for taking care of Duke and for letting us stay here. Cheers."

"Cheers," I say with an embarrassed smile.

We take a sip of our wine and place the glasses back onto the table. The pasta smells impressively tempting and we're soon digging in.

"Tell me more about your job," I say when I eventually take a breather.

"There's not much to it but I really like it. It's what I always wanted." A tired sort of smile crosses his face and I wonder what it means. I'm about to ask when he goes on, "Most of the time I make project speculations and apply coding rules. I visit and inspect building sites and review designs. I mean, I'd obviously prefer to be a professional golfer or an international spy, but this will do for now."

I smirk, shaking off my previous concern. "I'm thinking you're probably better off as a golfer. I can't picture you as a spy."

"Why not?" he asks seriously.

"Because you're not suave enough. Spies need to be well-rounded. They have to blend into places, speak different languages, dance…"

"Whoa, whoa, whoa," Ryan says, pausing his fork as it twists in his fettuccini. "I know how to dance."

I choke on my wine slightly as I swallow down my laugh. Ryan glares at me and I wipe my chin where some of my drink trickled down.

He drops his fork altogether. "I don't think I like what you're insinuating, Sullivan."

"Really? What am I insinuating?"

"You were scoffing at me."

"Did I scoff?"

"Yes, you scoffed when I said I could dance."

I join him in resting my fork down on the edge of my plate. "Okay, I feel bad telling you this since you've somehow made it to adulthood without learning the truth. Please know this comes from a place of honesty and friendship...but you are arguably the worst dancer in the entire world."

"What? I am an amazing dancer!"

Poor guy. He really has no idea.

"Okay, I was a kid the very few times we did dance and I have changed a lot since then. You know what? You need a demonstration." His demeanor is pure determination as he slides his chair away from the table. "And just know, once I start, I can't be held responsible if you faint. That has been known to happen to the women I take out dancing."

"That I do believe," I say in earnest. "But when these women did faint, was it because they were so utterly mortified or were they just laughing too hard that their bodies physically shut down? Or were you too busy bouncing around like a kangaroo on crack to notice?"

"Damn. You're in for it now, Sullivan." Ryan gets up and strides over to his computer that's on the couch, opening his music library and double clicking on his chosen song. A fast-paced dance tune fills the room as he turns back to face me and kicks his sneakers off one by one.

"Oh, boy," I say, "the shoes are coming off. Should I expect high-kicks?"

"There's no telling what you should expect. Once the lord of the dance is released from societal chains, he does whatever feels right."

"That sounds ominous."

"Ominously rhythmic and sensual."

Ryan moves into a standing leg stretch and I smile and shake my head. "You really have gotten so much weirder with age. What do they put in the water in North Carolina?"

"Mainly testosterone and Cheerwine." Ryan rolls his shoulders backward and forward and proceeds to pull his arms across his chest like a pitcher.

"A demonstration really isn't necessary," I say, raising my voice to be heard over the now-pumping music.

"I think a demonstration *is* necessary unless you admit that I have moves."

"Can't do it," I automatically respond.

"Say I have moves."

"Honor forbids it."

"Fine. Remember, you were warned." Without another word, Ryan claps his hands together. He whips a hip to one side with a shimmy-shake and I shut my eyes, refusing to watch the embarrassing dad-dance of a now-desperate man.

"Okay, you have moves!" I yell. "You have serious moves!"

I crack an eye open and see that Ryan is now frozen in place.

"Are you sure?" he asks, fully prepared to start dancing again if I change my mind.

"I'm sure."

He gives me a victorious smile before standing up straight, clicking off the music and returning to the table. "I knew you'd eventually admit the truth." He sits back down and takes a dignified sip of wine.

"You're deranged," I tell him, picking up my fork. "Can we have dinner now? Is the lord of the dance all tuckered out after that little display?"

"Dinner may continue. Dazzling a lady with my dance skills always makes me hungry."

Before I know it, we've finished our second glasses of wine, dinner is done, and I get up to start doing the dishes.

"Let me help you," Ryan says as he begins clearing the table.

We quickly get a system going where he scrapes the dishes and pots clean and hands them to me before I rinse and load the dishwasher. Five minutes later, the kitchenette is spotless and we're heading into the living room.

Duke is already sleeping in the bathroom as I sit down in my reading chair, bending my knees as my feet rest against the ottoman. Ryan settles himself on the couch and flips on the TV to watch baseball highlights. He used to sit like that in college. The only difference is, I would be tucked against his side with his arm around me, reading a book and feeling so safe that I'd almost always fall asleep.

"Can I ask you something?" I venture.

"If you're trying to find out what I charge for dance lessons, you should know that I'm industry-level. I cost more because I'm worth more."

"Obviously," I agree. "No, I was wondering…what did you do after we broke up?"

Ryan fumbles with the remote for a second as he turns away from the TV to look at me. "Why do you ask?"

Because I want to know. I want to know what happened to the boy I used to fall asleep with on the couch.

"Idle curiosity. I started writing for the first time a few months after."

Ryan puts the TV on mute. "I started working out a lot. I think people would have been impressed, but I also grew an off-putting beard, so they kind of cancelled each other out."

"I doubt that," I say lightly, "I'm pretty sure ninety-eight percent of the dating pool would vote 'yes' for a muscular bearded man."

"No, I'm not talking about a scruffy, emotionally-wounded

lumberjack beard. I mean a creepy, belligerent old-fisherman-blacked-out-at-the-end-of-the-bar kind of beard. Think Forest Gump in the last leg of his cross-country run."

"Those were highly effective visuals."

"I try my best. So, yeah, I went through a temporary werewolf metamorphosis while you jump-started your literary career. I guess one of us handled the split better."

"I think I would have started writing regardless if we broke up or not. You were just the springboard that made me move at a faster pace."

"How did you decide what to write?" Ryan asks.

I get more comfortable in the chair, pulling a blue fleece blanket up to cover my legs as I lean back into the cushions. We set a timer for the thermostat, so the room is already getting chilly.

"I was sitting on the stoop at my mom's house one day as I finished reading what felt like my millionth romance novel. I tried to imagine what I would come up with if I were a novelist and decided to write a chapter. I went inside and was done an hour later. I printed it out, gave it to my mom and she liked it."

"And a writer was born."

"After that I just kept going. I took it one chapter at a time and gave each one to my mom for feedback. It was nice for us. It was a good distraction from my dad."

Ryan smiles but it's not happy. It's regretful.

"It also felt amazing to have my mom enjoying something I wrote. She's never thrown a lot of praise my way, so I was basking in it whenever she would read my work."

"I'm sure she's proud of you now, though. You're a successful author, self-made and living in New York City. You're a great person. She probably brags about you all the time."

"I doubt it," I mutter, knowing too well how in her eyes, I still don't measure up.

"Why would you say that?" Ryan seems genuinely confused and in a strange way, it makes me feel better. He thinks I'm someone worth bragging about.

"It doesn't matter. She's just hard to impress."

"Sophie and I could do no wrong in our mom's eyes after my dad left. It was like everything we did had this perfect glow around it."

The room falls quiet until we hear Duke snoring with rumbling force. I never realized my apartment had such good acoustics. Ryan and I both grin at each other.

"When the divorce was getting finalized, my mom kept telling me that she and my dad met too young. She swore their marriage would have lasted if they started dating in their twenties instead of when they were sixteen." Ryan's gaze shifts to the floor before turning it back to me. "You think if we met now instead of in college that things would be different?"

My heart starts to beat faster. "Maybe. But if we didn't meet in college, you and I might never have spoken at the pre-wedding party."

"But we would have eventually met at the wedding," he says.

"True. I'd be stuck in my uncomfortable maid of honor dress and counting down the minutes until I could take off my heels and sneak on the sandals I stashed in my bag."

"You'd be having a mini-stroke about giving your speech. We'd sneak off to the bar right before to take the edge off."

"You'd be a bad influence on me."

"We'd have a great night. You'd talk more than you usually do."

"You'd talk less than *you* usually do. You'd show me a bunch of pictures of Duke on your phone to butter me up."

"I knew it would work since you seemed so sweet."

"And then the night would wind down."

"I'd ask you for your number."

"I'd tell you I don't normally give out my number, but I'd make an exception for you."

"I'd text you that night and tell you it was great meeting you."

"I'd wonder if you'd call me the next week."

"I'd call the next day."

"And that would be that."

"That would be that."

We look at each other, slipping out of our made-up reality and back into the one that actually exists.

I sit up in my chair, straightening out my legs and pulling the blanket up higher. "Or maybe we would have had a cordial first meeting at the pre-wedding party and nothing more. You would have hooked up with one of Cristina's work friends and we never would have spoken again."

"You might have met someone else in college and got married young. You'd show up to the wedding in your minivan full of Cheerios crumbs with your husband and five kids."

"It's very possible," I say. "I guess we'll never know."

"Guess not."

I take a slow breath, feeling a little light-headed and confused after our impromptu "what if" role-play. I pause for a second before clapping my hands onto my knees. "I think it's time to call it a night." I get up from the chair, pushing off the blanket and leaving it on the ottoman. "If you're compelled to perform any more jigs this evening, I'd appreciate it if you kept the volume down."

"I can do that."

I give him two thumbs up and walk towards my bedroom but stop midway, deciding to take off my sweater to leave in the living room for tomorrow. Facing away from him, I bend my arms behind my back and slip the sweater down. It's nearly off when my left sleeve somehow gets caught on the claddagh ring I forgot I was wearing on my right hand. My arm is now pinned tightly behind my back like I'm in a straitjacket.

How befitting.

I push my shoulder blades back in hopes of freeing my ring but end up feeling a piercing pain in my left shoulder. I can't help but let out a small yelp.

"What's the matter?" Ryan asks, immediately getting up.

"It's nothing. I'm fine." I desperately try to wiggle out of the sweater. I push my shoulder back again and suck in a loud breath from the sting.

Ryan is now standing behind me with his hands on my shoulders. "You're not fine," he says in a somewhat stern voice, gently tugging at my sweater. "What happened to your arm?"

I feel him slip his hand into my sleeve and over my wrist, twisting the ring around on my finger.

"It's just sore. I banged my shoulder a bit when I took Duke for his walk today."

I'm quickly freed as Ryan pulls the ring off my finger and the sweater down my arms, placing them both onto the coffee table. I turn around to face him and am surprised when he doesn't move away.

"Banged it on what?" he asks.

"It's actually a funny story." I try to get comfortable with Ryan's close proximity but it's easier said than done. "Duke and I were leaving my friend's apartment this afternoon when he got excited and kind of ran down the stairs full force."

Ryan's eyes remain locked on mine. "And he pulled your shoulder out?"

"No. I didn't fall or anything, but he dragged me along for a few seconds and I wound up crashing into a door."

My explanation earns me a pitying look. "I'm sorry, Sullivan. I should have told you Duke can get overexcited on his walks."

"It's fine. I probably won't even feel it tomorrow." I'm gearing up for my next retreat when Ryan turns me back around and pulls me towards him. "What are you doing?" I immediately ask.

"Where does it hurt? Here?" His hands slip under and past the neck of my shirt to squeeze the bare skin of my shoulders.

"You don't have to do that," I say, in no way wanting him to stop but also feeling somehow guilty.

"Will you relax? This is my fault. The least I can do is rub your shoulders."

I decide not to argue. It's just a shoulder rub. No need to fight it. I stare straight ahead at the row of books in front of me, thinking I'll rank them in descending order, but the titles all seem blurry.

Ryan shifts the top of my shirt over to one side, pulling it down to expose my left shoulder even more and rubbing the sensitive knot. It's starting to take more concentration to regulate my breathing.

After that, I don't know if I move backwards or he moves forward, but his chest brushes up against my spine and I can feel the firmness of his muscles through the fabric of our clothes. We're pushed up against each other now, so much so that I almost brace myself against the bookcase in front of me.

His hands slip down my arms and back up again, leaving a trail of sensitive heat everywhere he skims. He follows the same quiet rhythm and repeats it several times before his hands stop moving by my wrists. I look down as our fingers intertwine. I can feel his breath against the back of my neck, giving me goose bumps and making my shirt feel impossibly tight.

I'm nervous and curious and hungry to feel more and all of a sudden, Maggie's seduction list comes barreling into my mind.

If I were the shy, cautious version of myself, I'd thank Ryan for the massage and walk away. If I were the romance-novel version of myself, I would turn and face him. One of the actions on the list was to create physical contact. If I'm ever going to check that item off, the time is now.

My breath is shaky as I shift around to meet Ryan's gaze. It's as heated as mine and none of this seems real, like I'm living inside some nostalgically sexy fever dream. His fingers untangle from mine and his hands slide to the small of my back, scrunching the material of my shirt together in his tight grip as he pulls me closer. Being surrounded by him feels incredible. My hands skate up his arms and shoulders, barely brushing the surface until my fingers push into the hair at the nape of his neck. His eyes almost close as his forehead rests against mine.

"I've missed this," he says, his tone lulling and deep. "You have no idea how much."

No cynical inner voice whispers insults into my ear. No pangs of doubt or embarrassment scratch under my skin. My mind goes quiet. Blissfully quiet.

"I've missed this, too." I'm speaking in a breathy kind of voice that I've only ever written about.

One of his hands move to graze the curve of my waist while the other brushes up along my throat. His thumb rests just under my jaw to tilt my face upwards.

"We should stop," he says, even though he keeps on touching me.

"Then stop," I whisper.

He swallows but doesn't move. His hand grips my waist tighter.

I go up on the tips of my toes and brush my lips against his. He pulls back an inch with a shallow breath and I drink it in.

It's not enough. I'm impatient and agitated, a match scratching against a rough surface, trying to spark. I kiss him again, increasing the pressure. Ryan lets out something between a sigh and growl as he drags me forward, squeezing our bodies impossibly closer. I gasp and his tongue sweeps into my mouth. My stomach flips in all the right ways. I can't believe we used to do this all the time.

A minute passes but the sensations only get stronger. I want to melt into him. I feel like I might. His right hand moves from my neck to my breast as he kisses me with a hunger I'm just starting to remember. I'm as starved as him. I arch my back into his touch, feeling myself inching closer to a familiar precipice despite being fully clothed. We're both panting when I lean back a minute later, my eyes searching his.

And just like that, it's over.

Ryan steps back, suddenly holding me at arm's length, and the absence of his body heat makes the room unbearably cold. I almost shudder from the lack of it.

"I'm sorry," he quickly says. He's breathing like he just ran a mile while trying to pretend that he didn't. "I'm sorry, I…" He doesn't finish his sentence. His hands slowly fall away from me and a dazed expression remains on my face as I wait for him to offer some kind of reassurance. Anything. Nothing comes.

I step back as best I can on my wobbly legs. "I didn't mean to do that," I find myself saying. "I don't know why I did that."

"No, that was my fault. I got carried away."

I nod my head and Ryan looks around the room, looks everywhere except at me. I get a sinking feeling in my gut but I hide it well.

When he finally looks at me, he's resigned and almost disappointed. "I guess we should get some sleep."

What in the actual hell is happening?

"Yeah. Okay, good night."

I begin to turn around when I hear, "Sullivan, wait a second."

I pause, again hoping for some sense clarity. "What?" I ask.

He just keeps looking at me, saying nothing. I'm not convinced he knows why he asked me to wait. Silence stretches wider and thicker between us until his cell phone starts to ring on the kitchen table. I move towards it, planning on handing it to him when he steps in front of me.

"It's okay, I'll get it," he says. I watch as he picks it up and silences it before sliding it into his pocket. Feeling more awkward with each passing moment, I turn around and head for my bedroom.

"Thank you for tonight. For dinner," Ryan says to my back.

I pause in the doorway but don't look at him again. "You're welcome. See you tomorrow." I go directly into my room and shut the door, holding it closed and leaning forward, too shaken to move.

That was not a drill.

Ryan told me he missed me. I kissed him. He kissed me back, and then it was like nothing happened.

But it did happen.

I begin to feel oddly lethargic and change into my pajamas a couple minutes later, sneaking outside and moving in and out of the bathroom like a ghost to avoid waking Duke or seeing Ryan. Back in my room, I crawl into bed and pull the sheets up all around me as I roll onto my side to face the window. I nuzzle into my ice-cold pillow and allow one quick, sleepy smile as I almost immediately drift off to sleep.

11

I pick up the small piece of paper from my coffee table for the third time, still annoyed by its contents as I read it again.

Kara,
I took Duke for a walk before I left so he won't need another until I get home. I'll be back by two. Thanks.
—Ryan

Such a sweet love note. I toss it into the trash as I go into the kitchen, feeling slightly appeased when I see the new scone that's waiting for me on the counter. I scoop it out of the bag and gobble down half of it. Stress eating is warranted in this situation.

Every day, Ryan is more and more of a contradiction. He's mad at me, but he wants to spend time with me. He kisses me, and then pushes me away. He disappears this morning, but leaves me an edible reminder of how considerate he can be.

I move to the stove, ready to pour myself a much-needed cup of tea, when a cell phone alert from the front desk goes off. I put down my favorite mug that has *Her Ladyship* painted on the side and answer it.

"Hello?"

"Hi, Ms. Sullivan. Your sister is here to see you."

"Oh. Great, thanks, Nick."

I hang up but keep the phone in my hand. I'm surprised Jen is here. She usually never comes into the city anymore. I'm excited to see her, though...until I remember that Duke is currently sleeping on my bed.

Crap!

I run into my bedroom and look down at the cumbersome dog that's lounging on my pillows like he's Cleopatra. *Please, please let him fall asleep.* I quickly swipe open my phone and place it on the nightstand as soft as a feather, switching on the Celine Dion acoustic playlist that Ryan sent me before tip-toeing out of the room. I close the door so slowly that by the time it's sealed, Jen is outside and knocking.

I jog/leap over and swing open the door before she can knock again.

"Jen, hi!" My tone is a Pollyanna level of bright. "This is such a fun surprise."

Jen is instantly suspicious. "I was meeting one of my sorority sisters for lunch and decided to take a chance. You've been missing in action the past couple of days."

"Yes, sorry, work stuff. Come on in. Do you want something to drink?" My Stepford-Sister-smile remains in place as she crosses the threshold into the apartment.

"Some water would be nice."

I'm about to head for the kitchenette when I hear Duke scuffling around inside my bedroom. "Better yet," I say, moving back towards Jen, "why don't we go out? There's a restaurant a couple blocks away that has amazing water."

I sound insane even to myself.

"What? No. I just got here, and my feet are killing me."

"Right, sure." I give a nervous glance to my bedroom door, moving back towards the kitchen and opening the fridge.

"Did you drink that whole bottle of wine by yourself?" I hear Jen ask.

I look over at the counter and see the empty bottle of Riesling that Ryan and I finished off last night.

"Yeah, I did."

"Going a little strong for a weekday, aren't you?"

I replay the events of last night over in my head. "The alcohol was necessary." I close the refrigerator and hand her the water.

"If you say so. Just bear in mind that if this becomes an issue, I'm not visiting you at some fancy rehab facility upstate."

"I'm not an alcoholic, Jen. Relax."

She thankfully lets my potential substance abuse problem go and walks into the living room, plopping down onto the couch with a contented sigh. I follow after her, settling down into my reading chair.

"So…" I say, trying to think of small talk.

Jen takes a sip of water and looks back at me with a studying eye. "What's going on with you today?"

"What do you mean?"

"Something's weird."

"Nothing's weird."

"Yeah, you're being weird," she says. "What's wrong?"

"Nothing is wrong. I'm perfectly fine. How are you? You still puking every morning?"

"Yes, I still have morning sickness. Stop trying to change the subject. What did you do?"

"I didn't do anything."

"You're lying." She places her water onto the coffee table and sits back, crossing her arms. "Are you in trouble?"

"No," I assure her.

"Are you sick?" Tricky one. Physically no, but mentally, that's debatable.

"Nothing is wrong with me, Jen. You're acting crazy."

"I'm not acting crazy. I just know you and I know you're lying to me."

"I'm not lying to you. I swear, I have nothing to hide."

And this is the exact moment Duke chooses to start barking. The traitor.

"What was that?" Jen asks, her gaze now locked on my bedroom door.

"That was the neighbor's dog."

"It came from your apartment." She doesn't hesitate before standing up to investigate.

Are there legal ramifications for physically restraining a pregnant woman?

"I have thin walls. A concert pianist lives two units over and I hear him all the time. He's still struggling with Brahms's *Rhapsody in B Minor* but his Schubert is legit."

My sister walks past me towards my bedroom. I don't try to stop her. There's no getting in the way of a determined Jen once she's in motion. She opens my bedroom door and steps inside. I close my eyes and wait.

"Kara?" she asks calmly.

"Yes?"

"Why is there a humongous bulldog standing on your bed?"

I get up and join her in my room, accepting the fact that I'm sunk. "Someone left him at my doorstep in a basket this morning. I've decided to raise him as my own."

"Of course you did." She continues inspecting the room,

then peeks just outside to see Ryan's bag sitting beside the bathroom door. "And were these men's clothes left in the basket, too?"

Duke is pacing all over my bed, desperate to jump into Jen's arms if she would only open them to him. He's panting uncontrollably and staring at her, trying to send the message that if she doesn't pet him soon, life will no longer be worth living.

"The clothes are mine," I say.

"Really? You wear men's clothes now?"

"I lead a double life."

"Kara!" Jen shrieks. "Just tell me the truth!"

"Fine," I shout back. "Ryan is staying here. That is *his* dog and those are *his* clothes. He's staying here until Cristina's wedding is over and then he's leaving and that's it."

Silence ensues.

"Wait a minute. Ryan?" she asks. "As in college Ryan?"

"Yes," I admit.

"How did that happen?"

I look up at the ceiling before meeting her curious gaze. "I ran into him at Cristina's pre-wedding party. He's friends with Jason and that's how this all got started."

"So," Jen says, taking everything in, "he was the guy you were talking about with me and Mom the other night? The guy you were texting?"

"Yes."

She finally sits down on the bed and pets Duke. He drops backwards into her lap in exhausted relief. "I need to hear more. Start over and elaborate."

Jen swings her legs onto the bed and leans back against the cushioned headboard. Duke snuggles into her, having no intention of ever leaving her side again.

I groan and belly-flop onto the bed. It takes me a good half hour to get through the entire story, beginning at Cristina's party and ending last night.

"So you're still not over him," Jen says.

"Apparently not."

"And you need him to finish your novel."

"It would seem so."

She nods, mulling over my confession. "What's your next move?"

I let out a short, empty laugh. "My next move is no move. I'm remaining immobile."

"Unacceptable. Where's the list Maggie wrote?"

I begrudgingly get up from the bed and go over to my bedroom bookcase. I pull out my old tattered copy of *The Devilish Duke* and open it, finding the list folded up inside where I stashed it. I hand it to Jen and she reads it over.

"Okay, this is all doable. You already have one step marked off from last night and you can check off the *challenge him* step, too. From what it sounds like, all you two do is challenge each other."

"Exactly," I agree, "we challenge each other too much for our own good. I think I've aged ten years since he got here. I'm developing gout."

"You're not developing gout. Now I get to pick what you're going to do next."

"Why are you encouraging me? The last time Ryan was in the picture, you were glad I broke up with him."

"Yeah, but that was a long time ago and we were all a mess after everything with Dad. From what you told me, Ryan seems like he has his act together now. You should pursue this for real. You're not getting any younger, you know."

"I hate it when you and Mom act like I'm one birthday away from death's door just because you were a child bride."

"I got married when I was twenty-nine years old, Kara."

"Irrelevant! I'm just not good at this stuff."

"It sounds like you did a good enough job last night."

"Sure, and he flew out of here this morning like a bat out of hell." I try to keep the bitterness out of my voice, but I can't quite manage it.

"So he got a little spooked, big whoop. Know what you should do now? You should go out with someone else. Jealousy. I choose the jealousy step. Ryan needs some competition."

"I don't want to play any more games, Jen."

"You're not playing games. If anyone's playing games, he is. You're a successful writer doing what she needs to do for her career and you're also a single woman. There's nothing wrong with what's happening here."

I fold my arms behind my head as I look up at the ceiling. "Maybe."

"Try to make something happen for tonight and don't tell Ryan where you're going or when you'll be back. The less details you give, the better."

"Tonight might be pushing it," I say, scouring my brain for a dating prospect.

"You don't have anyone you want to go out with?"

Well, there *is* someone.

I grab my cell phone from off my bedside table and unlock it. Jen crosses her arms with a villainous smile as I switch off Celine and scroll through my recent calls until I find who I'm looking for. I hold the phone to my ear and start talking once I hear the beep.

"Hey, Maggie, it's Kara. I'm just curious to see if you met up with Kyle yet. I have a question about his friend Adam."

12

I do a spin in front of the standing mirror in the corner of my bedroom, watching my blue short-sleeved sundress rise and fall as I twirl. A few seconds later, I walk out into the living room feeling confident in my comfortable but fashionable wedge heels. My hair is washed and blown out, I shaved my legs above the knees and I'm wearing mascara. Basically, I'm a supermodel.

Ryan is sitting with his laptop at the kitchen table and I give him a quick smile before scanning the room for the boho purse I want to take with me tonight.

"You going out, Sullivan?" he asks, taking in my appearance.

I pretend not to hear him right away. "What'd you say?"

"I asked if you were going out."

"Oh, yeah, but I shouldn't be too late."

"Where are you going?"

"I'm meeting some friends for drinks." I find the bag I'm looking for on the hanging coatrack by the door.

"Nice. Where?"

Interested, are we?

"Just to a bar." Moving over to the entryway, I pull the bag down and take inventory of what's inside, trying to decide if I should bring my whole wallet with me or just my license and a credit card.

"I'm sure you are going to a bar," Ryan says, "but which bar?"

"Why do you care?"

"I'm just curious." He pauses. "Wait, are you about to commit a crime, Sullivan?"

I pivot around to look at him. "And why would you ask me that?"

"Because if you're getting ready to go take part in a complex bank heist, then you being vague right now makes sense. I would actually appreciate you leaving me out of the loop since I'm not trying to get shanked in prison for being your accomplice. But since you said you're not about to commit a crime, I'm not sure why you're refusing to tell me where you're going."

Well, being mysterious was fun while it lasted. It was a brief and shining moment—like Camelot.

"We're going to McFadden's. It's around the corner."

I zip my bag closed in a huff. I'm poised to leave with my hand on the doorknob when Ryan speaks again.

"I would ask which friends you're meeting but I'd hate to throw off your femme fatale persona any more than I already have."

His smug remark rubs me the wrong way and I turn back around. "To put you out of your misery, I'm meeting two guys and my friend Maggie."

That earns me a surprised look. I enjoy it.

"Oh, yeah? Is this a double-date thing?"

What's it to you, smart-ass?

"I don't know if I'd call it a date, but Adam seemed really interesting and cute so I wouldn't mind if it was."

Ryan's jaw tightens. "Well, have fun."

"Thanks," I say cheerfully. I exit the apartment without another word.

I've learned a lot about Adam in the past hour. He's an accountant, he grew up on Long Island, he wrestled in high school and, on his days off, he likes to watch reruns of *Seinfeld* and do crossword puzzles. To sum things up, he's lovely.

I have also learned several other things while talking to Adam. There are seven buttons on his shirt. No one has scored in the Mets game playing on the flat screen above the bar. A couple standing a few feet away is arguing over their plans for this coming weekend. And I have also learned, after stealing clandestine peeks at my phone, that I have only been here for an hour and ten minutes and it is way too early for me to go home.

It's not that I'm having a bad time; I'm just not focused. I should be giving Adam my full attention. He's good-looking, nice, he has a job and he doesn't give off any noticeable let's-see-if-you-fit-in-the-trunk-of-my-car vibes. By modern standards, he's the holy grail. Other single thirtysomethings would gladly club me over the head and walk over my unconscious body to get to him. That's why it's so unfortunate that upon further investigation, I'm not attracted to him at all.

He and Kyle have just walked over to the jukebox that charges a dollar a song when Maggie slides next to me at the cocktail table we're standing around.

"So, what do you think?" she asks.

"It's going okay."

"You hate him."

"I don't hate him," I clarify. "He's very nice."

"Calling a guy nice on the first date is the kiss of death. Did he offer you money to touch your feet? Does he train seventeen cageless parakeets on the weekend?"

"I don't think so." I chuckle.

"Lucky. Kyle does."

"Does he really?"

"No, but he did tell me he has a waterbed, and that's a deal-breaker for me."

"Really? I bet you'd get your sea legs after a week or two."

"It's possible but it's not a risk I'm willing to take."

"That's unfortunate."

"Devastatingly so," she agrees, picking up her wineglass. "At least you have your actual dream man back at your apartment. The only thing waiting at my place is bitterness and old age."

"That's not true. You see your dream man multiple times a year."

"The Phantom of the Opera doesn't count. Though he should count, since we're obviously in love, but the fact that I have to buy a ticket to see him every few months makes me feel dirty."

"Well, Ryan doesn't count either. So once again, it's just you and me."

"I'm good with that."

"Me, too." I lift my bay breeze and we tap our glasses together, smirking and taking a sip. I turn to look towards the jukebox where the guys are still searching through songs when I notice a lone figure sauntering into the bar from out of the corner of my eye. My breath catches in my chest and I have to fight back an ear-to-ear smile.

Ryan stands by the door for a few seconds until he spots me. His eyes lock on mine and he flashes me that sexy grin that makes me feel like a cavewoman. He's wearing worn-in jeans, a plain white T-shirt and a Carolina Hurricanes base-ball cap. Needless to say, Momma likes.

"Crap," I mumble under my breath.

"What?" Maggie asks, following my gaze to the door. She stares at Ryan for a solid amount of time until she looks back at me. "Stop. Is that Ryan? Is that him?"

"Yes, that's him."

Maggie gasps and turns back. "I honestly don't know what I was expecting but he looks like a modern American version of the prince from *Beauty and the Beast*."

"No, he doesn't."

"He fully does."

I manage to put a lid on my escalating giddiness as he makes his way towards us through the minor crowd. Maggie, on the other hand, does not.

"Sweet lord, he's walking over. What should I do? Should I sing?"

"Please don't sing."

"Whenever two people are about to admit their love for each other in a musical, they always sing. I should set the mood for you guys."

"Don't you dare."

Ryan is then at my side, resting his hands down against the table.

"Hello," Maggie sings. We both look at her and she starts nervously laughing. Uncomfortable situations were never her strong suit. "Hello," she says again, normally this time. "I'm Maggie. Sorry about the weird hello. I have a background in music."

"I can tell. You have a great voice. I'm Ryan."

And Maggie is back nervously laughing. "Yes, I know who you are."

"Oh, yeah? Has this one been trash-talking me?" he asks,

nudging his head in my direction. A waiter appears and Ryan orders a beer on tap.

"What? No, not at all." Maggie's trying to recover. Bless her heart. "I mean yes, Kara has mentioned you in passing but nothing out of the ordinary. You guys went to summer camp together, right?"

"College."

"Really? My mistake, I must have been thinking about her summer-camp boyfriend that we often discuss at great length. You, not so much."

Ryan smiles in a confused sort of way and looks to me for clarification. All I can do is shrug.

"Hey, Sullivan," he says softly.

"Hi." We hold eye contact for longer than we should and Maggie starts humming the opening notes to "Tale as Old as Time." I give her a warning look and she cuts it short, appearing guilty but satisfied as she glances back towards the jukebox.

"Yeah," she says, "maybe this isn't the best time for me to mention this, but our current suitors are now on their way back. Should I clear the area?"

"No, don't do anything," I tell her.

Kyle and Adam return to the table and Maggie immediately picks up her purse. "Hey, Kyle!" she says, a thousand times louder and peppier than she needs to. "You know what? I'm starving and I love dinner. Would you like to get dinner?"

"Sure," he says, giving a quick look over to Adam. "Are we all going?"

"Nope, just the two of us. We should go now, though, because I want to hear more about your parakeets."

"Parakeets?" he asks, confused, as Maggie grips his arm and drags him towards the door.

I'm now left standing inconveniently alone with Ryan and Adam. I'm trying to think of what to say when I feel Adam's hand on the small of my back. Ryan notices and squares his shoulders.

Awkward.

"Can I get you another drink?" Adam asks, leaning in close to my ear even though the bar isn't that loud or crowded.

I'm about to tell him I'm good when Ryan clears his throat.

"Right. Sorry, I should introduce you guys. Adam, this is Ryan."

Adam stretches his arm out around me. "Nice to meet you."

Ryan shakes his hand, saying, "Likewise."

After a nice painful silence, I realize I should probably start talking. I face Adam and try to explain. "Ryan is my friend from college. He's crashing on my couch this week until our mutual friend's wedding."

"That's cool," Adam says. "I wish I kept in contact with more of my friends from college."

"She's also my ex-girlfriend," Ryan throws in.

Adam straightens up. I force a smile. "Yeah, but he and I dated, like, way, way back in the day." Adam doesn't answer and I take a sip of my drink.

"It wasn't that long ago, was it?" Ryan asks.

"It was. It was ten long years ago."

"Really? It feels like yesterday to me."

I shift my stance away from Ryan and towards Adam, wondering if I can salvage whatever is left of our mini-date. Turns out, I can't. A minute later, he mumbles something about having to wake up early the next day. He gives me a quick kiss on the cheek and gives Ryan an uncertain high-five. I watch him leave the bar before turning an accusing look on my now-lone companion.

"What?" he asks, acting like we just had the most normal interaction in the world.

"Are you serious? What was that?"

"What was what?"

"You telling Adam that I'm your ex-girlfriend."

"I just told him the truth, Sullivan. You *are* my ex-girlfriend."

"From a million years ago," I complain. The waiter reappears, dropping off Ryan's beer and heading to the next patron. "And what about the other thing you said?"

"About it feeling like yesterday?"

"Yes. That was such a lie."

"How do you know it was a lie? Maybe to me, it does feel like yesterday. Yesterday especially felt like yesterday." He gives me a wink and I consider flicking him on his forehead.

"You're a real pain in the ass. Adam might have been my soul mate and now he's gone. I don't know how you're going to live with the guilt."

Ryan stretches his shoulders and leans down against the table. "It's nothing a little therapy couldn't fix."

"You should probably seek therapy regardless."

"That makes two of us. Guess I'll see you there."

He holds up his glass and I shake my head with a grin as we clink our drinks together.

Two hours later, I leave McFadden's feeling very happy, very energetic and very, very tipsy. Ryan seems looser than usual but it's hard to tell if he's drunk or not. His personality is too out there for me to distinguish the difference between drunken weirdo Ryan and baseline weirdo Ryan.

We're heading back to the apartment after we mutually—I stress, mutually—decided to pick up pizza.

"Did you ever think we would end up like this after we first met?" he asks as we turn up 41st Street. "Here we are, thirty-two years old and—"

"Um, excuse me, old man, you're the only one who's thirty-two. I'm still basking in the golden age of thirty."

"Forget about age. Did you ever think we'd be walking down the street with pizza ten-plus years after we first met?"

"That would be a no," I answer. "The first time we spoke, you thought I was a nerd reading a dirty novel."

"I did not. You thought I was a rude thief. I will admit, stealing your book wasn't my best moment, but I wanted you to talk to me."

"Why?" I find myself asking.

Ryan smiles. "Because when I walked into class and saw you, I thought you were the most adorable thing I ever saw."

I make a skeptical face but he goes on.

"I wanted to find out who you were, so I sat down next to you and bothered you until you talked to me. And when you did talk to me, I got you so worked up and angry by taking your book and...I don't know, I just couldn't stop looking at you."

"I'm sorry but that makes no sense."

"You were beautiful, Sullivan. You still are."

I don't take compliments well, so I ignore him completely. "I was so bratty to you that day."

"I deserved it. I was a jerk."

"True," I agree. "When you sat with me again in the next class, I was stunned."

Ryan catches my gaze and keeps it. "I think I was already in love with you by then. I just had to wait for you to catch up with me."

His words comfort and crush me. We both look forward.

"You didn't have to wait very long," I say.

Ryan's gaze falls to the pavement, a cloud seeming to come over him. "When we broke up, when you cut me off like that…I was messed up for a long time." Seconds go by until he speaks again. "You really broke my heart, you know?"

We stop walking as we arrive outside my building and I say the first thing that flashes through my mind. "You broke mine first."

Ryan takes in my words. Part of me wishes I didn't say them, but they're the truth. Maybe he needed to hear them as much as I needed to say them.

"It's surprising that we're still able to be friends now," he says, "considering what we did to each other."

"I'm sure a fair amount of former couples are able to stay friends."

"And you think they're the same as you and me? That they had what we had?"

I roll his question over in my head, hoping to find an answer that's honest but vague.

"I don't know," I decide to say. "Did you ever feel what we did with someone else?"

I can see his chest pitch up and down. I've probably overstepped but it's too late to take it back now.

"I haven't." His tone is sure and final, not at all in the quiet voice that would have come from me. "I never really wanted to feel that way again. That's why…"

Before he can finish, a car comes to a screeching halt at the corner. I gasp at the jarring sound as Ryan grabs my arm and pulls me behind him. Two cars are now stopped and are aggressively honking at each other when Ryan turns back to me, letting go of my arm.

I clear my throat and plaster on a smile. "Okay, I think that's a sign that we should go inside. We've both had a lot to drink so let's head on up and eat this pizza." Without waiting for a response, I walk into the entrance with Ryan falling in step behind me. Pizza makes everything better. Hopefully.

Once we're inside, I kick off my shoes and flop down onto the couch, finding Duke asleep under my desk. I'm toasty drunk so the freezing apartment doesn't give me immediate pneumonia. Ryan puts the pizza box on the kitchen counter and sits down in the reading chair across from me. He nudges his sneakers off as I close my eyes and sink back into the unbelievably comfortable cushions.

"Can I ask you something?"

I open my eyes to look at him. "Sure."

He hesitates before going on. "The last time I called you, when you finally picked up…did you mean what you said or was it a lie?"

I think back to the call and a heavy weight starts to press inside me. I told him I used to laugh at him—that I was happier without him—that he was a waste of time. I wonder now if my words from that day stayed with him as much as his words put down roots in me.

"Of course it was a lie," I admit. "After we broke up, all I thought about was going back to you."

"I wish you would have. Or I should have come back for you."

His statement almost knocks the wind out of me but I don't show it.

"It wouldn't have made a difference," I tell him. "Too much happened. It couldn't have worked." Ryan doesn't say anything and I take his silence as an opportunity. "Were you lying back then, too? Or were you really cheating on me?"

Ryan looks at me for a long time. "What do you think?" he asks.

"I don't think you would do that to me."

"I wouldn't," he affirms.

His words sink in, leaving me relieved but also enraged. He never cheated on me. He made it up. That lie touched every relationship I've had since him. I thought every guy I dated had a hidden agenda, that I wasn't enough for anyone. Why *wouldn't* someone cheat on me? I tortured myself for years imagining Ryan with another girl while I pined for him. And it was all for nothing.

"When I moved back to North Carolina after graduation, I used to talk about you a lot to my dad. I'd tell him how smart and funny you were and how much I missed you. He would make fun of me and tell me how bad I had it, but after a while, the more I would talk about you, the less he'd say."

I startle a little at his words. Parents usually love me. I'm shy and sweet and rarely a cause for concern. I run every interaction I had with Ryan's dad through my mind, but can't find any red flags.

"I could sense there was something going on with him, but I didn't know what it was. He started telling me that I shouldn't end up with the first girl I fell for. He said we were too young and it wasn't fair to you since you still had two years left of school."

I nod, not sure where he's going with this.

"I brushed it off in the beginning. I thought he was wrong and that we'd be okay. He kept going at me, though, saying it every time I brought you up. And then when things got rough between you and me, I started to think that maybe he was right. That I wasn't being fair and I was ruining things for you."

"But you weren't—"

"Yes, I was. You know I was."

I want to argue but my case is weak. I remember how central I made him to everything. If it was a day when he called, I was walking on air. If it was a day when he didn't, I was a mess. Good day or bad day, it was set by him. Not me.

Maybe that's the cost of finding love young. Everything

is new and overwhelming and chasing that sensation down is priority one. I think back to the girl I was then and I feel bad for her. I still have plenty of flaws, but I know who I am. I like who I am. I'm fulfilled by my job and my family and friends, and if love found me now, it would add to my life, not consume it.

"And all the time that my dad was giving me relationship advice, he was cheating on my mom. He convinced me to pull away from you and then he went and screwed us all over." Ryan looks at the wall behind me for a while before refocusing. "I haven't spoken to him since he told me the truth. Not for ten years."

I sit up fully then, feeling the color drain from my face. "What? Are you serious?"

"I was left with nothing and it was his fault. I couldn't just let that go."

My stomach is queasy and my eyesight blurs. I have a million things to say and words fall out of my mouth in a trembling heap. "Stop. You can be mad about what happened between your dad and mom and how he lied to you, but don't blame him for what happened between us. That was you and me. Just you and me. Your dad was clearly going through something, but I'm sure he thought he was doing the right thing when it came to you. Don't cut him out of your life. You'll never regret the times you talk to your parents, only the times you don't."

Ryan shakes his head with a lazy smile. "You're too nice for your own good."

"You're not listening to me!" I'm yelling now and his eyes turn nervous. I need to make him understand. I try to sound in control, but it's so hard. "Believe me when I say that there are few things on this Earth I wouldn't do if it meant I could have one more conversation with my dad. I regret every second I saw him without telling him what he meant to me, and I hate myself for every moment I could have spent with him but didn't."

I pick up the pillow next to me, not sure if I want to punch it or squeeze it or hurl it across the room at Ryan's head. I end up pushing it into my lap and moving my hands across the surface until I reach the corners.

I look up and Ryan is watching me like I'm an exotic creature he's found in the wild, untethered and mesmerizing and capable of mauling him at any second. He says nothing.

"You have what I'd kill for. I'm not saying you have to forgive him. Just promise me you'll talk to him. Promise me you'll try."

It takes a few seconds and the air turns thick between us, but Ryan slowly nods. "I will. I'll try to try, if that makes sense."

I nod as well as I lean back a little, lifting the pillow from my lap and hugging it to my chest. My heart rate returns to normal as the thermostat kicks the air to an even stronger level. The steady, cold breeze cools my flushed skin.

"I'm sorry I screamed at you," I say after a while. "Why do all our conversations turn dark and emotional whenever we drink together?"

"It's all the history, I guess. I kind of like it, though. Oddly enough."

I let out a grim chuckle as Ryan studies me from across the room.

"Were you mad that I ruined your date tonight?" he asks.

"Not really." I push my pillow back onto the cushions beside me, tucking it underneath my arm.

"Adam seemed like an okay guy."

"He was, but he's not what I'm looking for."

"What *are* you looking for?"

It takes me a few seconds to come up with a response. "I wish I had the answer for that."

"Someone like the guys in your novels?"

"Yeah, someone like that," I say with a wistful smile. "A dramatic whirlwind romance that takes the world and turns it upside down."

Ryan isn't smiling. He watches me for a good long while, silent and still. "I don't think I believe that. Even if you could experience what you write about, you would be way too uptight to do that kind of stuff, let alone enjoy it."

I take in his accusation and once again sit up straight. "That's not true. What happens in my books just doesn't happen in real life. If I could experience something like that, I wouldn't be too uptight to enjoy it."

"You're sure about that?"

"Yes, I'm sure."

"Okay. Prove it."

I think back on Ryan's words. "What do you mean?" I ask.

"I mean let's choose a book and we'll see if you can read it and act out what the characters are doing without you being too afraid to stop."

"You want me to read what's in a romance novel and then act it out?"

"Yes."

"And who am I supposed to act it out with?"

"Me, of course."

Ryan's proposition crashes over me like a cold, unexpected wave. "You're kidding."

"I'm entirely serious. This way, we can see who's right about your novels once and for all, or you can just admit that you would never really do any of the things you write about."

I continue to stare at him in total silence.

"I knew it," he says a few moments later.

And then my stubborn nature, strengthened by the alcohol, takes the wheel. "Fine," I say defiantly.

"Fine?" he asks. "Are you sure?"

I get up from the couch without hesitating. "Pick a book."

Ryan smiles. "How about the one you're writing now?" He strolls over to my desk and picks up the new steamy chapter I printed out only this morning. He flips through the pages with his thumb until he slows down to skim a particular section. "Last chance to admit I'm right, Sullivan."

I shake my head, feeling more determined than ever to test the boundaries.

"Here we go, then." He walks into my bedroom, still holding the pages. I slowly follow and find him standing beside the bed. I close the gap between us until I'm two feet away. He hands me the manuscript, pointing to the top of the page. "Start reading."

I look at him for several moments before my gaze falls to the paper. The words seem jumbled until they gradually begin to take form.

"'Robert turned the key and locked the door…'" My words trail off as I peek up to see Ryan watching me through hazy eyes. He steps forward and around me, walking over to the door, pushing it closed. The space around us seems significantly smaller as he returns to his spot across from me. Less air. More heat. I feel trapped but in such a good way. I look back down at the page and continue.

"'Charlotte stretched and arched her supple body across his bed, gripping the satin sheets in unbridled anticipation.'"

Ryan steps closer, slicing the distance between us in half. "It sounds like only one of us should be standing." His eyes go from the papers in my hand to the bed.

Having no idea what I just said, I look down and reread the

last line. *Charlotte stretched and arched her supple body across his bed, gripping the satin sheets in unbridled anticipation.*

I had to write unbridled anticipation, *right?*

Okay. It is officially game on.

I take the couple of steps needed to reach my bed and sit down on the mattress. I can't let him win. I won't. I slide back and lie back, holding the pages above me as I pick up where I left off.

"'Robert moved towards her...'"

Ryan clears his throat.

"What?" I ask, lowering the pages.

"Aren't you supposed to be arching and gripping sheets?"

"How can I do that when I'm holding a stack of papers in my hand?"

Ryan actually thinks about it. "You can arch a little bit and still hold the pages. Or you could at least grab the sheet with your other hand."

"What's the difference?" I ask.

"The difference is, we said we would see if you could live out what's in your books, and that's what's in the book. Our findings will only be accurate if you fully commit."

I send him a challenging glance. "Oh, and you're going to fully commit?"

"Hell yeah," he says.

I roll my eyes and wrap part of the sheet in my left hand. I give my attention back to the manuscript and find my place. "'Robert moved towards her at an agonizing pace, using every ounce of his self-control to keep from taking her that very second. Charlotte was equally tortured, and a frustrated moan slipped from her kiss-swollen lips.'"

I look up from the manuscript. Ryan steps forward and raises an eyebrow. He's daring me.

Saddle up, cowboy.

I close my eyes and unleash the best come-hither moan I've ever attempted. I don't want to toot my own horn, but I can see Ryan's shoulder muscles tense up in the aftermath.

I'm encouraged enough to continue, "'That was his undoing. Robert could wait no longer. His heart pounded in his chest as desire burst through his veins like liquid fire. He tore at his shirt, ripping it open in his haste to remove the unwanted garment.'"

I haven't even finished the last sentence when Ryan pulls his T-shirt over his head and drops it to the floor. My eyes lock with his, as they always do, and in that moment, I'm struck with a sudden sense of clarity. This isn't some fantasy and it's not my overactive imagination. Ryan is here. He's here and he's smiling and why shouldn't we do this if we want to? My nerves begin to fall away as I close my eyes for a brief second.

"Is me without a shirt on that scary to look at?" Ryan asks. "Or is it just too arousing for you? That, I'm willing to accept."

I open my eyes and glower at his smirking, half-clad form. Afraid that I'll stare, I move the pages close to my face—so close that the top paper folds down and bumps against my nose.

I straighten it out and read on, "'He needed her skin on his with nothing between them. Needed it more than he needed anything in his life. Without pause, Robert lowered himself onto the bed to lean over the perfect beauty writhing beneath him.'"

I move the pages away from my face, and Ryan pauses as he looks at me.

"Do you want me to stop?" he asks.

His question hangs in the air for what feels like forever until I shake my head no. I then concentrate on even breathing as he carefully lowers himself onto the bed. He braces his hands on the mattress, framing my face and pushing up so he's hovering above me. With the manuscript still in my right hand, I extend my arm to the side and continue reading.

"'Charlotte's excited breaths caressed Robert's cheek as he kissed her throat…'" My voice cracks as Ryan's warm mouth moves along the side of my neck. "'He worshiped all of her, every inch. He didn't stop until…'" My words are smothered as Ryan brings his lips down to mine, tender at first and then urging them open. My body feels close to igniting as our tongues touch and slide. I can't believe we ever bothered using them to talk when we could have been doing this instead. He breathes into me and takes it back. A moan from me. A growl from him.

It feels like I'm kissing him again for the first time—a stranger I've kissed a hundred times before. It doesn't take long until we both need more. Still holding the pages, I wrap my arms around his neck, desperately trying to pull him down to press his body where I want it the most. He doesn't give in. He stays positioned over me, his weight supported by his arms as he slants his mouth over mine, kissing me over and over. Deeper and longer.

He pulls back just enough that our noses are still touching. He's taking quiet but labored breaths as he slowly nudges his knee into the space between my thighs. "Keep reading," he says.

Desperate not to lose the friction, I hold the pages up with a shaky hand, finding my place. I blink as I attempt to decode the illegible words. "'"Don't," Charlotte moaned, practically drowning in the pleasure of it all. "Don't stop…"'"

I'm not sure who's talking anymore, Charlotte or me. I honestly don't care. Ryan's mouth is back on my skin, nipping at the base of my throat as I shift down against his knee, trying to ease the ache that's steadily climbing. I twist my free hand into his hair and pull. He attacks my neck with renewed hunger. I'm beyond intoxicated, and it has nothing at all to do with drinking.

"'Robert groaned against Charlotte's neck as he ran his fingertips up her thighs. With his kisses and hands, he urged Charlotte's trembling limbs around his...waist!'"

The exclamation point is all me as Ryan's hand slips under my dress and along my leg, pulling it up to wrap around his hip. His breath is as strained as mine now as his hand drifts from my leg to my face. He angles my chin up to kiss the underside of my jaw and keeps the delicious path moving from my throat to my shoulders to the top of my chest. His mouth moves lower as he tugs the neckline of my dress down until it's taut, almost ripping. I'm dizzy and burning but I force myself to keep reading.

"'"I have loved you since the first moment I saw you rolling around on that library floor," he whispered into Charlotte's ear. "Don't ask me to go. Stay with me. Tell me you want me, always."'"

"Enough," Ryan says, his voice breaking. The manuscript is torn from my hand and is sent flying across the room. He grabs the hem of my dress and bunches it at my waist, pulling it up even farther until it's off my body completely.

His mouth is everywhere and so are his hands, possessive but feather-soft. I'm nowhere near as graceful, clawing at his back and shifting all over like I'm delirious, which I am. My bra is gone and he's there instead, kissing and licking. I grip the back of his hair with no intention of letting go. Ever.

He asks if I have protection and I remember the box I keep in my bedside table drawer. I reach for the handle but end up pointing, and Ryan opens it himself. He sits back on his heels and pulls out a foil packet, almost ripping the box in two. He's red-faced with wild eyes. I made him like that. It's a heady feeling.

He's soon pulling down my plain white panties and throwing them across the room with my other clothes. He kisses me hard and he pushes me down farther into the mattress. His pants and boxers join the pile on the floor. The feel of his weight, the heat of his skin—I'm never leaving this bed.

He eases in, inch by blissful inch, until there's nowhere else to go. My eyes close and my head tilts back. I'm savoring every second. He rocks into me with an unhurried rhythm, his body reminding mine that he was there first, that no one else fits me like he does. I urge him on and he gives me what I want, moving faster and telling me to look at him, to keep looking at him or he'll stop. A slow-burning tension flares and stretches inside me, building and surging until I break and a sharp groan that sounds nothing like me tears from my throat. Ryan follows, pitching his hips forward and calling my name as his back arches and his muscles shake.

He goes slack a few seconds later and his cheek rubs mine. Our eyes find each other's and we both see the same thing even if we don't say it.

Everything has changed.

13

The room is quiet and calm as my eyes flutter open. I watch the steady rise and fall of Ryan's chest beside me, feeling the soft trail of his fingertips as he skates his hand across my arm. A maelstrom of questions scratches at the walls of my content state but I push them back. Nothing can touch me in this moment except for Ryan.

Despite feeling cozy and sated, I decide to go to the bathroom to freshen up. I shift and squeeze the hand that he's now resting on my waist before I slip out from under the sheet to sit up. My feet touch the ground and as they do, something occurs to me.

I'm naked!

I'm perched on the edge of my bed, stark naked, two feet away from Ryan, who now has a clear-as-day view of my bottom.

I immediately stand up and walk calmly but briskly into the

bathroom, even though I really want to hurtle myself across the room while covering my butt with a pillow.

Safely out of view, I close the door and turn the faucet on full blast. I rinse my face with cool water and remind myself that the heroines in my novels never feel uncomfortable after they've given in to their lustful desires. They revel in their newly discovered glory—their feminine power. They celebrate their freedom with complete abandon.

Me, not so much.

I exit the bathroom five minutes later with a towel wrapped around me, doing my best to avoid Ryan's gaze as I sneak back into bed.

I lie down and pull the sheet up, almost tucking it under my chin. Now fully covered, I unwrap the towel from around my body and toss it to the floor.

Ryan rolls over onto his side, pushing himself up on his elbow to look down at me. "Are you cold?"

"No," I answer.

"Sullivan?"

"Yes?"

"You do know that I have seen you naked many times before, right?"

I close my eyes and scrunch my face. "Unfortunately, yes."

"Unfortunately?" Ryan moves again so he's now lying on top of me. "Trust me, it's anything *but* unfortunate."

I cover my face with my hands and groan. "I can't have this conversation with you."

"Why not?"

"Because it's too embarrassing."

Ryan forces my hands away from my face, rubbing my wrists with his thumbs as he keeps them locked against the mattress. "You must have a real warped view of yourself."

I pull one of my hands free from Ryan's grip and run my index finger along a scar beside his ear. I never noticed it before. It's a bit Z-shaped and the skin around it seems pulled tight. "Where did you get this?"

"That," he says, "I got when I was walking home from the bar a few years ago. Some guy was getting mugged, so I jumped in and helped fight the other guy off. He got away with a cell phone and some cash and I got this."

"Really?"

"No," he answers, cracking a smile. "I had basal skin cells removed last year. The scarring was supposed to be minimal but the dermatologist wound up leaving the mark of Zorro on my face. I guess he didn't like me. And he really liked Zorro."

"I don't know why I take anything you say at face value."

Ryan tilts off to the side, now holding the bulk of his weight on his right shoulder. "I can be serious sometimes. Back home I'm considered a fairly serious guy."

"I doubt it," I say with a grin, brushing a lock of hair off his forehead—because I can do that now.

"How about this for being serious—since we broke up, barely a week went by when I didn't think back to the last time I saw you."

My stomach sinks. I think about getting up again. "We don't have to talk about this."

"I want to," Ryan says. "I've waited a long time."

I wish I could look away or leave the room, but I stay put and keep my eyes trained on his. "Okay. Go on, then."

Ryan takes a breath. "One of my biggest regrets was how I treated you towards the end of our relationship. I knew I was hurting you. You tried to tell me what I could do to make things better, and I just moved further and further away. I would do anything if I could go back and be there with you when you lost your dad."

I try to push my emotions into the background like I usually do when people talk to me about my dad. Smile and nod.

Dissociate and move on. "You didn't even know about my dad, plus we were kids back then. It's okay."

"It's not okay, though. And I know I apologized to you for how I acted when you broke up with me, but I want to apologize again now, as a man."

"It's really not necessary. We're different people now."

"Maybe someday we can go visit him together. I'd like to talk to him—tell him I'm sorry for not being there with you when I should have."

Unwanted tears well up in my eyes as I imagine visiting my dad's grave with Ryan. I hold them in. They sting but they're manageable. I try to talk but my throat is too tight.

As it is, I go to see my dad a few times a year and every Christmas morning. My mom doesn't know about that last part, but I'm always pulled there then. Maybe it's from thinking of how he always had his big video camera propped on his shoulder as Jen and I opened presents until we were teenagers. I don't want him to feel abandoned at Christmas. I've always visited my dad alone but maybe I don't have to anymore.

Part of me is afraid that bringing Ryan to see him is wrong. That my dad wouldn't want it. That he'd be disappointed in me again. I'm not sure how to feel but Ryan is watching me, waiting for me to say something to his painfully thoughtful offer.

"I'd like that," I eventually manage. I give in then and allow a couple of tears to fall even as I let out a small laugh. "I really thought we were done with all the emotional stuff for the night. Weren't we just joking about me being naked?"

Ryan wipes a tear away from the corner of my eye. "I didn't mean to make you sad. I've just had a lot to say to you for a long time."

"I know the feeling," I say, still attempting to absorb it all. "It means a lot to me."

Ryan kisses me, gentle and sweet. "*You* mean a lot to me. You always have."

My cheeks pull back in a grin as I roll onto my side. Ryan moves me back to fit snugly against him, tucking the top of my head under his chin.

"So," I say into the peaceful quiet of the room, "is this the wrong time for me to tell you that I want to see other people?"

I hear Ryan's quiet laugh against my ear. "Sorry, Sullivan, but that's not possible. You're mine now."

I smile to myself, thinking I probably always was his. I'm still smiling a few minutes later as I drift off into the most peaceful sleep I've had in years.

I wake up in an empty bed and with a pounding headache. Rolling off my stomach and onto my back, I massage my throbbing temples. Just touching my head is painful. I expected to feel the usual grossness after drinking too much last night but right now my body feels like I lost in a street fight.

Why am I so sore?

And then, a parade of images flashes through my mind. McFadden's with Adam, Ryan walking in, pizza, walking home, talking in the living room, Ryan with my manuscript, me, my bed, me on my bed, Ryan on me on my bed.

More images come—varying from bow-chicka-wow-wow to talking about my dad to Ryan whispering into my ear that I was his.

It would be easy to panic but I desperately hold on to the sensations from last night. How I had no regrets. How it felt right. And even though it's nothing new for me to wake up to an empty apartment, I can't help but feel like Ryan should be here. That I shouldn't be alone. And then I realize I'm not alone.

I look to my right and find Duke sitting directly next to my bed, staring at me stalker style, as per usual. A piece of paper is wedged under his collar and I sit up, holding the sheet to cover my torso as I reach out and take the note.

It reads:

Good morning, I already went for a walk and Papa Ryan is out getting breakfast. He said he'll be back very soon.

A huge smile spreads across my face.

P.S. He also told me to look away when you get out of bed because you're too hot for me to handle.

All thoughts of hangovers and embarrassment vanish as I break out laughing and lie back down. I extend my arms and hold the note up over my face to reread it. I'm satisfied when I have it memorized. I then let the small piece of paper rest on my chest on top of the sheet, staring up at the ceiling with my now ever-present grin.

I'm doing it again. I can feel myself falling for that wonderful idiot all over again and I can't stop myself. And what's worse, I don't even want to.

Twenty minutes later, I'm dressed in yoga pants and a T-shirt when I hear Ryan push the key in the apartment lock. I scurry into my bedroom, wanting to casually walk out once he's inside like I didn't hear him come in.

The door opens and closes, and I come out soon after, feeling strangely unsure and out of place in my own apartment. Ryan is standing in front of the kitchenette with two coffees and a bag with what I'm pretty sure is two scones.

"Hey," I say, looking to him for any sign of how I should be reacting right now. There are a lot of options on the table. I can pretend nothing happened. I can joke about it. Or I charge at him full force for an overhead lift, circa *Dirty Dancing*.

"Hey," he answers, placing everything onto the kitchen table. "How are you?"

"I'm good," I say. "Feeling perfectly normal and not awkward at all."

Ryan smiles. "Yeah, me, too."

"So...do you want to talk about last night?"

He rests his hand on the table, moving it this way and that way across the wooden surface. It's a nervous gesture and it makes me feel a degree more comfortable.

"We probably should. Do *you* want to?" he asks.

I pause and consider. "Not particularly, no."

"I just don't want you to think that I planned what happened last night. When I came to stay here, I had no intention that anything would..."

I wait for him to find the words to finish his thought but he can't. It's not hard to see what's happening here. He's having regrets. I should be feeling the same way. Last night was way more than I bargained for when I started this experiment, but still, I can't bring myself to regret it.

"Look, let's just not talk about it, okay? I'd really rather not."

Ryan still seems like he wants to say something but reluctantly agrees. He then reaches into the bag on the table and pulls out the scones I was hoping for. If I thought he was handsome before, it pales in comparison to how good he looks while holding post-coital breakfast pastries.

A minute later, we're sitting down at the table together, eating our scones and drinking our coffees.

"By the way, after breakfast, I have to pick something up for Cristina so I can bring it to the rehearsal dinner tomorrow."

Ryan takes a bite of his scone and sets it back down on his plate. "You want some company?"

"Sure," I answer, a little surprised. "You actually want to run errands?"

"Not really, but I'm worried that if I leave you alone with

your thoughts for too long, you'll go nuts thinking about what happened between us and you'll vanish into the night."

"I think you're way more likely to do that than me. Plus it would be difficult for me to vanish into the night considering it's midmorning."

"You're a wily lady, Sullivan. Who knows what kind of time-travel trickery you're capable of?"

Trying to hide my smile, I add a splash of skim milk to my coffee and give it a stir. "Just for the sake of conversation, where do you think I'm going to disappear to?"

"That's a good question. My guess would be that you'd take an Uber to New Mexico or bus to Indiana."

"What would I do in Indiana?"

"If I had to put money on it, I'd say you'd reinvent yourself, work hard, get accepted to Notre Dame, fight your way onto the football team and show the world that anything is possible if you believe in your dreams."

"So I'd have to change my name to Rudy?"

"That's implied."

I chuckle and take a sip of my coffee. "Do you ever make it through a significant stretch of time without watching or making reference to that movie in some way?"

"Um, no, nor would I want to."

"I get that. It would probably be terrible for you to miss your weekly cry."

"Tearing up in manly happiness after watching the most moving sports movie of all time is not the same as crying. And if you ever do meet a someone who doesn't cry at the end of *Rudy*, I suggest you run away as fast as you can because they one hundred percent have a treasure trove of dead bodies piled up in their basement."

"Is this how you talk to everyone or just me?"

"Just you, Sullivan. You're a lucky lady."

"So, when you said running an errand for Cristina, I was thinking more along the lines of buying pens or picking up computer ink."

"Meaning you thought we were going to Staples? I told you before we left that I was picking up Cristina's veil."

"Granted, but I just didn't think it would be this...bridey."

Anxiously glancing around the veil section of the fancy bridal salon we're now waiting in, Ryan looks as if he were dropped down and left to survive on an alien planet made solely of beige carpeting. Miles of chiffon, tulle and organza surround us from the walls. Some veils have sparkles, some have pearls, and for some inexplicable reason I want to touch all of them.

We shouldn't even be here right now, but somehow Cristina's veil didn't get packed in with her wedding dress when she picked it up yesterday. After having a mild heart attack, she called the salon and they confirmed it was still in the store and told her she could come pick it up whenever she was available. Problem was, Cristina wasn't going to be available until two weeks after she said "I do." She's with the florist at this very moment and is then going straight over to the venue for a final, comprehensive meeting, and will be prepping for the rehearsal dinner all day tomorrow.

Thus, here we are. And as overwhelming as the whole scene is, I still can't help myself from drifting to the nearest wall and moving my fingers along the delicate fabric of one of the veils. I can feel myself being lured deeper into the hypnotic bridal cloud that is ready to engulf me, but strangely enough, I'm okay with it.

"When I was little," I say, not turning around to face Ryan, "I wanted a veil just as long as Princess Diana's."

"How long was that?"

"One-hundred and fifty-three yards. Is it weird that I know that?"

"No, it sounds reasonable."

I smile and move along to a veil with antique lace trim as Ryan still stays frozen in place. "On one of the many bridal reality shows I watch, a girl had her deceased mom's name embroidered into the edge of her veil. I thought that was a nice idea I could use with my dad someday. That way he can still walk me down the aisle."

"You should do that then."

"Maybe I will. I guess I'll have to get married now." I shift around and find Ryan watching me with curious eyes. I'm about to move closer to him when a short salesgirl with a blond pixie cut suddenly enters the showroom.

"Would you like to try that on?" she asks, reaching for the lace-trimmed veil I was just admiring.

"What? Oh, no," I tell her, stepping away. "I'm not a bride,

I'm just here to pick something up. The manager went to get it for me."

"Come on, try it on. It feels so good. Sometimes, I wear one through my entire lunch break."

"Really?" I ask, inadvertently stepping back towards her and the veil.

"Unless my manager is here, like today. Then I can't. And I swear, on those days, I always feel significantly less alive. Okay, here we go."

Before I can stop her—not that I'm actually trying to stop her—my veil fairy godmother slips the bridal comb into the top of my hair and pulls the front tulle down to cover my face.

"There," she says, stepping back to appreciate her work. "I knew the antique lace would suit you. You have a bit of that old-fashioned glamour about you."

"Do I?" I'm set on believing her whether she's lying or not. Full disclosure, there's a solid chance I'm walking out of here with a veil to wear while sitting at home. This girl is a good saleswoman.

I have the distinct suspicion she's on the verge of selling me a festive tiara when the salon's phone rings.

"One sec, I'll be right back," she says.

I turn to the mirror as she skips back behind the counter.

"Okay," I say to my reflection, "I need to find a valid excuse to justify the purchase of this veil. I'm thinking I either use it for character research or I become an elegant beekeeper."

Ryan chuckles as he steps into view behind me in the mirror.

"What do you think?" I ask, quickly realizing just how important his answer is going to be.

"I think," he says, stepping closer, "you look incredible."

"Thanks." A smile crosses my face and I bite my lip to try to contain it. "Honestly, fashion designers need to figure out a way for people to wear these in everyday life. I feel like my entire gait has changed. Something about the comb going into your hair activates the spine to correct your posture to make you inherently graceful."

"Look at you, changing the future of fashion and making major medical breakthroughs. And here I thought our sexytime was going to be the most memorable part of your week."

"I'm a gifted multitasker."

"It would seem so."

I fluff the veil a bit in the front as I continue to watch Ryan's reflection behind me in the mirror.

"So, as a guy who's said he's trying to get married and have kids in the very near future, how does it feel to be in the presence of a veil-wielding lady? Are your hands clammy? Are you on the verge of buying a one-way ticket to Indiana?"

"I'm fine," Ryan says calmly. "Cool as a carrot."

"You mean a cucumber."

"No, I hate cucumbers. Carrots are delicious and they do great things for your vision."

I laugh and turn around as Ryan approaches. Despite claiming to be cool as a carrot, I catch a nervous flash in his eyes as he reaches out and grabs the bottom of the veil. I have to remind myself to breathe as he slowly lifts it up to uncover my face, pushing it behind my head to fall across my shoulders.

"I know this is sudden," he says, "but I have to ask you something. Kara Sullivan...do you want to take Duke for a walk with me when we get back to the apartment?"

I give my smile free rein as I take his hands. "I do. I do want to take Duke for a walk when we get back to the apartment. Do you?"

"I do," Ryan answers with a grin.

A second later, we jump apart when the store manager walks back in carrying Cristina's veil in a white garment bag.

"Here it is," she says, handing it to me while pulling off a note that's attached to the hanger. "Please apologize to Cristina for us and wish her a very happy wedding day."

"I will, thank you so much."

Mission complete. Breaking further away from Ryan and our strange wedding vow imitation, I hold the bag up high enough so it doesn't drag as I head for the store's exit. I'm halfway across the room when he forces a cough.

"Hey, Sullivan. Do you feel like your posture is uncommonly straight right now?"

I freeze and turn around. "As a matter of fact, I do."

"I thought you might."

"I promise I wasn't actually trying to steal the veil."

Ryan walks over, looking like he only half believes me.

"If that's the story you're sticking to, I'll go with it. But just know, I crack under pressure, so if the DA starts hammering me, don't be disappointed when I sing like a canary."

"Just help me take the veil off and we'll talk about your snitching ways at a more convenient time."

"Sounds good." Ryan reaches up and pauses. "Is there a release button I should be looking for here or is there a pull string?"

"What? Neither."

My head is suddenly yanked back and I wince as he tries and fails to remove the veil.

"Ouch! Just ease the claw out of my hair."

"The claw? That sounds violent."

"You're the one making it violent and you're giving me a bald spot."

"Hold on, I think I got it. Boom." Ryan eases the veil off and hands it to the manager. "All right, problem solved. I bet people accidentally walk out of here with veils on all the time, right?"

"Not really," she answers, completely immune to his boyish charm. "Your fiancée would be the first."

"My fiancée," he echoes uncomfortably, flashing me a worried look before turning back to face the manager. "Yes, I can see why you would assume that." She continues to stare at him with a stern expression and he slowly starts to walk backwards. "On that note, everybody have a great day. This is, by far, the best bridal store I've ever been to. I mean it, you're killing it. Mazel tov." His back hits the door, making the bells ring as he becomes even more flustered. He exits the store with a wave and I have to rush to catch up with him.

I find him waiting for me outside in the middle of the sidewalk and I take his hand as we start walking down the busy street. "So, not to make you feel bad, but did you just lose your mind in there?"

"I think so. A little bit, yeah."

"Was it because that lady called me your fiancée? It's really not a big a deal, you know. She seemed a bit on another level if you ask me."

He stops walking and our interlocked hands make me stop, too. I can tell he's rattled by the interaction. "It's not that…" He trails off. "These last few days have really been a jolt to my system. They've been amazing, so amazing, but they came out of nowhere and I don't know what I'm supposed to do anymore."

I feel my inner defenses crouch at the ready. The manager calling me his fiancée clearly made Ryan question things even more between us. Things are moving too fast and too soon. He doesn't want this much of me.

I swallow down my nerves and clear my throat, trying not to let my mind run wild. "I get it," I say.

"You do?" His eyes dig deep into mine, looking for something, but I'm not sure what.

"I'm just as surprised about all this as you are," I tell him. "And I know we've always struggled with finding a middle ground. With us, it's either zero or a hundred. Hate or…" I let my words fall away as I have the distinct feeling that I'm only making matters worse. Here he's trying to tell me we need to slow down and I almost dropped the L bomb.

He gives my hand a reassuring squeeze, urging my eyes back to his. "I just feel like for this to work, we need to get everything out in the open." Here it comes. He's done with me. Again. "I should have said something sooner. I should have told you—"

"Stop! You don't have to tell me anything," I interject, cutting him off. "That lady was crazy, so don't let what she said get to you. We're fine. Last night was…perfect. Let's not ruin it with thinking too much."

Ryan looks at me, saying nothing but squeezing my hand tighter. "I don't think us not talking is going to help."

"Maybe not," I say. "But just trust me on this, okay? Please?" We're still standing in the middle of the sidewalk. Horns and sirens blare in the street beside us as determined pedestrians pass us by. We barely notice.

"Okay," he eventually agrees. I nod and try to walk away but he only pulls me back again. "And just so you know, last night was perfect for me, too."

I didn't know how much I needed him to say that until his words weave through and around me in a uniquely intricate pattern. I give his hand a tug and he wraps his arm around my waist as we finally continue walking home. And as I pull him the slightest bit closer, I try not to pay too much attention to the fact that I'm starting to think of the apartment as *our* home, and not just mine.

It is now 7:15 p.m. and I'd be lying if I said I wasn't losing it a bit. After a relaxing afternoon of dog walks and writing, Ryan left a half hour ago, saying he needed to get supplies to cook us dinner.

It's dark out now and for some reason, our situation seems totally different out of the sheltered light of day. Days are for friends, nights are for friends who get freaky.

I have no idea how to act towards him when he gets home. Will things be different? Will he act differently?

I doubt he's overthinking things. He probably does this all the time. Not sleep with college girlfriends whom he once deflowered, obviously, but he's always had a better poker face than me. I'll deal with the situation either way. If it was a mistake, so be it. If it happens again, yeehaw.

I take a deep breath and almost choke on it when I hear my apartment door unlock moments later. Before I know it, Ryan is in view and my eyes go large at the sight of him. He shuts the door with the back of his foot and I can barely see his face over the tower of "supplies" he's carrying.

In his right hand is a beautiful bouquet of what seem to be wildflowers that are bunched together with a burlap sash. His left hand is holding three plastic bags filled with groceries. Then I notice what he's wearing. I bust out laughing, taking in the novelty apron tied over his shorts and T-shirt, depicting the muscular body of a Roman gladiator, bare-chested and wearing only a canvas loincloth and a sword. Ryan remains where he is, standing across the room with a shy smile.

"Big plans tonight?" I ask.

"What would give you that idea?"

"You just have a lot going on over there."

"Truth be told, I was planning on romancing a girl I used to know."

My insides flip in the best way possible. "That sounds like fun."

"It might be. She kicked me to the curb the last time we dated, though, so we'll see what happens this time around."

"Were you maybe a bit of an ass the last time you dated?"

"You know, I can't really recall but I think I might have been."

"And how about now?" I ask.

"I'm probably still an ass but hopefully I'm a little more tolerable."

Wanting to show him just how tolerable I do find him, I move to stand directly in his path, less than a foot away. I don't put up the slightest fight against my urge to place my hands on his chest, going up on my tiptoes and kissing him. He responds right away, slowly at first but then dropping everything to the floor. His hands find their way to the small of my back, pulling me close but still not close enough. Not nearly close enough. That's all the encouragement I need. I wrap my arms around his neck and kiss him again and again.

We eventually break apart, out of breath and smirking as we look down at the mess we've made. Flowers and food are everywhere. I don't have time to fully assess the damage before Ryan tugs me forward, drawing my eyes up to his.

"Are you nervous?" he asks.

I pause and think about it. "I don't think so," I answer. "Are you?"

"Honestly, I am. This still doesn't feel real."

I nod, knowing exactly what he means, barely believing I can look at him and touch him and talk to him like I am right now. Like this is how it's always been. Like we never stopped.

"When we broke up," he says, "I used you as motivation to succeed. I thought if we ever saw each other again, I would show you how great I was and you would regret not wanting to be with me. I did everything I could to push you out of my life but really I was keeping you in the center of it—and I was this bitter ex-boyfriend planet just orbiting around you all the time."

I have to smile before getting serious again. "When I saw you at Cristina's party, I thought I hated you. It was ten years later, but everything felt so raw because deep down, I still thought about you all the time. Anytime I wrote about love or want or pain in one of my books, I drew on those feelings from what we had. Bits of you and me are layered inside each one of my stories."

Ryan takes a moment. "So what you're saying is, you're not just using me for my body."

"Oh, no, I absolutely am. I just happen to like you as a person, too."

We both smile as Ryan leans down to kiss me with a gentleness that makes my head spin.

His hands soon drift around my waist to slip under the bottom of my shirt, lightly rubbing along the skin of my lower back. I do the same, sneaking my hands under his shirt and sliding them up along his spine. I feel the goose bumps there when I repeat the path down again.

"Maybe we should go into the bedroom," I say, already heading in that direction.

"Or we could stay here." Ryan pulls me back and moves his mouth to the curve of my neck, hot and insistent. I turn my head to the side to offer more. To feel more.

Through the haze that's becoming more intense by the second, I look around for Duke. I don't spot him anywhere, so he must still be asleep in the bathroom. How Ryan managed to end up with the world's most discreet wingman of a dog, I'll never know.

I feel bolder knowing we're alone and start to shift towards the couch. Ryan stops me again.

"Not there. Here." He looks down at the reading chair and a mischievous thrill shoots through me at the prospect.

"I've never done that in my reading chair."

The tips of his ears turn red and he looks at me with a hungry sort of smile. "I like having your firsts."

It feels like my whole body breaks out in a blush. He steps into me slowly, brushing my chest with his in his lethal ratio of desperation and devotion. Our mouths fuse together and I twist a hand into the back of his hair. His kisses start out tender but then turn frantic. He pushes a knee between my legs, grinding against me and forcing a needy whine from the depths of my throat.

He breaks away at the sound and begins to step backwards, pulling me with him until his legs hit the ottoman. He nudges it away with his foot and then there's nothing between him and the front of the chair. I tear at his apron and shirt and he makes quick work of my top and bra. Dragging him down for another searing kiss, I pull his tongue into my mouth and drink him in until I have my fill.

How can this be life now?

His hands drift down to undo the button of my pants and I move away the slightest bit, pulling them down myself along with my panties. Ryan digs a condom out of his back pocket and soon he's fumbling with his belt, tearing it open, and pushing his shorts and boxers to the floor. I'm pulled back flush against him a second later and his hands cup my bottom as I gasp and arch my back. Ryan sits in the chair, holding my hand and gazing up at me with lust-filled eyes.

Whenever we're both standing, he's so much taller—forever towering over me by at least half a foot. I've always liked our height difference, and I've always secretly liked the idea that he could toss me against the wall and have his wicked way with me if we ever felt so inclined. But now, looking down at him, I'm wondering if this way is better. He's staring up at me like I could tell him to do anything in this moment and he'd do it. It's a powerful realization.

Riding my newfound high, I crawl into his lap and straddle him in the chair, adjusting myself until we're lined up perfectly. I ease myself down little by little until he's fully inside and his head falls back with a groan. I'm never going to be able to read in this chair the same away again.

"Damn, Sullivan," he sighs, sounding breathless and drunk as I continue to slide myself steadily up and down. "How is it this good? How can you always feel this good?"

His words stoke a fire in the pit of my stomach, building it up to an almost unbearable level. My hands grip the back of the chair for leverage as I move faster and a little bit harder. Our bodies soon turn slick with sweat and his hand shifts from my chest to my center that's already starting to flutter. I keep my pace as his fingers go right where I need them, rubbing and pressing, and blood roars in my ears as I cry out. Ryan's free hand flies to the back of my neck and pulls me down, kissing me deeply and swallowing my every whimper. He thrusts himself up into me once, twice, three more times until he's the one moaning into *my* mouth, his eyes clenching shut as his arms tighten around me to keep us pinned in place.

We float along in silence after that as we struggle to recover. He leans back to look at me, his hair tousled and his breathing still heavy. I have the primitive urge to keep him this way for the foreseeable future.

"I'm never going to stop wanting this," he says. I can feel his heart pounding between us as we stay locked together. "It's not like this with anyone else."

I let go of the back of the chair to drape my arms around his neck. "No," I agree. "Not for me either."

"What do you think that means?"

We search each other's eyes for the answer until I lean down, hiding my face in the curve of his shoulder. "I wish I knew," I answer honestly. "I really wish I knew."

15

The next morning, we're in my bedroom after gorging on a breakfast of whole wheat toast, scrambled eggs and non-incinerated bacon. Ryan got me a scone but I'm saving it for later. He's sitting back against the headboard on the bed now, wearing boxers and nothing else as I sport one of his oversize T-shirts with a sweatshirt on top. I'm staging a novel for Instagram, a contemporary romance with soft but striking cover art. So far, I have the book lying on my windowsill and framed with twinkle lights. My curtains run along the edge of the photo and vintage book pages that I ordered online are scattered underneath. I look through the camera on my phone to check the lighting but there's still too much empty space.

"Are you excited for the rehearsal dinner tonight?" I ask, shifting around to check the room for something else to add to the picture.

"I guess," Ryan says, flipping on the TV. "I never understood the purpose of rehearsal dinners. I want to meet the first person who said, 'You know what, I'm nervous about this whole wedding dinner situation—we better do a walk-through the night before.'"

I grab my open laptop from off the bed and add it to the corner of the shot. "We're obviously not rehearsing eating. If they were getting married in a church, we would rehearse going down the aisle in order and things like that, but since they're getting married at the venue, we get to skip the work and just have dinner."

"Well, I think it's overkill."

"What?" I ask dramatically. "You have a strong opinion about something? That's so out of character for you."

"And if I didn't know for a fact that you love arguing with me, I would probably rein myself in until I knew I had you hooked. But, seeing as that isn't the case, I'm going to let my inner weirdo run free with the wind in his hair."

"Your weird inner self has long flowing hair?"

"Yours doesn't?"

I shake my head and turn back around to the novel. I can feel Ryan adjusting his seat on the bed to check my progress.

"I never knew so much work went into these pictures," he says.

"Most people don't. Bookstagram is time-consuming but intensely worth it. And the sense of community is magical."

"It sounds cool. So what do you think, should I moon the camera in the background? That'd be a fun Easter egg for your followers to find."

"That would be a no," I answer, looking over my shoulder. "But I *will* take your watch."

"Prude." Ryan slides the watch off his wrist and hands it to me. I check the image through my screen one more time and opt to place the watch just above and to the right of the book. I then stand on my bed to hover over the scene and start clicking away. I take about twenty pictures, altering my position every few shots so I'll have variety when I choose which ones I want to edit.

Once I'm satisfied, I plop down beside Ryan to start scrolling through my options when my phone starts ringing. Jen's picture appears and I accept the call.

"Hello?"

"Kara? Why are you wide-awake so early?" I lower my phone and look at the top of the screen to check the time. It's 8:15 a.m. Sex on the reg is really affecting my morning routine.

"I don't know," I say, bringing the phone back to my ear. "I had night terrors."

Ryan and I look at each other and I quickly remember that Jen knows about him. No made-up excuse was necessary.

"You what? No, whatever, okay, don't hate me, I had no idea she was doing this."

"What are you talking about?"

"Mom!"

"Mom?" I repeat.

"Mom is on her way to your apartment!"

"What?" I immediately leap onto the floor. "Why is she coming here?" Fear echoes in my voice as I run my fingers through my bed-tangled hair.

"Yesterday she told me she's been calling you and you haven't answered or called her back. I told her you were busy writing and I thought she was okay with it but when I called her cell a few minutes ago, she was already on the train."

"When did she leave?" I ask, holding my breath and entering full-blown panic mode.

"She got into Penn Station a few minutes ago. Depending on whether she's taking a cab straight to you or taking the subway to Grand Central, she could be there any minute."

"I have to go. Thanks for the heads-up."

"Wait, wait, Kara!"

"What?" I ask.

"Is Ryan still there? Are you guys together?"

"Yes, and I think so."

"Oh, my God! Did you have sex with him?" She sounds desperately curious and I'm too frenzied to lie.

"I did. Many times."

"I love it! Call me ASAP. I want to know everything, positions included!"

"Gross, no!"

"Please?"

"Fine, goodbye." I hang up the phone as horror continues to rock through my system. Mom could be knocking on the door at any given second.

Ryan smiles over at me without a care in the world. "Problem?"

"Yes, you have to get out."

"What?"

"Go, you have to go. Right now!"

I sprint to his side of the bed and grab his arm, trying to drag him into a standing position by force. "You have to get up! My mom is on her way here."

Ryan's mouth twitches up, ready to start laughing, and his nonchalance only fuels my anxiety. I give his arm a fierce tug and, thanks to the adrenaline now pumping through my veins, I'm able to pull his half-naked form out of bed with less effort than I anticipated.

"Are you trying to tell me you don't think I'm ready to see your mom again? Is it my outfit?"

I give him a frustrated look as I pick up some of his clothes from the floor and chuck them at him. Not appreciating his lack of urgency, I put my hands on my hips and glare at him, still only wearing his favorite college sweatshirt and T-shirt. His smile vanishes.

"Sullivan, you have never looked as sexy as you do right now." He takes a determined step towards me and I jump back.

"No way!" I yell, holding out my arm. "Don't even think about it!" He continues to advance, his eyes drinking me in. "I swear, take one step closer and I will maim you. I was a biter in preschool so I will not hesitate to fight dirty."

He stops walking. "Okay, I'm sorry, I can't control myself. You look way too good in that shirt. You should take it off. I'm a gentleman so I'll help you."

I manage a little laugh as I toss him his jeans. "Just take Duke for a walk, okay? A very long, far walk."

"How far?"

"Miami."

"I knew I should have packed his beach tent." I give Ryan a pleading look and he finally starts to put on his pants. "All right, we're going," he says indulgently. "How long do you think your mom will stay?"

"I have no idea. I'll call you when you can come back." I proceed to rush through the room like a tornado, looking for anything I need to hide. Ryan's bag, his clothes, his watch on my windowsill—they all need to go.

"Do you even have my phone number saved?" I hear him ask.

I grab my cell phone from the bed, unlocking the screen and tossing it to him. "Program it in for me."

He takes the phone and disappears into the living room as I check the bathroom. It's clear. I dart into the living room next and Ryan is sitting on the reading chair, tying the laces of his sneakers.

"Not to stress you out further, but is there a reason why you're getting so worked up over this?"

"I don't know," I answer, barely sparing him a glance as I start tidying up the space as fast as humanly possible. "I just need everything to look perfect. My apartment is one of the few things my mom actually likes about me."

I'm in such a state that I don't notice Ryan getting up. I actually almost forget he's there until he puts his hands on my shoulders and turns me around to face him.

"Okay, I need you to take a breath for a second."

"I don't have time—"

"Ah, ah, ah," he says cutting me off. "Just one breath, a deep one, looking at me. Ready, set, deep breath…"

He takes a long inhale and I find myself involuntarily doing the same, feeling my heartbeat slow down just the slightest bit.

"Now talk to me," he says. "Why are you freaking out?" His hands are still on my shoulders and are now applying comforting squeezes. It's nice. Really nice.

I force myself to stay put for one more second even though I'm still wondering if I should just stiff-arm him and move on. "It's hard to explain things with my mom. She's amazing and she's given everything she's had to taking care of Jen and me, but she's also very critical, particularly of me. And as much as I pretend like I don't care, I want to impress her. I always want to impress her but no matter what I do, she always finds fault with me."

"What else could she possibly find fault with? Besides you being a blanket hog and a terrible judge of men's dance skills, you're close to perfect."

I chuckle as my welling panic starts to dissipate, replaced instead with the typical sense of mediocrity that creeps in right before or right after I see my mom.

"She wants me to be the best version of myself, but the way she sees it. Fully confident, not as bookish, happily engaged to the heir of a Greek shipping tycoon."

"That specific?"

"More or less."

"Well," Ryan says, still methodically squeezing and releasing my shoulders, "a wise woman once told me that we'll never regret the times we talk to our parents, only the times we don't. And I know I'm the last person who should be giving you advice, but you're incredible, Kara. And if your mom doesn't see that, she's just not looking at you the right way."

A too distant sensation of feeling truly happy in my own skin starts to sprout inside me, and I bring my hands up to rest on top of Ryan's.

"Thank you for saying that."

"It's the truth. And don't you forget it."

I can't help myself. I lace my arms around his neck and pull him in for a kiss that's soft and sweet but still filled with the promise of what's to come later. He looks slightly dazed and almost shy when I pull away.

"Okay," he says, "and now Duke and I are going to get out of here before I say or do something stupid and ruin the moment."

"What could you possibly do to accomplish that?"

"I can't be sure. Something weird. And considering you're still wearing my sweatshirt, there's a solid chance it'd be inappropriate."

"I think I like it when you're inappropriate." My arms are still wrapped around his neck as I pull him in a little closer, bringing myself flush against him.

Ryan lets out a slow breath. "You are going to be the death of me, Sullivan."

I push him away with a playful smile. "Have a nice walk."

"Surprise!" My mother, wearing khaki dress pants and a pale pink top, kisses my cheek and crosses the doorway into the apartment.

"Wow," I say, feigning astonishment, "I can't believe you're here." I close the door and follow her into the living room.

Dear God, please let me pull this off.

"It's so good to see you," I go on. "I'm sorry I've been out of touch this week. I've been a little preoccupied with writing."

Mom sits down on the couch, placing her purse and a shopping bag down next to her. "I understand that you're busy and you have a deadline, but it'd still make me feel better if you kept checking in. You know I worry about you."

"Yes, I know." I sit down in my reading chair and try to ignore the flurry of risqué memories it now brings to mind. "Again, I'm sorry. I'll make sure to keep checking in from now on."

"Good. So has it been a den of productivity over here this week? Is that why you've been too busy to make a five-minute phone call to your mother?" My mom speaks two languages: English and guilt. If only she would harness her powers for good instead of evil.

"Pretty much," I agree. "Just wall-to-wall productivity."

"Well, that's good. I know you're cutting it close. Is there anything I can read yet?"

"Not quite but soon. I think you'll like it. It's another historical."

"I like everything you write and I like contributing, too. Speaking of, I got these for you." She picks up the shopping bag beside her and holds it out for me. I stand up from my chair and take it with a wary smile.

"Thank you." I reach into the bag and, one by one, pull out three tank tops, all made with thin material. I force my smile to hold. "These are great. Very thoughtful."

"You don't like them." Her voice is passive but lined with frustration.

"I think they're very *you*."

"You haven't even tried them on yet. The colors will complement you so well. Why don't you like them?"

"Because I don't, Mom. I like T-shirts and sweaters and tops you can't see through."

"Return them, then," she says, crossing her legs and looking around the room. "The receipt is in the bag."

A familiar twinge of disappointment settles inside me. "I don't mean to sound unappreciative, but you always buy me clothes that you know I won't wear."

"Lesson learned. I won't buy you clothes anymore."

"Mom, come on," I say, waiting until she finally looks at me. "Why does it have to be like this? I love seeing you and spending time with you, but every time we get together our talks always turn snappy."

"You're the one who gets snappy. I'm just trying to encourage you."

"Encourage me to what?"

"To improve yourself. To venture out of your comfort zone."

"But why do I have to improve myself?" I sigh, feeling like we're going round and round all over again. "You act like I'm some miserable crone wading through a swamp just because I don't live your lifestyle and dress the way you want me to."

"All I'm trying to do is help. When you lived at home, you always felt insecure wearing anything that wasn't three sizes too big. To this day you practically wear the same stretchy pants and sweater every time you come over. Am I supposed to see you struggling and do nothing?"

"I'm not struggling, though. I'm happy with myself. I know eating extremely healthy and exercising a ton has helped you deal with a lot of painful stuff, but it's not for me. Just because I like to wear comfortable clothes doesn't mean I hate my body."

Mom gets quiet and I hope my honesty didn't make her feel bad. I've always used humor as a shield to hide how much her words can hurt. I've never been vulnerable with her about this before. Her silence leaves me feeling exposed and nervous and I debate whether I should have said anything at all.

"I only want what's best for you, Kara," she eventually says.

"I want you to find real love and get married and have a family and it's going to be so much harder for you to get there if you're not confident within yourself. Losing your dad made me see how fast life goes by and I don't want you to waste any more time."

I take a second and her words sink in, heavy and honest. "I know that you love me and you're coming from a good place, but your opinion means so much to me. I'm never going to be fully confident or think that I'm good enough until you do, too."

Mom looks at me and I have the intense instinct to say that I'm kidding, that I haven't been grasping for her approval for most of my life and she should forget everything I just said.

But I say nothing. Instead, seconds pass by in silence until Mom folds her hands in her lap.

"I never meant to hurt you," she says. "You and Jen make me proud every day and if I didn't make that clear, then that's my fault. I'll try to do better."

It's not often that my mom offers an apology, and to be honest, it kind of freaks me out.

"It's okay," I quickly reply. "I'll be better, too. If I layer up those tank tops I bet they'd look great…with a sweater."

Her cheeks pull back in a smile and I exhale a breath of relief. I've always been terrified of confrontation. If we ever had an actual argument, I'd probably run out of the room screaming.

"And how are you doing?" I ask.

"Me? I'm fine." I keep looking at her and for the first time in a long time, I see a crack in her steel demeanor. "You know," she goes on to say, "I have my good days and my bad days."

"I'm the same way."

In the blink of an eye, I'm swarmed with memories of my parents together. My dad was playful and my mom was strong. He joked and she laughed. He danced with her when she turned the radio on in the kitchen. She doesn't turn the radio on anymore.

"How do you do it?" I find myself asking. "How do you recover from losing someone you love so much?"

"You don't," she answers. "I haven't. I just have to believe that I'll see him again someday, and then all the waiting will be worth it."

I take a breath at her words. "That's a really beautiful thought."

"Use it in your next book," she says with a grin.

It gets quiet after that but not uncomfortable. I'm about to offer her a cup of tea when the sound of Beyoncé's "Crazy In Love" starts blasting through the room, leading us both to exchange matching expressions of confusion.

"Is that your phone?" I ask in disbelief, while also being incredibly impressed.

"What? No, it's not my phone."

I get up and follow the sound of the music until I find my cell phone lit up on the kitchen counter. The word *Beefcake* flashes across the caller ID screen.

Oh, that bastard.

I'm feeling a mixture of rage and amusement as I answer the phone. "Hello," I say sweetly.

"Hey, you like my ringtone?" Ryan's voice is light and easy. He's going to catch an elbow to the chin when he gets back.

"I'm sorry but I'm busy right now." I smile at my mom as she eyes me suspiciously.

"Duke says hi. He also says that he's tired of walking."

"Well, tell him it's good for him. I have to go now. You have a great day."

"Wait, wait, I have to ask you one more question. It's really important."

"What?"

"Are you still wearing my sweatshirt?"

"Okay, bye!"

I hang up and focus back on my mom, unable to stifle my smile as I put the phone down on the counter. I try to act neutral as I return to the reading chair.

"Who was that?" she asks.

"That was the census bureau."

I can tell she doesn't believe me but she still sits back with a shrug. "So have you started packing yet?"

"Packing?"

"Kara Marie Sullivan," she says with clear disapproval, "do you mean to tell me that you are leaving for Italy in a matter of days and you still haven't even started packing yet?"

Packing. Italy. Crap. Is it horrible that I forgot about that?

"Okay, so I haven't packed yet, but it won't take me that long."

"Packing for a weekend getaway wouldn't take long. You're leaving for six months. Six months, Kara. How couldn't you have started yet?"

"I don't know," I mumble. "I guess I got distracted."

"Distracted by what?"

Nothing in particular. Just all the filthy, passionate, awesome secret sex I've been having with my ex-boyfriend.

"Work stuff," I say, my voice sounding pitchy. "Switching back to Italy, though, I meant to give you this last week." I hop up from the chair and walk over to my desk, opening a drawer and pulling out a folder. "I did some early prep work for Jen's baby shower since I'll be gone during the planning time. Jen loves Beatrix Potter so I figured that can be our theme. I got some invitation samples for you to choose from and I printed out pictures of the decorations I'm going to buy. I'm thinking I'll order things little by little while I'm in Rome and have them sent to your house."

I hand Mom the folder. She opens it up and looks through

each invitation and picture. "This all looks great. I'm surprised you got all of this done already."

"Yeah, well, when you find out that you're actually a sub-par writer who can't finish her work on time, it's shockingly therapeutic to shop for baby party decor online."

My mom laughs and tucks the folder into her bag.

An hour later, I'm in the clear. The sneaky daughter gods have smiled upon me and my mom doesn't suspect a thing, other than her thinking that I'm losing my mind, but that's nothing new. I should feel guilty about lying to her, but she'll find out about Ryan and me soon enough.

"Now, I know tomorrow is going to be hectic, but you could still text Jen and me pictures of all you girls in your dresses. And you better call me the next day to tell me all about the wedding."

"I will, I promise."

My mom smiles before kissing me on the cheek and heading for the elevator. I close the door behind her and my mind slowly drifts back to Italy. How could I have forgotten? I've been looking forward to this for months, years even. All my hard work has brought me to this trip. How is it possible that for even one hour it slipped my mind?

Ryan.

That's how it slipped my mind. Between him and my deadline, I've been able to think of little else. Ryan is this surprising, amazing force that is back in my life and it's starting to get hard to remember what it was like without him.

But what about Italy? Do I really want to pack up and leave for six months now? We'll be right back to where we left off in college. Am I willing to risk what we have all over again?

I have to decide what to do. I have to tell Ryan.

Soon.

16

The three long tables at Cristina and Jason's rehearsal dinner are half-filled with guests as Ryan and I enter the private wine cellar at Del Frisco's restaurant. The Edison bulbs dangling overhead cast an orange glow over the space, complementing the hundreds of wine bottles that are pristinely shelved behind the solid glass walls surrounding us. It feels like we're in an upscale cave stocked with booze and I have to say, I'm into it.

Ryan and I look at each other, our eyebrows going up, mutually saying *fancy*.

He gives me a quick wink before we walk deeper into the room, which is filled but not crowded with about thirty people. I hear a happy shriek and suddenly Cristina is grabbing me by the shoulders and giving me a fierce hug.

"I'm getting married tomorrow!" she almost sings.

"Yes, you are," I say, stepping back and handing her the garment bag with her veil. "And you're going to need this.

I swear I only wore it around my apartment for a few hours and then one time to the gyno, super fast."

"Totally understandable. Jason, come here," she calls across the room before turning back around. "Seriously, thank you so much for picking this up. I almost lost my mind."

Jason appears beside Cristina. I give him a beaming smile and am confused when he looks at Ryan and me with jumpy, uncomfortable eyes.

"Hey," he says, sounding like he's talking to a medical professional instead of his two biggest fans.

"Well," Cristina chimes in, "you two look very sweet standing side by side. I was sure one of you would bury the other before the wedding but I'm glad I was wrong. Don't they look good together, Jason?"

"Yeah, super great," he agrees. He then turns to Ryan, still seeming jittery. "Hey, man, can I talk to you?"

Ryan barely says, "Sure," before Jason pushes him off to the side and follows after him.

Cristina looks away from them and back to me. "I don't know what's going on with him. He's been stressed out about Ryan for days."

"Really?" I ask, looking over her shoulder.

"Yeah, but forget about Jason," she says, pulling my hand and making me concentrate on her. "I've been so busy with wedding stuff, but I want to hear every detail about what's been going on with you and Ryan. I kid you not, when you guys walked in, you looked in love."

"We did not look in love," I assert.

"Yes, you did, and I will die on that hill if you try to convince me otherwise. I watched you two coming down the stairs and you were straight-up dirty smiling and trying not to look at each other. If I wasn't someone who was also in love, I would have thrown food at you in disgust."

I think about denying it but decide against it. "What kind of food?" I ask instead.

"The kind of food an angry mob would throw. Maybe cabbage."

"That's actually really creative. I like the backstory behind your choice."

"Thank you. Okay, go, tell me everything." She crosses her arms and steps closer to me, trying to get comfortable.

"There's not too much to tell. I think we're together."

Cristina's eyes light up. There's no way she's not inwardly planning double dates for the rest of our lives and arranging marriages for all of our hypothetical children.

"Remember, this is all very new," I remind her. "I have no idea how things are going to pan out, so don't get carried away."

Cristina rubs her hands together. The don't-get-carried-away ship is already long-gone and has set sail for the Baltic Sea.

"I won't, I definitely won't," she promises. "This is all just so incredible, though. Never in my wildest dreams did I think my best friend would date my future husband's best friend. Can you imagine the family vacations we can go on together?"

I start to smile despite my hesitation. Family vacations together would be nice…

No! Stop this!

"Okay, let's not get ahead of ourselves. No one is getting married here besides you. Who knows how long Ryan will stay interested in me anyways?"

"Why do you have to put yourself down like that?" Cristina demands. "You're a successful, funny, beautiful woman. Any guy would be lucky to be with you."

"That's very nice of you to say but also very unnecessary."

"Apparently it is necessary. Do you remember when we first met?"

"You mean the best day of our lives?" I tease.

Cristina and I were both waitressing in a pub in Chelsea in grad school. The food was average, but the clientele was almost always drunk, so no one complained.

"I was crying because it was Valentine's Day and Warren dumped me for my Swedish roommate who claimed to be a ballerina even though she wasn't even good."

"I remember," I say. "That guy was lame, and Astrid never once reacted to any of my *Center Stage* references. It was highly suspicious."

"I know, but I was heartbroken and insecure, and you told me that Warren would regret leaving me because I had true grace and I was a thousand times better than my troll of a roommate."

"Not to veer off topic, but I'm still convinced that your roommate actually was a troll. I did a report on Scandinavian folklore in high school and she checked a lot of boxes."

"Can you please focus?" Cristina places her hands on my shoulders. "What I'm trying to say is, now it's my turn to pump you up and tell you that *you* are the one who has true grace... Plus you don't even have a troll roommate so there's no way Ryan will ever fall out of love with you."

I try to disguise my confusion, but I don't do a good job.

Cristina shakes her head and rests her hands on her hips. "That inspirational speech made so much more sense in my mind. Just don't sell yourself short, okay?"

I sigh and give her a hug. "Why didn't you just say that in the first place?"

"I tried but I'm a numbers person. You're the word weaver."

"I know," I say as we step back. "I love you, my numbers person."

"Love you more, word weaver."

We both look over and find Ryan and Jason still locked in an animated conversation.

"What do you think those two are talking about?"

"No idea." I take in Ryan's stoic face as he continues to listen to Jason before I turn my attention back to Cristina. "So, is there anything else I can do for tomorrow? Anything I can help you with?"

"Not really," she says. "Just be at my apartment no later than 9:00 a.m. The hair and makeup people will be there and we'll all take turns. I'll have bagels and fruit and mimosas so don't worry about having breakfast. Overall, I anticipate zero stress."

"Zero stress, that's what I like to hear. Do you mean it?"

"Absolutely not. One million percent, I'm going to be manic."

Out of nowhere, Jason and Ryan appear back at our sides.

"Hey, hi everyone." Jason is forcing a smile as he grabs Cristina's hand. "Babe, we should go sit, I think. The food is getting cold."

"What are you talking about? The food isn't even out yet." She looks around at the very foodless tables with not a waiter in sight, save for the ones serving champagne.

"I know it's not out yet, but it's coming."

"What is the matter with you?" Cristina asks.

"I just need to sit down, honey. My feet hurt and I have to save my strength for tomorrow. Plus, I feel gassy."

Everyone takes a step back.

"Okay, that was a bit of an overshare, babe. Let's not forget that this is our rehearsal dinner."

"I know it's our rehearsal dinner but I'm feeling definite movement in my body, so I suggest we sit down before I accidentally fumigate this entire room."

"Okay, okay," Cristina mutters, "so thrilled to be marrying this pillar of class tomorrow." She looks over apologetically at Ryan and me. "I guess we're going to sit down. We'll catch up again later."

Cristina and Jason walk off to the head table and soon everyone is circling around, looking for their place cards. Shock of the century, Cristina seated me next to Ryan.

"What were you and Jason talking about?" I ask him as we sit down.

Ryan's expression shifts from pensive to blank. He flattens his tie against his shirt before tucking his chair in closer to the table. "Just about how much I suck, basically."

"What? Why would he say that?"

"It's not his fault. I told him I would do something and I didn't." He keeps fiddling with his tie and it makes me want to grab his hand and pin it down.

"Was it groomsman stuff? In case you haven't noticed, I'm a pro bono wedding planner extraordinaire. Whatever it is, I'm sure we can fix it."

"It's not groomsman stuff." I'm ready to press him further when he reaches around the back of my chair and drags it forward until our seats bump together. "How about we have a good time tonight and I'll explain everything when we get home?"

His close proximity makes me a little loopy but not enough for me to ignore the slight uneasy feeling that's growing in my stomach.

"Is it—" I don't get chance to finish as a trim, towering man unceremoniously drops into the empty seat beside Ryan. His brown hair is messy in an intentional way and the suit he's wearing seems tailor-made. The watch on his wrist looks more expensive than my first two cars.

"Remind me never to be a groomsman again," he says in an inconvenienced tone. "I almost forgot all about this thing."

"I figured."

"What's there to rehearse anyways?"

"I said the same thing."

Watching him and Ryan talk, I recognize the man as his friend from the pre-wedding party. I think his name was—

"*Bonjour, mademoiselle*, my name is Beau." He reaches out and takes my hand in a steady grip. I can tell he likes to moisturize.

"*Bonjour*," I say with a hesitant smile, "I'm Kara."

"You look very beautiful tonight, Kara. That shade of blue you're wearing is particularly alluring with your deep brown eyes."

"Do not hit on her," Ryan says. "She's self-sufficient and doesn't have any incapacitating self-esteem issues so you wouldn't like her at all."

"That's a shame. Your skin tone and my height would have made for exceptionally superior offspring."

"I said don't hit on her."

"I'm not hitting on her, I'm stating genetic facts. This guy always has such a bad attitude."

"I haven't noticed," I say jokingly.

"How I've been able to stay best friends with him for so long is beyond me. I just have too big a heart."

"How am I the one with a bad attitude?" Ryan asks. "You're the one who got us thrown out of our hotel room."

"Tell me you're not still whining about this. God strike me down for forgetting to serenade your dog with Celine Dion's greatest hits while simultaneously petting him to sleep on the second night of the full moon."

"All you had to do was play the playlist."

"If I hear you say 'play the playlist' one more time, I'm going to buy the rights to every one of those songs and destroy their original recordings in a fire."

"That would make zero difference whatsoever. There's billions of copies of them around the world."

"And I will make it my life's work to delete them all."

"You guys are fun," I say with a grin.

Beau and Ryan's relationship is a bit surprising. Beau comes off as very metro—well groomed, well dressed, ready to mingle and probably drives a sleek little sports car. Ryan is happiest in jeans, wants to be home with his dog and has driven nothing but a pickup truck since he was sixteen.

"How long have you been friends?" I ask.

"Since kindergarten," Beau answers. "Ryan came in the first day of school wearing camo shorts and cowboy boots and kicked everyone in the shins, including the teacher."

"I did not kick the teacher," Ryan clarifies, "I hissed at her. There's a big difference and I couldn't help that my shyness was misinterpreted for aggression."

"As you can imagine, I've been a mentor to him through the years. He's always been there for me, so our friendship is one of my top priorities… And I think Cristina's morally questionable coworker just walked in, so it was nice talking to you both. Farewell."

Beau is out of his chair and is crossing the room before I can even say goodbye.

"Well," I say to Ryan. "He seems like a handful."

"Yeah, he's pretty much nuts. He has severe shiny ball syndrome but he's a good guy."

"I liked him. It's nice seeing you annoy someone other than me for a change."

"All he had to do was play the playlist."

I stifle a groan and roll my eyes. "Hey, I forgot to ask you, what are you going to do about Duke tomorrow while we're on wedding duty?"

"All taken care of. I booked a dog-walker for him four

months ago. The guy is really sought-after so I had to get him early. We've already FaceTimed a bunch of times so Duke could get used to the sound of his voice."

"A sought-after dog-walker?"

"I found him through a highly vetted dog-walking company. He's going to visit with Duke, walk him twice, play with him, feed him—essentially, he's going to offer complete physical and emotional support."

"Lovely, and this is all happening inside my apartment?"

"That is correct." He pauses as I give him a pointed look. "So, I'm just now thinking that I probably should have run this by you."

"Probably," I say.

"That makes sense. I'll tell you what, if anything is damaged or stolen, I will apologize profusely and pay half the value."

"You wish."

"You drive a hard bargain. Hopefully you'll mellow out a bit when me and Duke move to New York."

I freeze, feeling like my chair has suddenly fallen out from under me. Ryan looks as shocked as I do, if not more so. I don't think he meant to say those words out loud, but they're out there now. "What was that?" I ask as calmly as possible.

He doesn't move a muscle. He looks like he's entirely afraid but is trying not to show it. Seconds tick by until he turns to me, seeming to make a mental decision. "I said, when I move to New York, I hope you adopt a more relaxed lifestyle. A stressful environment is very detrimental to Duke's personal growth."

My heartbeat drums faster and faster. It takes real effort to keep my voice level. "Just so we're clear about what's going on right now, are you asking to move in with me?"

"I mean, I think that's the goal, eventually, but I figured I would get my own place with Duke at first." I stay quiet. He keeps going. "I could sign a year-long lease or maybe I could sublet for a few months. I'd have to find a job here first anyways. That could take a while. I know Duke and I are a lot and obviously this is all happening quickly, but I don't want us to do long distance again. I feel like we should give this a real shot and if moving to New York is what that means, then that's what I'll do, if you want me to."

He's rambling. He's hard-core rambling and I have to smile as I try to wrap my head around the situation.

Ryan swallows, a look of adorable anxiety crossing his face. "Is that smile from thinking about how maybe you could potentially want the same thing, or was it more of an all-right-I-now-need-to-change-my-name-and-number-and-start-a-new-life-in-a-foreign-land kind of smile?"

My entire body fills with so much petrified excitement that I think it might spill out of my ears. "It was the wanting-the-same thing bit."

"That's good to hear." Ryan's hand slips into mine under the table. His eyes are bright and his ears are red and I suddenly get Maggie's penchant for bursting into song. "I guess second time's the charm."

"That's not a thing."

"It is now." He picks up a champagne flute from off the table and gestures at me to do the same. "Cheers, Sullivan."

I tap my glass to his with a reckless smirk, delirious in my own happiness and giving zero thought to anything else outside this moment. "Here we go again."

Having been home from the rehearsal dinner for a half hour, I've come down from my Ryan-wants-to-move-to-New-York high long enough to realize that I have to tell him about Italy. As in now. I'm a pile of nerves and I have no clue how he's going to react.

I get up from the couch when he walks into the apartment with a none-too-happy Duke huffing and puffing behind him from their before-bed walk.

"Hey," I call out, holding my hands behind my back as Ryan unclasps the leash.

"Hey. You look comfy."

I look down at my soft gray pajama pants and my emerald T-shirt.

"Yeah, whenever I have to get all dressed up for something I morph back into my true form in a matter of seconds once I get home. It's my superpower."

"I like it," he says, seeming distracted. He's breathing heavily but quickly as he crosses the room to me, so much so that I grab his hand.

"Are you okay?" I ask.

"Yeah, I'm fine." I know he's not. I sit back down on the couch and pull him down beside me, watching as he rubs sweaty palms against the front of his pant legs.

"You look on edge," I say.

"I know, I'm sorry." I try to smile and twist my hands together in my lap. Ryan notices. "You seem a little on edge yourself."

I tug him closer. My grip is tight and my eyes are worried. "Honestly, I kind of am."

"I am, too," he admits. "I know I said at the rehearsal dinner that we'd talk about everything when we got home, so now is as good a time as any. Let me start by saying I—"

"Can I talk first?" I ask, interrupting. "I mean, it's nothing crazy but something important slipped my mind and I think we should discuss it. In retrospect, I should have brought it up earlier, but I didn't and now...yeah."

"Okay," Ryan says hesitantly, seeming confused.

"Right. So a few months ago, I was having a bit of a tough

time with writing. I had just gone through my breakup and I was looking for a change of scenery, so I decided to take a trip."

"Oh, yeah? Where'd you go?"

"No, I didn't go anywhere then. I booked a trip that I'm going on soon. Two days after Cristina's wedding. To Italy."

Ryan moves forward on the couch, turning in towards me. I can see the underlying concern in his eyes. "How long are you going for?"

I pause. "Six months."

Ryan's face falls. My heart is pounding one second and slowing the next. Stopping and starting at the same time.

"Six months?" he asks.

"I've always wanted to take a big trip to Europe and when I booked it, I thought it was the perfect time to go. I figured I would relax, I'd write, I'd travel. All that good stuff."

Ryan sits back on the couch. "Sorry, I'm just taking this all in. You're leaving for Italy in two days and you're not coming back for six months?"

"Yes." I keep twisting my fingers together.

"So were you and me a kind of fun, goodbye fling?" His tone is light, but I know there's more fear to his words than he wants to let on.

"No, not at all," I say, inching closer. "I honestly didn't know what this was until you said what you did at dinner tonight. The thought of you moving here made me so happy and then I felt terrible because I didn't tell you about my trip."

Ryan swallows and nods.

"But this doesn't mean that I don't want to be with you. There are other options to consider."

"What kind of options?"

"Well, option one is that I go to Italy as planned. We can FaceTime every day and maybe you can even come over for a vacation if you can get time off work." I lean forward and grab the paper I hid under a book on the coffee table. "I printed out a brochure of the apartments I'm staying in. I'm sure you'd love it. It can be your first trip abroad."

I hand him the folded-up paper, giving my best travel-agent smile. Ryan looks at the front cover but doesn't open it.

"And option two?" he asks.

The room goes quiet. I can hear Duke's heavy breathing from my bedroom.

"Option two...I don't go." I search Ryan's eyes for what he could be feeling but can't find anything definitive. His emotions are blurry, silhouettes swimming under a thick sheet of ice. "What are you thinking?" I ask.

"I really don't know."

"Are you mad?"

"No, I'm not mad. I'm just processing everything." A few seconds pass until he stands up and walks towards the kitchenette. His steps are heavy until he turns around to face me, his hands resting down on the frame of a dining table chair.

"How would you feel if I decided to go?" I ask.

"I'd miss you. I'd be scared that what happened between us before would happen again."

"And if I didn't go?"

"If you didn't go, I'd feel guilty and worried that you were missing out on something you wanted because of me."

His words confirm that there's no winner in either scenario. No obvious choice.

"I should have brought it up sooner, but I wasn't even positive if you were into me or not until fairly recently."

"Are you serious?" Ryan walks closer to the couch but doesn't sit back down. "Since the first second I saw you again all I've been doing is trying not to throw myself at you every second of the day."

My heart feels heavy, beating faster still. "Why did you try not to?" I ask.

It's hard to swallow. My mouth feels dry. I'm poised to speak again when Ryan's cell phone vibrates in his pocket. He pulls it out and looks at the screen before silencing it. He then slides it back into his pocket and sits down on the couch beside me.

"You need to go on this trip," he says.

"I don't." The thought of him wanting me to leave suddenly makes me want to stay. "What if what we have goes away again?"

"It won't. Six months is a long time, but we can handle it." He takes my hand and moves his thumb over my fingers. "We've already made it ten years without each other. Six months will be like a long weekend for us."

"Is that what you really think?" I ask.

"Yes. It won't be easy, but we'll get through it. We'll be okay."

I nod my head, moving forward to wrap my arms around his waist.

We'll be okay.

He thinks we're going to be okay.

I wish I believed him.

The next morning, I wake up again to an empty bed. It's quiet. No running shower water or murmurs of the TV in the other room. I sit up and Ryan is nowhere to be seen. My apartment, which would once seem perfectly normal in this state, now seems deserted.

I get out of bed and walk into the living room. Duke is resting on the floor next to the ottoman as Ryan sits in my reading chair. He looks up at me with a small smile that doesn't reach his eyes. I return it with one of my own as I cross the room, standing beside him and rubbing the back of his neck with my hand. "Good morning."

"Morning," he answers.

"I have to head over to Cristina's to start getting ready soon. You're meeting Jason and the guys at the hotel, right?"

Ryan nods. He looks tired.

"Are you feeling all right?"

He takes my hand from his neck and squeezes it in his own. "I'm fine."

I walk around the chair and sit on his lap, pushing my hand into his sandy hair that always looks darker when we're inside. He nestles me close and inhales against the top of my chest through my T-shirt.

"You don't seem fine. Are you upset because today will officially prove that Jason loves Cristina more than you?"

A grin tugs at the corner of his mouth as he nudges at my chin with the tip of his nose. "Who told you?"

"Lucky guess," I answer.

We sink deeper into the chair and he brushes the front strands of my hair off my face as he kisses me. Despite his gentleness, he still seems somehow absent.

"Are you sure you're…" He cuts me off with a searing kiss and I'm lulled into a state where I forget my worries. Right now, in my head and my heart, nothing exists outside of us.

17

Cristina and Jason's wedding is more beautiful than I ever could have imagined. The venue, Manhattan Penthouse on Fifth, seems perched above the world, with the arched windows revealing jaw-dropping views of the Freedom Tower to the south and the Empire State Building to the north. Flowers and candles are everywhere, mixing seamlessly with the elegant but modern decor.

The ceremony drifts by, smooth as a dream as Cristina floats down the aisle to *Canon in D*, played live on a solo acoustic guitar. Jason has noticeable tears in his eyes as he watches her walk towards him, and I can only thank the Lord that I wrapped tissues around the base of my bouquet because I needed every single one plus twenty-five more.

They recite traditional vows and I try not to melt as Ryan steals looks at me as they speak them. I can't stop from thinking that maybe, one day, this could be us—that we could have this.

After the ceremony, we take pictures in the street, working through the cocktail hour. We pose in every scenario humanly possible and then some. Ryan and I are never paired together since I'm matched up with the best man, Jason's balding but very nice older brother. At one point I stand next to Ryan for a group shot and he holds my hand behind our backs, leaving me feeling as nauseously excited as I did the first time a boy held my hand in a movie theater when I was thirteen.

Cristina and Jason are now having their first dance as all two hundred and eighty guests circle the dance floor, smiling and catching the eyes of their dates—enjoying watching how in love they are.

I'm about to go on the hunt for more tissues when I feel a familiar hand on the small of my back.

"What's the verdict, Sullivan? You think they'll make it?" Ryan's breath is warm on my ear as he leans in close. He smells like shaving cream, whiskey and home.

I keep watching Jason and Cristina and breathe in deep. "Of course they'll make it."

"What makes you so sure?"

Their romantic song reaches its final notes and the fifteen-piece band slides right into another romantic slow number. One of the singers invites all couples onto the dance floor and Ryan silently slips his fingers through mine, pulling us into the mix. I link my arms around his broad shoulders as he holds my hand and waist. We leave zero room for the Holy Spirit as we both instinctually step closer, swaying and spinning to the soft melody.

"I'm just sure," I say. "Jason and Cristina both know what they want and they know who they are."

"That must be nice."

"What makes you say that? You don't know who you are?"

"I used to think I did. I was positive I was exactly who I was supposed to be."

"And then what?" I ask.

"And then, you." Ryan gives me a twirl and I try to channel my inner Ginger Rogers as he pulls me back in. I probably look closer to Big Foot. "When I went out with the guys the day we got our tuxes, Jason and Beau told me I was different. They said they had forgotten I was funny."

"Ouch."

"Honestly, I wasn't even offended because they were right. After we broke up, I think I went into a kind of survival mode. I'd go through the motions with everything, but nothing felt as good as it should. And now I don't know if I'm going back to who I used to be or if I'm changing into someone different."

"Maybe you're just acting like who you really are."

"And maybe that only happens when I'm with you."

The music fades out, the song ending. I can tell Ryan wants to kiss me as bad as I want to kiss him, but we both hold back. There are too many eyes around us, and too many questions would follow. Instead we stand there, in the middle of the crowded dance floor, grinning and looking at each other with an intimacy that only we can see.

The band whips into a lively salsa song next, and Ryan takes my hand, leading me back towards the tables.

"I'm going to head for the bar. You want a champagne or are you trying to get wild with a bay breeze?"

"Let's just go full throttle and start with a bay breeze. You only live once."

"I like where your head's at, Sullivan. I'll be right back."

I sit down at our assigned table and take a much-needed sip of water. Looking at the delicate calligraphy on the place card in front of me, I chuckle when I see that Cristina once again seated me next to Ryan. Good thing we're at the point we are in our relationship. If we weren't, we'd probably be royally peeved with the arranged marriage my best friend is trying to force us into.

I'm just beginning to scan the menu tucked into my napkin when a woman I don't recognize approaches our table, scrunching down a bit to check the place cards. She looks like a beautiful Southern belle with a bright floral dress and voluminous red-blond hair styled flawlessly over her left shoulder. Her makeup is YouTube tutorial caliber, and I mean that as in she makes the tutorials, not watches them. Something about her looks familiar but I can't place it. She still hasn't found her name when she almost reaches my side.

I get up with a smile as we make eye contact. "Hey. I'm Kara."

"Hi," she answers, seeming relieved. "It's so nice to meet you. I'm sorry to walk around looking lost, but I'm trying to find someone. I originally couldn't make it tonight, but I was able to move things around last-minute."

"Well, you're in luck because I can probably help you. I'm the maid of honor, so these seat assignments have haunted my dreams for weeks."

"Aw, you're such a good friend. I'm Madison." She holds out her hand and I stand up to shake it. As I do, the world seems to slow down around me. My stomach twists and tightens to an excruciating point.

Her name rings out in my head, soft at first, then louder and louder until it's deafening. Madison. Madison. Ryan's Madison.

Madison is still shaking my now-trembling hand as she looks past me and flashes a radiant smile.

"There he is! Just excuse me for one second."

Don't turn around. If you don't see it, it won't be real.

I wish I could listen to my own warning, but I can't. I turn around to watch Madison happily fling her arms around Ryan's shoulders as he stares back at me with a look I've only ever seen the day I left him.

My insides lurch.

Ryan untangles Madison's arms from around him and turns his eyes from me to her. "What are you doing here?" he asks.

"I cut my business trip short so I could surprise you. Did I?"

"Yeah, you did." Ryan walks over towards me and Madison follows. My chest feels like it's being stretched paper-thin. A million questions rush through me at once. "Kara, this is Madison."

Madison. Madison. Madison. I'm getting a splitting headache. Madison reaches out to me again, this time with her left hand, and I almost collapse backwards.

"Wow," I manage to force out, my voice shaking. "That is a beautiful diamond ring."

She pulls her hand back to admire the ring herself before moving to rest it on Ryan's stomach. I feel the world splitting in two and I want to fall into the gap.

"Thank you so much," she says sweetly. "We only got engaged a couple weeks ago. We haven't really told anyone yet. Just our families."

I think she's still talking but I can't make out what she's saying. I'm so dizzy and I hear this ringing sound and I might cry. I think I should walk away now, out of the room or out of the state.

"Okay, great to meet you but I have to go check on something."

I turn and leave without another word. Ryan is saying something but it's so hard to hear him over the ringing in my ears.

Calm down. Focus. Get to the bridal suite. You'll be all right if you can get to the bridal suite.

I cross the length of the reception hall as the people move

past me at an alarming rate. Everyone's spinning, all in a blur. The music is blaring and I'm sweating.

I hit the hallway and I know I'm almost there. The bridal suite. Quiet. I pass the coat check closet that isn't in use and open the door that only the bridal elite can open. It closes behind me with a thud.

I look around at the tufted settees and empty champagne glasses and remember all of us sitting in here an hour ago. We toasted Cristina and Jason, and Ryan brushed his knee against mine. No one knew but us.

Oh, we were a secret all right. I had no idea how big of a secret we were.

I move to the center of the white marble floor and turn when the door opens. Ryan. He shuts the door and it feels like a too curious zoo-goer has stepped inside my tiger cage. No one would blame me if I ripped him to pieces.

"Kara." He's trying to be calm, but I hear the fear in his voice. It pulls me out of my daze and now I'm focused. Out for blood.

"How long have you been with her?" I ask point-blank. "If you say you've been together since we broke up, I think I might actually kill you."

"No. No, of course not. She got a job on the West Coast right after you and I ended things and we never spoke again after that. We only reconnected a year ago."

It's strange. I've written about heartbreak for a long time. I've used words to dance around it, to flame the fire of pain in my readers to make them connect with a story, but this, what I'm feeling right now...my words never scratched the gory surface.

"Have you been talking to her while you were here? When do you call her, when you take Duke for his walks?"

There's a long pause. I can feel the color draining from my cheeks.

Ryan nods.

I shake my head and start pacing the room, barely breathing. "I can't believe I did this. I can't believe I let this happen all over again."

"Kara, I'm sorry. I'm so sorry. I swear I was going to end things with her as soon as I got home. I would have done it over the phone but that seemed wrong since we're..." His words break off.

"You're what?" I demand, already knowing what he means. "Go ahead and say it. Say it really loud so you can hear just how big of a dirtbag you are."

Ryan swallows. "Since we're engaged."

Man, this hurts. I might throw up. I need to get out of here. I try to leave but he's already in front of me, grabbing my wrists. The feel of his hands on me makes me want to claw my skin off. I pull myself out of his grasp and take a step backward.

"I knew I shouldn't have done this. I knew being with you was wrong, but I didn't care. This is what I get. This is what needs to happen to people like me."

Ryan doesn't say anything. He just stands there. He looks so lost.

"Why did you say all that garbage about wanting to move here and be with me? Were you setting me up?"

"What? No, I would never do that."

"Yes, you would! You told me that first night after dinner you wanted to. You dreamed about it, remember? Revenge on the girl who dumped you in college. Did it feel as good as you imagined?"

"No! Please listen to me—I'm so sorry for not telling you the truth but you have to understand what things were like with

Madison and me. We weren't madly in love. We didn't have an elaborate engagement. We were together for less than a year, but she kept talking about how all her friends were married and having kids and that we needed to take the next step. She asked me to marry her, knowing how I felt, and I said okay. I didn't have a reason not to. She picked that ring out herself."

"But you bought it for her! You agreed to be engaged."

"What else was I supposed to do? I started dating someone. She was nice and she cared about me, and she wanted to get married, so I went along with it. I had no idea I would ever see you again or that you would still want me."

"What were you supposed to do?" I echo disbelievingly. "How about not act like you're single and that you want us to be together while you're secretly engaged?"

"I made a terrible mistake, Kara. I should have ended things over the phone. I should have driven to her company retreat and told her face-to-face. I wish to hell I did. We've only been engaged for two weeks. We don't even live together." His eyes are pleading but I don't care. He can't justify this. I wrap my arms around my stomach as he goes on.

"I knew from that first night when we almost kissed that I couldn't marry her. All our calls this week felt forced and awkward and I know she could tell—that's probably why she's here right now. I couldn't tell her I loved her. I said we needed to talk when I got back. I promise everything was called off in my head—all I had to do was tell her in person."

"Screw your promises! And what? Now you're ready to ditch perfect, nice Madison who cares about you so much and who can't wait to marry you? Does she mean that little to you?"

"No, she's just…" He struggles to find the words until he says, "I have tried to move on from us. I tried but no matter what, I always looked for you, for what we had, in every person I've dated since you left, but it doesn't work. It *can't* work because they're not you. No one will ever be you and you're the only person who is right for me."

He tries to move towards me, but I only move back.

"Is that supposed to make everything better? You say something romantic and I pretend this never happened?"

"No. I don't know." Ryan shifts around and runs his hands through his hair, pulling at it before facing me again. "I wanted to tell you. I promised Jason I would. I tried to do it a bunch of times but something always went wrong or you'd tell me not to say anything and I'd panic. No matter what, I was going to tell you after the wedding tonight but I never should have let it come to this. I was a coward. I knew that if I told you the truth, you would want me to leave and I didn't want to leave you. I can't. I know I'm technically engaged—"

"You're not *technically* engaged, Ryan. You ARE engaged! Are you detached from reality?"

"And what about you, Sullivan?" he asks, suddenly stepping closer. "You're the one who conveniently forgot to mention that you're leaving the country for half a year."

"Don't you dare compare my trip to you being engaged." I actually consider hitting him.

"I'm not comparing them. I'm just saying—yes, I messed up on a colossal level. I should have told you the truth. I shouldn't have let anything happen between us until I broke things off with Madison. In almost every aspect of my life I'm a logical person, but when it comes to you, I lose my mind."

Ryan moves to approach me again but then thinks the better of it.

"I told you we should keep our distance. I thought if I stayed away from you until after the wedding I could get my head straight and sort everything out, but then all of a sudden there you were at Jason's and I was being shoved into your apartment whether I wanted it or not."

"This is all real compelling but it still doesn't explain why you're a spineless sociopath!"

"What should I have done, Sullivan? Should I have blurted it out right off the bat? I know, I'd walk up to you when I first saw you at the party and say, 'Hey, remember that girl I used to be friends with who made you completely miserable? The same girl you were convinced I cheated on you with? Yeah, I'm engaged to her now. You still want to catch up over drinks?'"

I shake my head and say nothing.

"I couldn't have told you then. You would have instantly hated me, and from the moment I saw you all I wanted was to talk to you and be around you 24/7. In the space of one night I morphed back into the desperate twenty-year-old who was obsessed with you in college and who would do anything to keep you near me regardless of the consequences. I knew I was lying and I knew what I was doing was wrong but I couldn't stop because stopping meant letting you go and I'm incapable of doing that. I always was."

"I swear, if you don't stop saying that all this happened because you care about me *so* much, I'm going to rip my ears off and shove them down your throat."

"I thought I'd be able to tell you the truth without anything physical happening between us. I thought we'd spend some time together and then I'd explain my situation and deal with whatever happened in the aftermath. I'd break up with Madison as soon as I got home, and hopefully you'd be willing to talk to me again when you saw how serious I was about you. Maybe we'd be friends for a while before we became something bigger. We could start fresh."

"Then why didn't you do that?" I yell. "You seem to know

exactly what you should have done, so what made you decide the better option was to drag me into a love triangle that I would never willingly choose to be a part of? You set us up to fail!"

Ryan steps back at my words. He swallows and sits down on one of the settees, leaning his elbows on his knees and covering his face with his hands. I have the horrifying instinct to comfort him but keep my feet planted to the ground.

He eventually lifts his head up, looking straight ahead and seeming torn apart.

"I thought I could do it," he says quietly. "I thought I could be around you and keep my emotions in check, but I couldn't. Being near you like that, staying in your apartment and seeing you every day, it felt like I was living out a fantasy that I've held on to for ten years, and I didn't want it to end. I was afraid telling you the truth would ruin everything we started to build, but by not telling you, I didn't just ruin it. I demolished it."

I feel my lip starting to quiver and I look away as I swipe at a renegade tear. "You really are a great salesman. It's almost like you believe everything you're saying."

"That's because it's true! For the past decade I've sworn that I was going to do things different from my parents. I didn't want a relationship with crazy ups and downs. I was going to marry someone calm and steady and who didn't expect or want some wild, over-the-top love story. I know that's not what sells in your books but that's what solid, stable families are built on."

"If that's the life you want then go for it! Don't act like I'm the one who ruined your plans."

"But you did!" he shouts, once again on his feet. "I had everything I thought I needed. I was with someone who wanted the same things as me, and after seeing you just once, I was ready to throw it all out the damn window. And the whole time, you didn't even have the decency to tell me that you were going to be gone for six months."

"Stop with the excuses! What are you looking to hear from me, Ryan? Yes, you're right. Me not telling you about Italy after being unofficially back together with you for less than a week fully makes up for the fact that you have a fiancée. No worries, we're even now."

"It's not about us being even. I'm trying to explain that you and I weren't just messing around before I went off and got married. From the second I walked into your apartment there was only ever going to be you for me. I was never going back to Madison. I was never going to love or want anyone but you. You mean the world to me and I would give up everything in a heartbeat if it meant that we could be together."

"Right. You'd give up everything except for the truth." Ryan stays quiet as I go on, "Well, you don't have to worry about lying anymore because we're over. I had a good life without you for ten years and I'll have a good life again after you leave." I feel like my throat is closing. My eyes fill with tears and I let them fall.

Ryan growls in frustration and moves his hands to cup my cheeks. "What do I have to do to convince you that I want to be with you?"

"Nothing," I say, pushing his hands off me. "It's just like you said, our relationship is what I write about in my books. Up and down and falling in and out of love. Everything that happened between us was fiction. None of it was real."

"Stop! It *is* real!"

"No, it's not," I say. "And you know what? It's totally fine because I was faking everything, too. I just needed you for an extra boost so I could finish my book. Why else would I have invited you to stay at my apartment?"

"I don't believe that." The tremor in his voice tells me just how much he *does* believe it. "And even if it's true, I don't care."

"It is true. I used you and you used me. We can both walk away with a clear conscience."

"No!" Ryan yells. "I know this—what we have is real. You have to listen to me." He grabs me by my shoulders, nearly shaking me. He sounds crushed. Everything about him is begging me to accept that this is somehow all okay. "I love you."

He loves me. Ten minutes ago, those words would have filled me to the brim with happiness. All they do now is drive home how selfish he is to say them to me in this moment. He's giving me everything I dreamed of now that it's impossible for me to keep it.

"How can you say you love me when you put me in this position? If I forgive you, I'm weak and a home-wrecker—if I don't, I'm stubborn and spiteful. I lose either way and you've somehow made it my fault."

I move back again but Ryan only follows, matching me step for step.

"Kara, I know I handled everything the wrong way but please don't punish me for having a past. I want to be with you, not her. You shouldn't make a life with someone just because you can. I get what my dad was talking about now."

"Yeah," I say bitterly, "and now you're nothing but a pathetic cheater, just like him."

I want to take the words back as soon as I say them. I'm sinking to a level I didn't know I could reach. Now I hate myself *and* him.

Ryan is immobile. He looks broken. "I guess you're right," he says softly.

I cover my face with my hands, stifling a sob and wiping under my eyes. "I'm sorry. I shouldn't have said that but I'm pretty sure I'm in an altered state right now."

Ryan gives me a pitying look and moves forward, reaching for me. I don't know what comes over me but I fall into his embrace, tangling my hands into the back of his tux. Heat radiates off him and into me and I can feel his heart pounding against mine. I move my face back to catch my breath and before I can inhale, Ryan stoops down and kisses me. His lips are insistent and soothing and they convince me to forget about breathing.

For a second it feels right and good, a protective bubble inside a moment that is all sick and wrong. Then he squeezes me tight, so tight that the pressure jolts the last ten minutes back into my body like an electric shock.

"Don't!" I beg, pushing him away. My face flushes red with anger and pain and the sharpest disappointment I've felt since my dad. "You need to go. You have to let me go."

He doesn't move, just stares at me. I can see he wants to wake up from this nightmare as much as I do. A minute goes by before he seems to acknowledge or accept what is happening.

"Listen to me," I say, "we are not going to ruin Cristina's night. We're going to go back out there and pretend that none of this happened and then we will never see each other again. Do you understand?"

He doesn't answer.

"I'm going to stay at Maggie's tonight, so after the wedding go to my apartment and get—" My voice starts to quake just from saying his name in my head. I take a breath. "Get Duke and your stuff and leave."

Ryan nods, staying quiet for almost a minute.

"I'm going to miss you so much, Kara." His voice is strained. It's hard to hear him and I wish I didn't. "You were all I ever wanted."

"I can't do this," I say brokenly. "Please go. I'll come out in a few minutes."

I don't look back as I walk into the bathroom connected to the suite and close the door. I sink to the floor and push my head down against my knees.

Minutes pass and I finally hear the bridal suite door open, then close.

I peek outside and Ryan is gone. It takes a solid twenty minutes until I'm together enough to get back to the reception.

When I walk inside the candlelit room, I attempt to detach. It's a useful skill to have. I used to do it well. I'm walking aimlessly, not really sure where I'm going, when Maggie appears in front of me wearing a black tea-length cocktail dress.

"Sorry I'm late," she says. "I was on the phone with Hannah. Turns out she's not loving her new Connecticut life as much as I hoped. I didn't miss dinner, did I?"

Maggie can barely finish her question before I lock her in a bone-crushing hug. The temptation to crumble to pieces is impossibly strong but I know I have to push it back. I step away and give a cautionary swipe under my eyes with the tips of my fingers.

"What's wrong?" she asks nervously.

"It's bad," I answer, my voice shaking despite my best efforts, "but I can't talk about it now. I need you to help me."

"I will. It's okay, I will." Maggie is using her therapist voice, soothing and melodic even without instruments. "Do you want to sit down? Do you want a drink?"

I shake my head, not sure what I want or need when I twist around and see Ryan and Madison in a far-off corner, deep in conversation. She places a hand on his arm, because why wouldn't she, as they continue to talk. I let out a small whimper and turn back around to Maggie.

"All right, it's okay," she says, rubbing my arms and looking over my shoulder. She scans the room until her eyes stop moving and fill with ice-cold fury. A few seconds later, they return to mine and immediately soften.

"I have an idea. How about we dance for a bit? I bet if we burn off some energy, we'll both feel better." She pulls me towards the dance floor, positioning us deep in the crowd where only other dancing couples are in our line of vision.

"What if dancing doesn't work?" I ask her.

The band is playing at a near explosive level and Maggie swings my arms up and down, puppeteering me into moving to the beat.

"If this doesn't work, then we murder Ryan in a kitchen stairwell and flee to Switzerland. Easy peasy."

She says her solution with such a sweet air that I have to laugh.

I spend the rest of the night drinking and dancing and holding Maggie's hand, refusing to acknowledge that Ryan isn't there—hasn't been there since he left the reception three hours early with someone else.

The next morning, I enter my apartment wearing flip-flops and my bridesmaid dress. A beautiful soft pink Grecian gown that no longer looks flattering with my puffy eyes and pale complexion.

I walk past the kitchenette and my eyes find a bakery bag I didn't notice yesterday morning. Knowing exactly what I'll find, I reach inside and pull out a scone that's cold and stale. I drop the empty bag onto the floor and toss the scone into the sink beside me without looking. I'm not even rattled when I hear it smash into a glass that's waiting to be washed.

I glance around the living room, and even though all traces of him are gone, the whole space is haunted by Ryan. He might as well be standing next to me. I walk back over to the door and lock it, feeling utterly and chillingly numb.

18

"I'm getting married."

Charlotte's words split through Robert like the swipe of an ax. "I beg your pardon?"

"To Edward Brinton, the Marquis of St. Clare. He's an acquaintance of my father. The wedding will take place as soon as possible."

Robert was unable to disguise his confusion as every muscle in his body tightened. He studied Charlotte, finding her cheeks pale and her eyes puffy and bloodshot. "I don't understand," he said.

"It's quite simple, really. Our dalliance has come to an end. I would have thought someone like you would be well-versed in these matters."

"If something is wrong then tell me. I can fix it."

"There's nothing to fix. It's true, I have enjoyed your company for the past few weeks, but it's now time for you to leave."

Silence stretched for what felt like a lifetime until Robert stormed forward to stand barely an inch away from Charlotte.

"I don't give a damn if you want me to leave! I'm gone for two days and I come back to find you engaged to some old letch? What the devil has happened?"

Charlotte pushed violently against Robert's chest, forcing him back and gaining some distance. "George is gone!" she cried. "Father sent him away and he won't tell me where he is or if he's all right and he won't tell me anything until I marry Lord Brinton."

Robert shook his head as anger hammered through him. "This is ridiculous. I'll talk to your father and put a stop to this at once."

"No!" Charlotte's voice was desperate. "If I interfere, Father will keep George where he is and I will never see him again. If I go along with what he wishes, he will let him live with me at Lord Brinton's estate after the wedding."

"I would marry you tomorrow if your father is so determined to have you gone. Why is he forcing you on Brinton?" Charlotte didn't answer and Robert's patience wore thin. "Answer me!" he roared.

"My father owes a fortune to countless creditors. He was on the brink of ruin when Lord Brinton offered to pay off his debts in exchange for my hand. He's already dispensed with half. The rest will be seen to once we are married, along with a generous annual allowance."

Robert advanced on Charlotte again, moving to stand a breath away from her. "And what about us? What of the other night? You expect me to step aside when you may already be carrying my child?"

Charlotte turned, dropping her gaze to the drawing room floor. "The odds of that occurring are very slim and I doubt it would matter much to Lord Brinton. Such things have happened before."

"They do not happen to me!"

"Robert, please! This is my fault! I let my guard down. I was with you when I should have been looking after George and now he's gone." Charlotte nearly fell apart then. She wanted to go to Robert so badly. She almost did, but George's face flashed through her mind and stopped her dead in her tracks.

"I must insist that you leave," she instead said, her voice firm despite her anguish. "I will not risk my brother's safety. Not for myself and certainly not for you…"

What I love the most about living in a foreign country is the total anonymity of it all. I don't know anyone. I can walk down the street dressed like a total slob and I won't bump into a single person I know. Not that I'm walking around Rome looking a mess, but still, knowing that I can is extremely liberating.

I've been here a week, staying in my rented apartment in the Della Vittoria District of Rome, and at this point, I'm leaning towards staying indefinitely. It's been done before. People have picked up and disappeared to live a fabulous life abroad. Leaving New York behind for a villa in Italy sounds more than mysterious and sexy to me.

Because mysterious and sexy is absolutely how I'm feeling these days. I wake up, eat, write, eat, sightsee, shop for food or other things (but pretty much just food), eat, send out emails, watch a movie, write, then sleep. Yeah, it's downright indecent over here.

The email section of my day takes a good chunk of time. I get daily updates from Cristina, Jen and Maggie. And, of course, my mom demands I write to her every day.

I'd like to say that my emails are a pleasant escape, but there's always an elephant in the room, or rather, an elephant in the email. I obviously told Maggie what happened with Ryan as soon as we left the wedding. She was enraged and understanding and instantly offered to have her cousins break his legs—that's what you call best-friend status.

When I spoke to Cristina the following day, she vowed bodily harm against Jason for not telling us Ryan was engaged. As it turns out, Ryan filled him in the day they went out for their tuxes and shoes, thus explaining his rehearsal dinner weirdness. Jason made him swear to tell me the truth and was under the impression that he did. Even knowing that, Cristina was still ready to go on the warpath but I begged her not to hold her new husband responsible for someone else's actions. He was only doing what he had to for his friend, which I know she would have done for me, times a thousand.

I convinced both Maggie and Cristina that the best way they could help me move on was to never bring up Ryan again. They agreed and as much as I'm glad that they've respected my wishes, it's hard to talk to them about what's going on in my life when I refuse to acknowledge one of the biggest current aspects of it. I wish I could be more open about it all, but it's like something inside me is out of place. I feel like a bike with a wonky chain, jammed and rusted and going nowhere.

Maggie's emails are the most in-depth, but I end up writing the least to her. She tells me about work and the problems her sister is having with taking care of their grandma. She wants my advice and wants to know what I'm doing and how I'm feeling, how I'm *really* feeling, and the more she wants to hear from me the more I want to pull away. Maybe it's easier to write to Jen and Cristina because they stick to more surface topics. Maggie mows over surface topics with a dump truck. She remembers everything and wants to talk deeply about it and all I want to do is forget.

As for my novel, writing is going…okay. I have three weeks left before my deadline and I'd like to say I'm making significant progress but that would be a gross exaggeration. I'm tooting along little by little, but the ending just isn't coming to me. Everything feels uninspired and lackluster and I don't know how to fix it.

On the plus side, my Instagram game is absolute fire. My balconies make for killer backdrops and I buy antique trinkets and fresh flowers from a nearby market for staging. I even took a thirty-minute train ride outside of Rome to Tivoli so I could visit Villa d'Este, a 16th-century villa that's open to the public. It has show-stopping gardens and fairy-tale-caliber fountains and thank goodness I brought three books with me that day. I shot each of them in locations more idyllic than the next and my posts have been blowing up.

Sightseeing is a welcome distraction and the highlight of my days. With my handy-dandy Italian Metro card, I pick a destination almost every afternoon and hop on the Metro after lunch. So far, I've been to the Coliseum, the Spanish Steps and the Trevi Fountain twice.

I can't get enough of that freaking fountain. I could sit there and stare at it for hours. The best is seeing it at night, all lit up with the smell of the running, splashing water flowing through the air. It's swoon-worthy—that's the only term that captures it.

I'm contemplating where I'll visit today as I sit on my favorite bench near the back of my apartment complex's cobblestoned courtyard. I may or may not be eating pizza marinara for breakfast—which is cheese-less pizza—but that's beside the point.

The city is fully awake with the early morning commute dying down as tourists take to the sidewalks, ready to dive into the best of what Rome has to offer. I blend easily into the background as the courtyard becomes more populated and I have to say, I like going unnoticed—being alone. That is, until I find that I'm no longer alone.

The figure now standing two feet in front of me is tall and imposing, blocking out the sun that was just keeping me perfectly warm. I squint as I look up and it takes a moment for me to see anything other than a silhouette.

Once my eyes adjust, I find that my sunlight stealer is a man. His auburn hair contrasts sharply with his fair skin and I can't quite make out the color of his eyes. He seems to be in his midthirties, but his dark denim jeans and navy polo shirt give nothing away in the age department. I continue to look at him as he glances down at me.

"Excuse me, I'm sorry, but are you eating pizza?" He has a British accent, which would explain his paleness. He looks at his watch and I'm unable to answer since my mouth is still filled with the aforementioned pizza. "You do know that it is only a quarter past nine in the morning?" His voice sounds aged. Maybe he's older than I thought.

As it happens, I'm not particularly in the talking mood, especially not with complete strangers who insult my pizza, so I look around the courtyard to start plotting my escape. *"Mi dispiace,"* I then say in my best Italian accent. *"Non parlo inglese."*

He gives me the once-over. "You don't speak any English?" I continue to look at him with a puzzled expression. "Right. *Mi scusi,*" he amends.

I scour my head for a proper response and come up with, *"Va bene."*

My Italian must be passable because the stranger gives me a hasty nod farewell. With his stiff posture and his hands pinned behind his back, it comes out looking more like a bow as he straightens up and walks past me, reminding me of a character from a Regency novel. Maybe my next romantic hero will be a dashing but snooty redhead. I mull the thought over as I take another bite of my apparently inappropriate breakfast.

My meal is disrupted once again a couple of minutes later when I'm approached by two older women wearing wide-brimmed straw hats and fanny packs. They may as well have American flags wrapped around their shoulders. I immediately love them.

One of the ladies steps right up to me. "Hello, dear. Do you speak English?"

"I do," I say with a smile. "Can I help you with something?"

"Oh, wonderful! Yes, can you tell us where the closest Metro stop is?"

She thrusts a street map of Rome into my hands and I'm able to find our location easily enough.

"Okay, we're here, so if you go a few blocks this way and then make another right, you'll find the Cipro station." I trail my index finger along her route to give an additional visual.

She beams at me in gratitude. "Wonderful! Thank you so much."

"You're welcome. Have fun."

The ladies are off to the races and I have to grin as I watch them rush away. I remember the excitement I felt on my first day in Rome. It must be nice to travel with a friend, though. The exhilaration of exploring a new place could only be amplified when you're sharing it with someone you care for.

Deciding it's best not to dwell on that particular subject, I take my last bite of pizza and stand up, brushing my hands together to dust off any loose crumbs, and start walking through the courtyard. Then I freeze. The redheaded pizza-hater is directly in my path, just a few feet away. His hands are still clasped behind his back as he looks at me with an amused expression.

I'm going to go ahead and assume that he just heard me speaking in perfect English. I act without thinking and do a quick curtsy. *"Scusi,"* I say, bustling past him and bounding into my apartment building.

Once inside, I step into the old-fashioned elevator through the two little doors and press my floor number. The lift roars to life and I drop my head back against the glass-and-wood-lined wall.

Yes, Kara. You just curtsied.

I wake up the next morning feeling sluggish and go directly to the pizzeria around the corner to get breakfast. I greet the middle-aged female storeowner and place my usual order, asking for a small slice of pizza marinara in my self-created mixture of Italian, English and sign language. I think she's used to me by now but finds me tedious. I grab a bottle of water from the display fridge as she wraps my pizza in thick white paper and hands it to me with a strained smile. I pay for my food and exit the store.

I didn't sleep well last night. I barely wrote. I'm restless and agitated, enough so that I decide to punish myself by skipping my sightseeing trip this afternoon in favor of an extra writing session. If I get something done, I'll treat myself to a gelato.

By the way, the chocolate is better here. It just is. I managed to find the authentic gelato, the kind that is stored in metal tins and covered with matching metal lids and, no joke, I felt like I'd died and was then reborn with the sole purpose of eating more gelato.

With the promise of elevated ice cream somewhat easing my pessimistic mood, I walk back into the courtyard with more pep in my step. That pep vanishes, however, when I find that my cozy little bench is occupied. Occupied by none other than the redhead from yesterday, who is now sitting quietly, eating a large slice of pizza.

I walk over to stand in front of him, blocking his light just as he did to me the day before. "This scene feels vaguely familiar," I say.

He glances up at me with an unconcerned look. "*Mi dispiace*, no English."

"Well played." I sit down next to him and rip open the paper that is keeping me from the carbohydrates I so desperately need.

"Oh, I'm sorry," he says as I take my first bite. "I thought you didn't speak English."

I nod and chew until I'm able to talk. "I may have been faking that a little bit."

"Really? A little bit?"

"Just a tad."

"You may not believe it, but after hours of thought and multiple diagrams, I managed to piece that mystery together for myself."

"What a letdown. And here I thought I committed the perfect crime."

"It couldn't be helped. I watched an impressive amount of *Inspector Gadget* growing up, so detective work has always been a keen interest of mine."

"You're an *Inspector Gadget* nerd? I can only hope that you're referring to the original cartoon and not the movie."

"Do I look like a monster?"

We both smile a bit and each take another bite.

"So what brings you to Italy?" he asks a while later.

"I'm sorry, please don't take this the wrong way, but why are you even talking to me? You didn't seem like my biggest fan yesterday."

He doesn't appear at all fazed by my words. "Yes, I'd like to apologize if I sounded a bit harsh about that. My tone always comes out more serious than I'd like it to. It's good in business but problematic while attempting friendly conversation."

I say nothing and he goes on, "I thought you seemed interesting. Plus, you appear to be as antisocial as I am, so that's always helpful."

"You're very chatty for an antisocial person. Speaking to strangers takes the *anti* out of *antisocial*, thus making you social."

"I just prefer not to eat outdoors by myself. Much as I personally don't mind it, I'm growing a little tired of people looking at me like I'm a dangerous drifter."

I somewhat get his point. I recall receiving some suspicious glances myself the past couple of times I went out to dinner alone.

"So you're suggesting we eat breakfast together so we can stay antisocial without looking antisocial?"

"Precisely."

"Okay," I find myself agreeing. Why not? When in Rome, do as the similarly withdrawn non-Romans do.

He answers me with a very faint smile. "Good."

For the next few minutes, we continue to share the bench, sitting and eating our pizzas in silence. It's only when we both finish and stand to leave that he speaks again.

"For the sake of our burgeoning friendship, I should tell you my name is Liam." He extends his hand and I don't hesitate to shake it.

"I'm Kara."

"Kara," he repeats. He gazes at me for a brief moment before he does his token nod/bow and walks away.

A few minutes later, I head back to my apartment with a small smirk, contemplating how, in my own outlandish, hermit-like way, I just made my first friend in Italy.

19

Since our conversation almost three weeks ago, Liam and I have eaten breakfast together every morning, and our meals have now evolved into breakfast followed by midmorning walks. As each day goes by, we seem to claim more and more of each other's time. Yesterday, Liam went on a morning bike tour of Rome with me. Two days ago, I visited the Borghese Gallery with him. Neither of us mind the company. Much as I glorify my cloistered antics, I would probably go crazy if I didn't have Liam around to talk to.

He was quiet at first, but continues to surprise me, randomly asking me questions about my life or spurting out a story from his childhood. I tell him about New York and how I'm a novelist. He knows I'm struggling with my latest book but isn't aware of how far I've let it go. He doesn't push me and I'm grateful. Our conversations bounce back and forth, easy and weightless with zero gravity.

Today, we've decided to walk to Vatican City. We're about

three quarters of the way there when I ask, "So, are you missing home yet?"

"Not particularly," he answers.

"How about your friends? Do you talk to them a lot via text and whatnot?"

"I do sometimes but not a lot. I think I take my vow of silence more seriously than you do."

"You? Take something seriously? Impossible."

We soon find ourselves in St. Peter's Square. Near the obelisk in the direct center, we maneuver past tourists and tour groups who follow smartly dressed guides as they hold up flags to keep people from getting lost. Getting lost in a crowd is easy here. Maybe that's why I like it so much.

"If you had to pick, what would you say is your favorite place to visit in Rome?"

Liam clasps his hands behind his back and thinks for a moment. "The Catacombs."

"Why?"

"Because it's morbid."

I give him a snarky smile as he watches me from the corner of his eye.

"And what's your favorite place to visit?" he counters.

I don't even have to think about it. "The Trevi Fountain. I go to see it at least once a week."

"I should have guessed. The Trevi Fountain is a very romantic place. The architecture, the water, all of it is very inviting for a dreamer, such as yourself."

"How can you be so sure I'm a dreamer? Maybe I'm a cut-and-dried, no-nonsense realist like you."

Liam actually smiles without holding back for once and the aftermath leaves me a little dazzled.

"Right," he answers, "a no-nonsense realist romance author."

"Fine," I concede. "Maybe I am a dreamer. You sound like you disapprove."

"Of daydreaming? I wouldn't say I disapprove, entirely. I just think that time can be spent in a more constructive manner."

"You think so? Tell me then, did you go see the Trevi Fountain?"

"I did," he answers.

"And what did you think?"

"It was what I expected."

"Did you throw in a coin?"

"What does that matter?"

"I'm curious. As someone who looks down on dreamers, I think your answer will be telling. So, did you throw in a coin, yes or no?"

Liam pauses. "I happen to carry a lot of spare change."

"I knew it," I say, satisfied. "Your high and mighty cynical self threw a coin into the Trevi Fountain and made a dreamy, dreamy wish. No need to be ashamed, it's perfectly natural."

"Fine. Maybe I did throw a coin in but I wasn't happy about it, and I certainly didn't think that it would alter the course of my life."

"You have a very pessimistic point of view."

"So I've been told. When I was young, my nanny actually quit because she said I was too depressing to work with."

"Did she really?" I ask disbelievingly.

"No, turns out Nanny Louisa just had hip issues, though she did tell me I was a very somber eight-year-old."

I shake my head with a little laugh as we continue walking. Liam is much stranger than he originally let on. I like it.

Twenty minutes later, we've left Vatican City and are each enjoying a gelato as we head back in the direction of our apartments. I got chocolate in a cup and he opted for vanilla. A more boring pair could never be found.

"I feel like we should talk about our love lives," he suddenly says.

I quit shoveling gelato into my mouth long enough to look over at him. "What made you think of that?"

"Nothing in particular. We've just been friends for a few weeks now and I realized we've never talked about that part of our lives before. It seemed a little strange."

"I guess it is a little strange," I say, already dreading where this is going. "How about we start with a couple of warm-up questions first?"

"Sounds sensible."

I have a trillion questions, but I don't want to come off as too eager. "Okay, what's your job?"

"I started a web development firm that was recently acquired by a large corporation. I'm taking a leave of absence before I go back to work under the new management. Though, as of right now, I'm not certain whether I'll return to the position at all."

"What's making you hesitate?"

"I quite like being my own boss. I don't know if I can go back to answering to someone else."

"Makes sense," I say. "You're a little young to have started your own company, no?"

"Says the thirty-year-old with seven novels under her belt."

"Trust me, you'd be far from impressed if you knew my current situation."

"What do you mean?" Liam asks. He seems like he genuinely cares.

I take a hefty spoonful of gelato and wish I never brought it up. "Nothing, I'm just having a hard time finishing off the book I'm working on."

"Are you under deadline?"

"That I am," I answer hopelessly.

"When is it?"

Tomorrow. A chilling wave surges through me but I don't feel it like I should. I should be horrified. Desperate. But I'm not. I'm resigned. Disconnected.

"Soon," I tell him.

Liam regards me with calm confidence. He has a solutions air about him—a quiet authority. I bet he'd flourish in a hostile work environment.

"What's changed with this novel?" he asks. "Are you out of ideas or is there something else?"

"I think it's a mixture of both."

"I don't know if this makes sense with writing, but something that always helps me when I'm feeling stuck or unfocused is to set myself up in the same situation I was in when I last had success."

"What do you mean?"

"Well, this obviously applies more for when I'm coding than when I'm in corporate situations, but some of the best work I did was when I was in university. I'd be in my room, blasting music through my headphones, cut off from everything. So now, if I really need to get something done, I lock myself in my office, put on my headphones and blast the same angst-filled music I listened to when I was in school. I'm almost always able to finish what I need and the caliber of my work somehow improves."

I eat another spoonful and consider Liam's advice. "Name one angsty song that you loved."

He smiles and says, "'Disarm.'"

"Smashing Pumpkins?" I ask disbelievingly. He nods and I shake my head. "And you think you know a guy."

"So, what situation are you in when you're best able to write?"

My stomach drops as Ryan fills my brain, rolling through

like a fog. He slips under doors and over walls and if I let him pour in like this, there will be no getting him out again. I focus on Liam's eyes to distract myself. They're ice-blue but still warm, like tropical beach water that you only see in pictures.

"My process is similar to yours," I eventually say. "I'm alone and I listen to music but more light stuff. I have a playlist of all the scores from romantic movies."

"Sounds sprightly."

"Quite sprightly. Okay, next question. What made you come to Italy?"

"I'm here on holiday."

"Yes, but you could have gone on holiday anywhere in the world. Why Italy?" I can tell Liam is uncomfortable but I let the question stand.

He stirs his vanilla gelato around a bit, looking off into the passing crowd before he says, "Sentimental reasons." I'm about to dive in with a follow-up question but he beats me to the punch. "My turn. Why are you here alone?"

Because the person I was in love with is already engaged. Because I was so picky in my twenties that I tossed away good guys who deserved more of a chance than I gave them. Because I'd rather stay home with my books than go out into the world and feel like I don't measure up.

"I just am. I haven't stopped working since I graduated from college and it's hard to find Mr. Right when you're almost always encamped in your apartment, trying to meet a deadline."

Liam seems to accept my answer, though I'm sure he knows there's more there.

"How about you?" I ask. "Why are you here alone?"

Liam pauses, his gaze dropping to his gelato before he looks back up at me. "I'm here alone because I didn't think my wife would care to join me after our divorce."

My eyebrows pop up. "You were married?"

"For two years. Pathetic, really." He's trying to laugh it off, but I can tell just how affected he is.

"It's not pathetic."

I can't help but suddenly see Liam through a different, softer lens. Guarded as he is, there was a time when he trusted a woman enough to fall in love with her—to propose to her—to marry her.

"We don't have to talk about this if you don't want to," I say after a bit. "This is all really personal stuff."

"No, oddly enough, I don't mind. This is one of the first times I'm willingly talking about my divorce and it feels… interesting."

"Interesting?"

"I guess verbalizing your feelings is beneficial, after all. It appears I owe my mum an apology."

I laugh quietly, thankful that the mood has been somewhat lightened.

"And before we finish up with today's conversation, I have one last thing to ask you."

"Go for it," I say.

We stop walking just outside our courtyard.

"Would you like to have dinner with me tonight?" he asks.

I'm taken off guard by his question and end up squeezing my Styrofoam cup a little tighter. Even though I've spent almost every morning with Liam for the past few weeks, we've never ventured into dinner territory and I'm surprisingly nervous of disrupting our normal routine. But still, I don't see any reason to say no.

"Sure," I answer. "What time?"

His face remains indecipherable but relaxed. "How about eight o'clock?"

"Eight it is."

With our plans secure, we enter the courtyard with easy

smiles, but the air between us feels different. It's not as care-free and there's the slightest hint of tension and I'm not sure if I like it. I shake it off as best I can as I go into my building and Liam crosses the courtyard to go into his.

I take a nice long shower once I'm inside and check my email as I sit at the dining room table. I'm happily swimming in an oversize T-shirt with a towel wrapped around my dripping hair. I get to Maggie's email last and find it unusually short, just one line asking me to call her. I look at my phone but don't pick it up. I'm not ready to connect back with reality. Not yet.

Opting to email her tomorrow, I instead decide that I'm going to finish my novel right now—or at least write something. Anything. I end up sitting at the table for a solid hour and imagine smashing my laptop into the floor every five minutes. I'm a day away from my deadline. A day away from jeopardizing so much of what defines me. My career. My reputation. I have to prove to the publisher and myself that my best work isn't behind me, but with every passing second, that outcome seems less and less likely.

I need to write. I need to finish. I type out a sentence and delete it. I force out a paragraph and delete it. I rub my hands over my face and leave them there, leaning my elbows against the desk. My mind is clouded with thoughts of fighting my way to safety but all I'm doing is digging my own grave. Soon I'll be down so deep that the sun will disappear, replaced instead with layers of dirt and cold, wet air.

I shake my head and try again, typing and typing until I've filled an entire page. My fingers fall away from the keyboard until I bring them back to the mouse a few seconds later to highlight everything I just wrote.

Delete.

20

A little after eight, Liam and I are seated at a cozy restaurant that's within walking distance of the Trevi Fountain, but not close enough to be a tourist trap. Being this close in proximity to my favorite place in the world, I'm itching to travel the distance and stare at it for no less than three hours.

"Perhaps after dinner we'll go see your fountain," Liam suggests over his menu.

I smile and nod, knowing he must have chosen this restaurant due to its location.

A handsome Italian waiter with slicked-back hair soon comes over to greet us and finds us ready to order. We're somewhat plain and picky eaters and both order rigatoni Bolognese. The waiter hates us. He does, however, brighten up when Liam orders an expensive bottle of white wine. Once the wine is poured, Liam sends the waiter away with a regal nod of his head and raises his glass, prompting me to do the same.

"What shall we toast to?" he asks through a small grin.

He looks ten years younger, more like his age of thirty-four, when he smiles like that, and my mind starts to go a little sideways. I unconsciously move closer to the table as I wonder if I could ever see him as more than a friend despite my initial uncertainty.

"To us," I say, "and to our antisocial comrades throughout the world."

"Poetry if I've ever heard it."

We tap our glasses together and savor our first sips. Much as I've tried to enjoy red wine since I've been here, I'll always prefer white. I'm glad Liam concurs.

Setting my glass down in front of me, I wait a very appropriate ten seconds before I begin my assault on the bread basket in the middle of the table. The bread is toasted to perfection and drizzled in olive oil, and Liam soon snags a piece for himself. He knows the deal. Our best conversations always require devouring carbs.

"Do you consider us good friends?" I soon hear myself ask.

Liam appreciates blunt questions and chuckles mid-chew.

"I do. Not many people can manage to put up with me on such a regular basis. Our companionship is quite the phenomenon." He takes a sip of wine and leans back in his chair. "Why? Do you consider me a good friend?"

I take a sip of my wine as well, answering his question with my glass still in my hand. "I do. I like how nothing is forced with us. We don't talk if we don't want to and we only see each other every day because we feel like it. It would be easy for us to ditch each other. I think it's nice that neither of us wants to yet."

"Neither of us wants to *yet*? Does that mean you may potentially be ditching me in the near future?"

I smile and shrug as I take another sip. "Who knows? You'll just have to stick to your A-game to keep me enthralled."

"I'll do that," he says, drinking more of his wine as well.

Two glasses each later, our food arrives and the timing couldn't be better. I'm beginning to feel loopy and some sustenance is needed. We dig into our meals and it takes a minute or so for either of us to come up for air.

"You've been here for about a month, haven't you?" he asks. I nod and take another bite. "Do you ever miss home?"

"Sometimes, but I try not to think about it."

"How do you not think about it?"

I rest my fork down in my bowl and scoot around a bit in my seat. "I try to keep occupied. I cook or watch a movie or write."

He seems to think about my reply as he lifts his glass to take a somewhat ample sip. I raise my eyebrows at his unusual lack of restraint.

"Do *you* ever miss home?" I ask, trying to seem less curious than I am.

Liam looks down at the wineglass he's now rotating in his fingers. "Do I miss home?" he repeats. "No, I don't miss home. Why should I miss home or anyone there when I doubt any of them miss me?"

When our eyes meet, I can see the sadness there. He looks away and reaches for the nearly empty wine bottle, pouring out the last drops into our glasses.

"Enough with our morose questions. Now, what say you and I get drunk?" He lifts his glass up for a toast and I bring mine up to meet his.

If Liam is going to indulge then I am, too. I down my glass in a very unladylike gulp. He smiles and signals the waiter over to order another bottle.

Two hours later, we finally make our way to the Trevi Fountain and I have, in the meantime, come to the conclusion that we should be drunk all the time. Liam insisted on buying every postcard he could find of the Pantheon from multiple souvenir shops on the way over, swearing he was going to create a mural replica to scale. I laughed so much I almost cramped up. If I had any idea he was this entertaining once you got a few drinks in him, I would have insisted on boozy breakfasts from the get-go.

We situate our tipsy selves directly in front of the fountain, and I only have one rule as I stand before hundreds of years of history.

Do not fall in.

Thankfully, there are stone benches for viewers to sit on parallel to the fountain, and we quickly throw ourselves down onto the nearest one, getting comfortable and leaning back. It's somewhat uncommonly deserted tonight, just a handful of groups here and there, and I can't help but enjoy the moderate quiet. I stare straight ahead, allowing myself to relax as I lose myself in the absolute magic that is the Fontana di Trevi.

"Do you think there's anything in the world more beautiful than this?" I ask in a lazy voice.

Liam looks forward as well with a languid smile. "No. I don't think so."

I'm not sure what prompts me, but I ask, "Did you once think there was?"

After a loud exhale, Liam wraps his arm around my shoulder and pulls me close to his side. "At one point I did."

I feel an all too familiar twist in my stomach at his words. The longing for an enchanted something that's not there anymore. My head feels heavy and the crook of his arm is as welcome and warm as a pillow. "Do you wish you could go back to when you did?"

"I'm not sure," he says after a while. "I'm quite happy where I am now."

"Will you tell me about her sometime?"

Liam smiles down at me. "You're very perceptive when you drink."

I nestle more deeply into his side, wrapping my own arms around his waist. "I'm always perceptive. I just only let people know it when I'm drunk."

Neither of us says anything else after that, simply enjoying the quiet and the view. We stay just as we are for a good thirty minutes before heading home.

When Liam and I get back to my apartment, I don't think anything of the fact that we're holding hands. We have since rallied from our calming time at the fountain and are now in the boisterous midst of our second wind. I show him around, giving him a tour of the dining room, the kitchen and the living room.

"Didn't you say you had two balconies?" Liam asks.

"Yes, I did," I respond proudly.

"Well, so far I've only seen one."

I have to think about it before I realize that I forgot to show Liam my bedroom. "Oh, duh. This way." I stride down the hallway until I reach the end and swing my bedroom door open. I enter while Liam hesitates at the threshold. "Come in," I say, sitting down on my bed.

I flick my shoes off and sigh in the comfort of my feet's sweet release. Liam walks around me and goes out onto the balcony with his hands buried in his pockets.

Now blissfully barefoot, I hop off the bed and follow him outside. He's leaning forward, his forearms braced against the wrought iron railing as he looks out onto the street.

"Two balconies, indeed. I'm quite shown up."

I smile and lean down onto the railing as well. "If you're ever feeling balcony deprived, you're always welcome to come over and share."

Liam's laugh is so faint that it seems to drift off on the open air. "You're very unique, Kara. I've never met anyone quite like you."

"Thanks, I think."

He turns his head and looks over at me, still leaning forward. "It's a good thing."

"Well, that's good, then."

He shifts his body to face me then and tucks a loose piece of hair behind my ear.

"Do you miss her?" I ask. For some reason, I can't stop wondering about her, about the woman who, to Liam, was more beautiful than the Trevi Fountain.

"Yes," he answers, stepping forward until our bodies are touching. "Do you miss him?"

I take a breath at his question. "No."

"It must be lonelier that way," he says softly.

I can't make myself respond. I only continue to look at him, hoping that if I stay still, then maybe I can keep it together. I'm searching his eyes when his hand reaches out to cup the back of my neck. I don't move as he slowly, gently lowers his head and brings his lips to mine.

I close my eyes and let him kiss me, thinking maybe all of this happened for a reason. Maybe I was supposed to come here and meet Liam. Maybe he and I can fix each other.

I pull my face back, taking a breath as I desperately try to picture the future I could have with him. We wouldn't have to be alone anymore. We could make each other happy. I look and I look but it's not there.

No matter how much I try to push them away, buried feelings start to flare up and churn inside me at a debilitating rate. I don't stop Liam when he lowers his head and kisses me again. I lean in. I reach up. I do everything I can to give myself over to the moment, but I just can't do it. All I'm thinking about is whether Liam is seeing someone else when he closes his eyes and kisses me. I wonder if he sees *her* in his mind right now, just as I keep my eyes clenched shut and see nothing but Ryan's smiling face.

Liam's hand moves to the small of my back and pulls me more tightly against his chest. For some reason, the movement triggers all the parts of me that are broken and touch-starved, breaking me down and exposing me in a way that I've been fighting to avoid. I instantly pull away and bury my face in the front of his shirt, feeling like an absolute failure as I start to sob.

Since the day Ryan walked out of that bridal suite, I've done everything I can to force him out of my mind—pushing my detachment skills to the breaking point and beyond. And now, after going on one of the best dates ever with an actual modern-day Mr. Darcy, I'm holding on to this poor guy for dear life like the emotional train wreck that I am.

Liam seems unsure of what to do but soon starts stroking my hair. The tears won't stop. Maybe they never will. I'm not sure how much time passes when I feel him bend down towards my ear.

"I know I'm rubbish at this romance business but it's nothing worth crying over."

I laugh, knowing he can't truly believe that I am wailing in his arms because of him.

"No, Liam, you're wonderful. This is all me." I sniffle from my runny nose and sincerely hope the shirt he's wearing isn't expensive. "I just feel like I'm stuck, and I can't move forward. I mean, here I am with you and I'm wishing for someone else. Who does that? Who doesn't go for the hot British guy?"

"I typically don't, if that makes you feel better."

I smile despite myself and step out of Liam's arms. "Before I came to Italy, I was with someone. I met him in college but then I didn't see him for years. And then last month, I saw him again, and everything was so different, but it was the same, too. I still cared about him so much."

I pause to wipe the bottom of my nose with the back of my hand like a post-tantrum four-year-old. "But he ruined it. He was engaged to someone else the whole time we were together. That's not what love is supposed to be like—that's probably what my dad would say if he was here."

A fresh wave of tears hits and Liam hugs me, waiting it out.

"And even after everything I still miss him *so* badly. All I want to do is see him and talk to him." I shake my head, ordering myself to tone it down. "Something is wrong with me. You should run before it spreads to you and I make you even more complicated than you already are."

"I think it would be a near impossible feat," he says. I look up at him and he wipes a stream of tears off my cheek with his thumb. "What a motley crew we are," he says, jutting out his chin to gesture to the street below. "What do you think? Should we toss our passports to the wind and wallow out here forever? I'm not much of a weeper, but I'm convinced I could imitate the sounds successfully."

I laugh and lean into his side. Liam's smile is somewhat vacant as he looks ahead once again. Whatever it is that he's seeing, the street or a memory, it makes him sigh before taking my hand and leading me back into the bedroom. We collapse onto my bed, both of us exhausted after our tumultuous night of drinking, breakthroughs and my emotional breakdown.

A few minutes later, I roll onto my side and find Liam resting with one arm behind his head as he looks up at the ceiling. Moonlight slits in through the open window and crosses his face, making his blue eyes even more striking against his fair skin. He's attractive and strong but he's so much more than that, too.

I exhale with regret and relief as I acknowledge that Liam is in every way the classic romance novel hero. But for some stupid, illogical, inexplicable reason, I just can't write him in as mine.

He falls asleep shortly thereafter while I remain restless and wide-awake. Careful not to disturb him, I slither out of bed and pass through the darkened hallway until I reach the dining room. I sit down at the table and open my laptop, doing the one thing that brings me home no matter where I am.

"Good morning, Lady Destonbury, Mr. Thomas Flincher, at your service."

Having hardly slept in over a week, Charlotte smiled as best she could at the gangly but well-dressed man who stood opposite her in the Greenspeak drawing room.

"It's a pleasure to meet you, Mr. Flincher. If you're looking for my father, I'm afraid he's in London, preparing for my upcoming wedding."

"Oh, no, my lady, I am here specifically to see you."

"Really?" Charlotte had no idea what a solicitor would want with her, but she asked the gentleman to be seated nevertheless. Mr. Flincher pulled several papers out of his travel case and laid them neatly in his lap.

"I have here very specific legal documentation that I was empowered to explain to you on behalf of my employer. The first matter we should discuss is the order awarding you full guardianship of your younger brother, Mr. George Destonbury."

Charlotte's eyes went wide as saucers. "I beg your pardon?"

"To my knowledge, your brother was recently visiting a school along the Scottish border but is now on his way back to Greenspeak."

Charlotte's hand flew to her mouth as relieved tears flooded her eyes.

"I do apologize," Mr. Flincher quickly said. "I didn't mean to distress you."

"No." Charlotte nearly laughed through her blinding happiness. She knew where George was. He was safe, he was well and he was coming home. "I'm sorry, I'm just… Do go on."

Mr. Flincher handed Charlotte his handkerchief before looking back down at his stack of papers. "As to the next order of business, I have further documentation leaving sole control of this property, Greenspeak Park, to you until your brother reaches maturity, at which time the estate will pass directly to him. A new property manager has been selected to assist you and is prepared to begin his duties pending your approval."

"I don't understand," Charlotte said, frantically trying to listen through her shocked state. "Were these documents drawn up by my father? Have you seen him?"

"I have seen him, my lady, and I assure you everything is perfectly legal. It is my understanding that your father is taking up residence in a smaller estate in Ireland."

"Ireland?" Charlotte repeated, astonished.

"Lord Destonbury wished me to relay his regards to you and your brother. He also sends his apologies for the cancellation of your engagement and assures you that time will heal your undoubtedly bitter disappointment."

Charlotte could hardly breathe. George was hers. She wasn't marrying Lord Brinton. Her father was gone. It was all almost too much to bear. "Mr. Flincher, are you at liberty to tell me how all this came to pass? Have you been my father's solicitor for very long?"

"What? Oh, no, I only met your father the day I finalized these documents and witnessed his signature. I've spent the entirety of my career under the exclusive employ of the Westmond family."

And then everything suddenly made sense.

This man worked for Robert. Charlotte felt as though the world had fallen out from under her as she attempted to retain her composure. "I see. And did Mr. Westmond include a letter addressed to me? Was there any message he wished you to relay?"

"No, my lady. He said everything was settled between you the last time you and he spoke."

Charlotte's heart sank to the floor as she forced a smile.

"Yes, thank you, Mr. Flincher."

I write until four in the morning. My eyes are burning, my back is bent, I'm a touch delirious, but I keep working. I run out of steam right before I reach the finish line. The last chapter. The happy ending. It's right there, but I can't reach it. I check my inbox and Sam has sent me five URGENT, SOS emails.

Time is running out.

Writing without Ryan hasn't been easy. If he was here, I might have been done. My manuscript might have been sent off weeks ago and in years to come, he and I would remember how he helped me through my toughest project. How our team won. When he's with me, my writing runs riot. When he's gone, it all stands still.

Sitting in the early morning darkness of my dining room, I think back to Liam's suggestion of setting myself up for success. If I wanted to do that, Ryan would have to be here. It's impossible, of course, but there might be another way.

Maybe he *can* help me one more time and we can finish this book together. I know what I'm about to do is nuts, but normalcy hasn't been hitting any home runs for me lately.

Screw it.

I get up from my chair and tiptoe back down the hallway to my bedroom. Liam is passed out in a deep, drunken sleep as he sprawls out on my bed like a starfish, and I quietly pull the door shut.

Slipping back down the hall, I stop midway and go into the bathroom, looking at myself in the medicine chest mirror. I'm tired and solemn and fully committing to my decided course of action. I take a step over and reach into the shower, turning it on as high as it can go. I pull the curtain closed but leave the door open. Returning to the dining room, I stand in front of the window air-conditioning unit. I look at it for some time until I reach forward and turn it on to the coldest setting, full blast. The icy air pours out and cuts into the skin on my arms. I let the chill soak through me until it hits my bones, and I sit back down in my chair with my laptop on the table.

A writer's imagination is a powerful thing. We feel what our characters feel. We hear people talking in our heads. We allow ourselves to be carried off and whisked back again from strange and beautiful places. It's surrender and it's something not quite sane and I need to let it happen to me now.

I need to picture a new reality—a reality where Ryan is here. I take a deep breath and clear my mind.

The shower water is still running. Splashing and misting, I can almost feel the steam. Ryan originally planned on showering tomorrow morning but after we went sightseeing, drank too much at dinner and walked farther than we expected, he decided not to wait.

He loves Italy as much as I do. The plane ride was…trying, but we got through it. He took something for his motion sickness, we watched *Rudy* twice on my iPad and he squeezed the life out of my hand for the full nine hours. Still, we made it.

I can't believe he was able to take more than a month's leave from work. He wasn't kidding when he said he never took days off and I'm so thankful that he didn't. He has one week left before his flight home and tomorrow, we leave for Sorrento, a beautiful town along the Mediterranean.

I check my email confirmation from the hotel we're going to stay at, and check-in is at one o'clock. Another SOS email from Sam catches my eye and I wince a little bit. She is going to kill me. I've been so busy gallivanting around Rome with Ryan that I still haven't written the last chapter of my novel. I need to wrap that up now before I become her worst client and she hates me forever.

Final chapter. Time to give Charlotte and Robert the ending they deserve. I take a confident breath and try to look inwards, drawing on all my feelings from this last amazing month as I move my hands to the laptop keys.

I remember Ryan waking me up this morning—his hand in mine, his mouth leaving soft kisses on my neck. I remember the cooking class we took yesterday—half the class had their eyes on him, but he only had his eyes on me. I remember him standing behind me the first time we saw the Trevi Fountain—my back pressed to his warm chest as he wrapped his arms around my front, whispering into my ear that life could never be better than this.

I take all the love I feel for him and send it from my heart, through my arms and out the tips of my fingers. I start to type, knowing what Ryan said was true. Life really couldn't be better than this.

21

Last month, I finished my novel by the skin of my teeth. My minor psychotic break/serious imagination exercise where I pretended Ryan came to Italy proved successful, and even though I cried for an hour straight once I was done, my last chapter turned out just how I needed it to.

I've definitely turned a corner of some kind. After a year of nerves and guilt, I forgot what it felt like not to have a deadline follow me around like a menacing shadow. Suffice to say, I'm happier now, but I still don't feel like my old self. I'm starting to question if I ever will.

Liam and I spend even more time together after our first and last date. We're keeping things strictly platonic, both agreeing that as convenient as it would have been for our friendship chemistry to translate to romantic chemistry, it just isn't there. I'm thinking my mid-makeout cryfest took care of that on Liam's end and for me, our dreamy balcony kiss felt like little more than a prolonged face high-five. Tragic but true.

At least we made personal progress. Liam isn't as uptight as he used to be and I'm attempting to let go of some pent-up feelings. He talks more about his future and I reveal more about my past. We're both just more relaxed in general.

It's coming on the end of month two of my trip and I finally start telephoning everyone back home instead of emailing. I call my mom first and she's thrilled to hear from me. Things have noticeably shifted between us since our open conversation at my apartment. She's not on the offensive. I'm not on guard. We're talking and enjoying each other in a way that feels brand-new, yet so familiar, and I hope it stays this way forever.

Cristina is next and she can barely contain her excitement when I call. She gives me even more details about her honeymoon in Turks and Caicos and explains how she's taking home ovulation tests since she's trying to get pregnant, like, yesterday. I didn't know so many elements came into play when making a baby, but apparently you only have a twelve-to-forty-eight-hour window to make it happen, and hoisting your hips into the air like a fertility acrobat after doing the deed really helps your odds. I'll have to ask Jen if she partook in these Cirque Du Soleil conception techniques.

Now it's time for Maggie. I can't wait to hear her voice and tell her everything that's been going on. Excited energy ripples through me as I press the call button and wait for her to pick up.

"Hello?"

"Hey, Maggie. It's me!" Silence follows and I wonder if we got disconnected. "Maggie?"

"Oh, hey," she says. "What's up?"

Her words would be totally normal in other circumstances but right now, they feel jarring. She doesn't sound happy to hear from me at all.

"Are you okay?" I ask.

"I'm fine."

"You don't sound…like yourself."

"Really? How do I sound?"

My heart starts to race and I have the sudden intense urge to duck back inside my emotional bomb shelter. "You seem different, I guess—are you mad at me?"

"Why would I be mad at you?" she asks in a clipped tone.

My hand gets clammy and I wipe it along the side of my pants. "I don't know. Do you want to tell me?"

"Sure. I actually would have loved to have told you a while ago, but this is the first time you're calling me in two months."

"I haven't called anyone," I offer weakly. "And you and I have been emailing."

"I realize that, but we went from speaking almost every day for years to you not calling me for months. And yeah, you emailed me, but your emails might as well have been automated responses. You sound like a bot in every single one."

"I don't know what you want me to say, Maggie. I'm sorry, I didn't know you felt this way."

"You didn't know I felt this way because you didn't talk to me! I have a life, too, Kara. It's not just you. I have things going on and I have problems and sometimes I really needed to talk to my best friend. It would have been awesome if she didn't bail on me for months at a time."

"I'm sorry," I say again, already knowing it's not enough.

"My grandma fell down the stairs last month. She broke her hip and her wrist and she's holed up in the hospital until further notice. They say the recovery time will be extensive, if she even recovers at all."

Maggie's email—the one where she asked me to call and I didn't. My stomach is queasy and the back of my neck is burning. I give my ever-present guilt full permission to hollow out an even deeper hole in my chest.

"I'm so sorry. Are you okay?"

She doesn't say anything. The line goes quiet until I hear her suck in a breath, and I can tell she's getting emotional but is trying to hide it.

My gut clenches. I might cry. I want to say a million things but nothing comes out.

"Is this all because of Ryan?" she asks after a moment.

I squeeze the phone closer to my ear. "I don't want to talk about him."

"It is, then. Do you realize that you emotionally checked out—that you, a grown woman, didn't verbally communicate with your friends or family for months because of a bad breakup? Do you hear how crazy that sounds?"

I want to answer that I do hear how crazy it sounds. That the truth of how I dealt with things blared around me so often and so loud that all I could do was run from it. But it wasn't just about Ryan. Yes, he played a big part in it, but I was also running from the stress of my deadline, from myself, from all my doubts and from life as a whole. I didn't want to talk about my problems and so I chose not to talk at all. I hid and I pulled away from everyone—especially her. Probably because deep down I knew she'd be the first one to call me out on my cowardice.

"Look," Maggie goes on, "Ryan had a fiancée and he didn't tell you. That was such a crappy thing for him to do, but should it really be unforgivable when he was clearly in love with you?"

My eyes scrunch a bit at her almost-justification of Ryan's actions.

"Obviously, it's unforgivable. He was lying to me the whole time. He was cheating."

"He wasn't cheating on *you*. He was yours first and he was only engaged to that girl for fourteen days. It's not like he was married with kids. He sounded heartbroken over hurting you, plus, he explained why he did what he did."

"Explaining it doesn't make it okay."

"It doesn't have to be okay, but it also doesn't mean you should use him as an excuse to shut yourself off from the world—from the people who love you. All we've ever done is be there for you and it's not fair. You know it's not fair."

My eyes fill up with tears. I hate that I let what happened with Ryan affect the other relationships in my life. I want to get over it. I want to move on but I can't. I want to forget but I won't.

"I'm sorry," I say brokenly. "I know I'm a terrible person, but I still can't believe what happened. I was the other woman, Maggie. That's all I am and that's all I was to him and I got exactly what I deserved."

"Kara." Maggie's voice is troubled but firm. "Don't talk about yourself like that. That's not what you are and there's no way that's what you were to him."

"That's what I feel like." I try to gather my thoughts, but everything gets lost in a teary haze. "I knew what I was doing was wrong. I knew he was never supposed to be mine, but I didn't care because I loved him so much. I still love him *so* much. I keep disappointing my dad over and over again and this is my punishment."

"What are you talking about?"

"I'm the reason my dad is dead! I fought with him and maybe he wasn't looking and if it wasn't for me, he might still be here. And even after all that, I went back to Ryan again and I want to go back to him now. I betrayed my dad twice over and I'm still betraying him to this day."

"Kara, stop!" Maggie's voice holds so much weight that

it seems like the only real thing in the world. I cling to the phone like a lifeline.

"You need to listen to me," she says. "What happened to your dad was not your fault. He wasn't chasing you and Ryan into the road and he wasn't thinking of you and walking into traffic. He was crossing the street and an old man hit him. It was a horrible accident and nothing else."

I keep the phone pinned to my ear and cover my eyes with my free hand. Tears spill down my cheeks. My face feels so hot and red that I think I might burst.

"You have to let your guilt go now. When you think about your dad, not about how he was the last time you saw him, but how he always was, do you think this is what he would want for you? Do you think he would want you emotionally mutilating yourself because in your mind, you let him down? Is that how you want to honor him?"

"No," I say, mewing like a child as I keep wiping away tears.

"You never have to forget him, you just have to release the pieces that hurt. Love is the part of him you get to keep."

I let my tears roll and roll until they start to slow, tapering off one by one. My eyes sting and my throat feels hoarse and Maggie waits with me all the while.

"Did you just do music therapy on me without the music?" I eventually ask.

I catch a little laugh from her end of the phone and it's the sweetest sound I've heard in a long time.

"You're right," I tell her. "I've been an awful friend. You've always been there for me, always, and I bailed on you. I'm so sorry and I understand if you hate me."

I wish she was here. I wish I could look her in the eyes and tell her how wretched and unworthy of her friendship I am. Needing to move, I get up from the couch and pace the room.

"I don't hate you," she says. "I'm partially to blame. I should have told you how I felt sooner instead of bottling it up and exploding."

"If you give me the chance, I swear I'll make it up to you."

"Of course I'll give you the chance. Nobody's perfect, least of all me." She waits a few seconds before going on. "I'm sorry I was harsh with you. It's okay that you're still hurting. I'm sure Ryan is, too."

I try to think of him for a second but I'm too exhausted. "I doubt it," I say. "For all we know, he could be married by now."

"I think we both know that he's not." I lean my forehead on the living room wall as Maggie pauses. "Maybe you should call him."

No. No. No. No. No.

"I can't. Too much has happened."

"You can't call him because you don't want to, or you can't call him because you're afraid?"

I think about lying but I know there's no point.

"Both," I say, closing my eyes. "Please don't ask me any more questions about him. I'd much rather hear about you. Which hospital is Grandma Noreen staying in? I'll tell Jen to have Denny reach out to make sure she's getting the best treatment. Or maybe he knows someone who works in the hospital. Also, what's the address? I'm going to send Noreen a care package. And you. And your sister. Every day. Forever."

"All right, relax, gift lady. Grandma is in a great hospital and is being treated like the queen that she is. I think her doctor has a crush on Hannah. She won't admit it yet, but I know she likes him, too."

"Well, that's good, right?"

"Sure. He's nice and young. And if it helps get Grandma extra attention, I'm all about pimping Hannah out. Teamwork makes the dream work."

"Yes, it does," I say through a small smile. "Thank you for forgiving me."

"You'd do the same for me in a second. I love you, you emotional hermit."

"I love you more."

"Can I ask you one more thing, though? And then we won't talk about that topic any more today."

"What is it?" I ask hesitantly.

"If the roles were reversed, if you were with someone you weren't in love with and then you got the chance to be with Ryan again...would you have been able to hold back? Or would you have slipped?"

I take a deep breath. "I don't know," I answer.

But I do. In my heart, I know.

A few weeks later, I'm heading back towards my apartment after a solo guided tour of St. Angelo's castle. Liam didn't feel well this morning so I'll make sure to check on him later. For now, all I can think about is having a shower, a snack and one mother of a nap. I'm halfway through the courtyard when I hear someone calling my name.

I turn around to spot Paolo, my favorite stocky, middle-aged Italian who is the manager of the apartment complex. He's bounding out of his little office/hut near the front gates of the property, carrying a small package in his hands.

"*Buongiorno,* Signorina Sullivan. I have a delivery for you." He hands me an unaddressed package wrapped in simple brown paper.

"For me? Thank you. I mean, *grazie.*"

Paolo smiles at my effort and heads back to his office. I think about waiting to open the package until I get inside but I was never one to do well with suspense. I pull at the string holding the wrapping together and the paper easily falls away.

My knees nearly buckle.

I am now holding a black leather journal with a photo of me, Ryan and Duke glued to the cover.

The book is smooth and heavy in my hands and I don't know how or why it's here. What I do know is that the strongest force on earth couldn't wrench it out of my hands right now. Whipping the book open, I find a piece of stationery folded inside. I tuck the journal under my arm as I open the note with trembling hands.

Kara,

When I left New York after Jason and Cristina's wedding, I knew that I'd single-handedly destroyed what would have been the best thing in my life.

Nothing is the same anymore. Days drag and nights are even slower and the memories of us hurt as much as they heal. All I think about is being with you again. I imagine going to the party that first night and doing everything different. I'd tell you the truth. I'd do what I needed to do back home, come back to New York and prove to you that I never stopped loving you.

I replay how I handled things over and over in my head and I want to go back and shake myself. I mean aggressively shake myself. I hurt two women who did nothing wrong and who deserved so much more than what I gave them. For that, I will always be ashamed and deeply sorry.

You were right in what you said to me at the wedding. I was using how much I wanted and loved you as an excuse to justify my actions, but I don't have anyone or anything to blame but myself. I was scared and selfish. I betrayed your trust by not telling you the truth and I made what we had look like a lie when it's the only real thing I've ever known. I stole a week and lost forever.

But the thing is, I still can't give up. I can't stop hoping that we'll find our way to each other one more time. You have lived in the back of my mind for ten years. You never left. You've always been there with your books and your humor, and even when half of me would try to move on, the other half would hold on to you even tighter. You're the best part of who I am and who I want to be, and when you feel something like that, it can't be wrong.

What happens next is entirely up to you and this is where the journal comes in. Since a novel is where our story started in college, I couldn't help but see it as a fitting symbol of our relationship. But as you can tell by the blank pages, our book isn't finished. I'd like for you to write out our story and when you're done, no matter the ending, please send it back to me. I put my address in the inner flap. If you don't want to or if you throw this book away, I'll understand. But if I ever do get to see this journal again, I hope, more than anything, that I end up reading a romance.

Loving and missing you,

—Ryan

P.S. If you're wondering who's watching Duke while I'm on this trip, you should know it's my dad. We're not back to how we used to be, maybe we never will be, but I'm trying. I won't break my promise to you. If you take one thing away from this letter and forget the rest, let it be that.

Great, so someone sprinkled water all over my letter. No wait, that's me crying. Again.

I'm sad and relieved and so homesick for Ryan that I could die, and how dare he send this to me! But Ryan also said he was on a trip. *Wait. Is he here?*

I bolt for Paolo's hut a second later. I've never run track a day in my life but now I'm thinking that maybe I should have.

"Paolo!" I yell, my hair falling in disarray in front of my face as I fling myself onto the reception desk.

He's waiting for me and smiling, resting his chin on his fist as he leans forward on the counter.

"He told me you come here yelling. He knows you very well."

"He who?" I ask, out of breath. "Was this hand-delivered?"

"*Si.* Signore Ryan came this morning. He ask for you, he wait a few hours, he give me the package, then he go."

"He go?" I all but shriek. "You mean he's gone gone? Is he coming back?"

I've never seen Paolo look so smug as he does in this moment, reaching into the left breast pocket of his gray blazer. He pulls out an envelope and hands it to me. "He leave this for you."

I snatch the letter ungracefully out of his hand. *"Grazie."*

"Prego."

I step away and tear the envelope open, pulling out the folded sheet of paper and I once again see Ryan's handwriting.

Kara,

To answer the questions you're probably asking: Yes, I flew over twelve hours to deliver this letter and the journal. Yes, I am now flying over fourteen hours to get back home. No, I did not take anything on the plane to make it easier for me. Yes, I got sick. A lot. And yes, I would fly this trip a million times over if it meant we might be together again. I love you.

—Ryan

My hand with the note falls to my side and I don't know where to turn or look or think. I just stand there, staring blankly ahead as my mind spins and spins like some sketchy carnival ride. I stand there for all of ten seconds until I'm once again charging at Paolo's hut.

"When did he leave? Paolo, when did he leave?" My tone is demanding and almost volatile, and Paolo's self-satisfied demeanor shifts on the spot.

"Non no so," he quickly answers. He fumbles around with his cell phone on his desk until he gets a handle on it and checks the time. "Five minutes? Maybe ten?"

I don't wait around to question him further. I turn on my heels and run out of the courtyard, heading in the direction of the busy intersection two blocks away. I run and run and I don't loosen my death grip on the journal the whole way. Reaching the intersection, my lungs are on fire and my heart is pounding. I scan the area around me, looking up and down the street until I turn to the taxi stop across the road, on the other side of the intersection. And then my heart feels like it stops altogether.

Ryan.

I see him. He's here. A quiet, elated laugh jumps from my throat and I bring my free hand up to cover my mouth. He's totally different and exactly the same. Jeans and a T-shirt and his Hurricanes baseball cap, but I'm no longer gazing at him through rose-colored glasses. Maybe that's the difference. Of course, I see the cowboy I perpetually want to jump, the guy who understands me—who understood me from the beginning and always wanted more—but I also see the man who offered me the world and then brought it crashing down all around me.

I take a step back, letting myself fade into the bustling crowd while keeping Ryan in my line of sight. He looks pale. Not even the Italian sun could cure his motion sickness completely. He's next in line at the taxi stop and he readjusts the strap of his travel bag over his shoulder as another cab pulls up to the curb.

He's going to leave.

Panic races through me and my feet pull me forward. All I have to do is call out his name. The intersection traffic is loud, but I could be louder. Call out his name and he stays—do nothing and he goes. I try to speak but my throat seems to close. I don't know what's right anymore.

He opens the back seat door and it's like I'm watching a movie right before the cliffhanger resolution. I should be a lead character but I feel like a passive viewer. Ryan looks up over the car to the corner that's parallel to where I'm standing. Is he looking for me? Hoping I'll come tearing out through the crowd to ask him to stay?

I remain motionless, drowning in my own indecision. Maybe he'll see me and I won't have to choose anything. His eyes will land on mine and all our issues will melt away—won't be anything more than a bad dream.

I wait and I look and I move forward a small step more, thinking that if it's meant to be, he'll see me. If it's meant to be, he'll find me.

But he doesn't.

With a final pull at his travel bag, he ducks into the car and closes the door. The taxi pulls away and I still don't move. My stomach drops as I wonder if I just made a life-altering mistake. Maybe. Or maybe I just saved myself from another brutal heartbreak in the making. Still not knowing which side the coin will fall on, I disappear deeper and deeper into the crowds, silently hoping that I'll disappear completely.

22

After I don't appear in the courtyard for our usual break-fast the next morning, I'm not surprised when I hear knocking at my apartment door bright and early. Still in my pajamas, I cross the faux white marble floor of the entryway and pull the door open, finding Liam outside. He's holding our pizzas and looking concerned.

"I don't know what happened, but I do know that only something horrific would keep you from breakfast."

"Come in," I say, pushing the door back and stepping aside.

"I have to warn you, the pizzas are now cold and slightly soggy. I don't think that will stand in your way, but I feel mor-ally obligated to tell you."

"I'm not deterred in the least."

"I expected as much."

Ten minutes later, Liam and I are settled in the living room. The space is minimally decorated with just a couch, a coffee table and a chair in front of the TV that I never watch. It's on par with what you would expect from a pre-furnished apartment. Occupying the not-quite-as-comfortable Italian version of my reading chair, I've just finished explaining why I'm moping around inside instead of sitting out in the sunshine. Liam sits at one end of the brown upholstered couch and is holding the journal, minus the letter, which I just told him about.

"Well," he says, leaning forward to place the journal on the rounded coffee table in front of him, "and who says people don't make grand gestures anymore?"

"I wish Ryan didn't make this one," I mutter, pulling my knees close to my chest.

"Liar."

Liam continues to regard me in that problem-solver way of his. "So just to clarify," he goes on, "because he didn't make magical eye contact with you in a highly dense and somewhat chaotic intersection during rush hour...you believe that was the universe saying you shouldn't be together?"

"It was an emotionally trying moment and I needed a tiebreaker."

"Wow. You're worse off than I originally thought."

"Let's not throw stones, okay?" I rub my tired eyes with the tips of my fingers and tuck my hair behind my ears. "I don't know. Part of me wishes he never came. Then things could have gone on as they were."

"Right. And you could have felt vindicated as you mucked off into your lonely existence. Trust me, I speak from personal experience when I tell you it's not as appealing as you think."

"I just want things to be over, one way or another."

"They can be," Liam says simply. "Forgive him."

I pause and take a breath. "I don't know if I can."

"That's fine, too. Toss the journal and carry on without him."

The thoughts of letting Ryan go or forgiving him seem

equally impossible. My face must reflect my emotions, prompting Liam to go on, "Listen, Ryan is either a liar who showed his true colors, or he's a good person who made a mistake. Whether you chose to work through this with him or not, you're taking a risk. You just have to decide if the risk is worth the reward."

"Ugh," I groan, tilting my head up towards the ceiling before looking at him again. "What would you do?"

"I'm not going to answer that. I've already messed up my own life beyond repair. I don't need the fate of your future resting on my conscience as well."

I give him an unappreciative but understanding nod. "Fair enough."

"I will, however, offer you a small bit of advice if you swear you won't hold it against me."

"I swear."

Liam leans forward and clasps his hands together. "When making an important decision, I find it's useful to think about the life that you want to have. Sit and visualize it, and ask yourself if the choice you're about to make will help you or hinder you in getting to where you ultimately want to go." I think he's about to go on when he sits back again. "That's it. If you require any further assistance, I'll have to charge a modest fee."

I chuckle and stretch out my legs, placing my slippered feet down onto the floor. "I can't really afford unnecessary spending at this point, but I appreciate your words of wisdom."

Liam pushes his palms against his knees and stands. "Well then, seeing as this will most likely be a day of reflection for you, I suppose I'll get going. Will we be back to business as usual tomorrow?"

"That we shall."

"Excellent. Until tomorrow." With that, he walks out of the room and disappears into the hallway. A few seconds pass and I still don't hear the apartment door open or close. I get up to investigate when Liam reappears back in the living room doorway.

"Sorry, before I go, can I make one small request?"

"Sure."

"If you do fill in the journal and you include your time in Italy, can the literary version of me be a bit more muscular and have a tan? I've always wondered what it would be like to have a tan."

I smile as Liam turns and leaves without another word. The apartment door closes shortly thereafter and without meaning to, I move to the coffee table and pick up the journal. I also bring my hand to the outside of my pajama pants pocket, where Ryan's letters are safely tucked away.

A few minutes later, I'm sitting at my dining room table with the journal open to the first blank page. I have no idea what to write or if I'm going to write at all. Maybe I'll fill it cover to cover and keep it for myself. Maybe I'll throw it away. Maybe I'll hold it tight to my chest as I take a direct flight to North Carolina.

No matter the content, I have to write something. I can't keep going on the way I am. Here in Italy, I'm in this beautiful limbo. I'm living but I'm not. I'm growing but I'm stunted.

I close the book and look at the picture on the cover. Ryan took it the morning of the rehearsal dinner when we had just finished up with breakfast. We're in our pajamas, laughing in pain and nearly falling off the couch as Duke scrambles between us, his paws digging into our stomachs.

I run my fingertip along the surface of the photo.

This isn't what the cover of a romance novel should look like. It isn't passionate or dramatic. It doesn't show off a scantily dressed hero and heroine, embracing each other with a lush backdrop. It's less. It's more.

I close my eyes and think back to Liam's advice. I do what he says. I try to clear my head and imagine the life that I want. It's not easy, my mind is a jumbled place with endless chatter, but I somehow manage to find quiet. Calm. I picture my life five years from now, envisioning the highest and truest version of myself, living a life built on contentment from the ground up.

I see myself and who's there with me and my eyes snap open as I look down. As unprepared as I am to admit it, the life that I want is a mirror image of the photo staring up at me. Terrified acceptance fills my consciousness and for some reason, in that moment, memories of my dad flood my mind and heart.

I wonder what he would say if he was here, what he would want me to do. I think of him smiling. I think of him hugging me. I hear his voice saying he loves me and that he's not far away. He tells me he wants me to be happy. That's all he's ever wanted.

I start crying in earnest but there's joy there, too. I cover my face with my hands, wanting to see my dad so much that I can hardly breathe. I sit back a while later and wipe my face with the sleeve of my T-shirt. I know that I grieved for him in all the wrong ways. I know that all he feels for me is love. And even though he can't be here physically, now I know where I can find him.

I take a deep breath and let my newfound freedom rush through me, returning the courage that I've held back from myself for far too long. I stop thinking. I stop worrying and questioning and without second-guessing, I open the journal, pick up my pen and start to write.

I can't believe I'm leaving Italy. Six months have flown by and I'm now decrepitly dragging my two massive suitcases out of the cobblestone courtyard.

Liam notices my difficulty and steps forward to help, grabbing them by their handles and loading them into the waiting cab. My heart feels heavier than my overstuffed luggage as I watch him, knowing just how much he's changed things for me.

"Is that all of it?" he asks after closing the trunk and walking back over.

"I think so."

"You have the journal?"

"Yes." I reach into my tote bag and feel around for the large sealed envelope holding the journal. "It's addressed and ready. Once I get home and talk to him, I'll take it to the post office and off it will go."

"I'm glad to hear it. I can already picture you riding off into the sunset with Ryan as I gallop into my own wasteland of a love life, most likely on a sickly donkey."

I shake my head and step forward to pull Liam in for a hug. I feign a crying sound and tighten my arms when he tries to pull away.

"You know, for someone with as much bark as you, I expected a tougher skin."

"I'm all talk," I say. "You should know that about me by now."

"I do," he assures me, "and I also know that you'll be fine once you're at the airport and on your way."

I lean back to look up at him. "Your flight home isn't for another week. Are you going to have pizza in the mornings without me?"

"Not a slice," he answers solemnly. "It wouldn't be the same."

"How will you survive?"

"I'll have to rely on croissants and your bittersweet memory to sustain me."

I begrudgingly let him go and step back.

"I wouldn't change anything, you know. If I stayed in New York, I wouldn't have come here, and I wouldn't have met you. I would do everything exactly the same."

"Really? You'd do *everything* the same?"

I give him a knowing look, fully aware that he still thinks that I should have stopped Ryan when he came to Rome. I can see why. Watching Ryan drive away was a physically painful experience for me, but I had to take these last few months to heal and to really understand what I need and want. Stopping him four months ago would have been great in the moment, but who's to say where we'd be today if we rushed into things again. I almost called or texted millions of times but stopped myself. I didn't want to ask him to wait for me. I didn't want him to put his life on hold. If I get home and he still feels the same way, we can start over. Not as a continuation but as something entirely new and based on who we are now.

"No comment," I eventually answer.

A small grin pulls across Liam's cheek. "I wouldn't change anything either. You're a very peculiar girl, but you've made a real difference."

"A real difference in what?"

"Everything," he says simply.

If that response doesn't warrant another bear hug, I don't know what does. I throw myself into his arms for a final time before getting into the cab. Once inside, I fasten my seat belt and roll my window all the way down.

"I'll miss you," I say as Liam steps closer. "And I've changed my mind. You can have pizza without me tomorrow if you want to."

He flashes me a roguish smile, holding his hands behind his back and allowing me a good long look at him standing as he did the first time we met.

"I always intended to," he says.

My jaw drops. "You jerk!"

Liam laughs as my taxi pulls away from the curb at a typical, crazy Italian speed. "Soft spoken until the very end," he calls out. "I'll miss you!"

23

I feel an absolute rush as I get out of the yellow cab in front of 5 Tudor City. It's a cold October day but there's so much excitement bursting through me that I don't feel chilled in the least. The sounds of sirens, the people, the traffic, heck, even the smells…everything about New York sends my heart into a flutter.

I'm soon pulling my luggage off the elevator and power walking over to my door, feeling full-on butterflies as I thrust my key into the lock. I wrench the door open and step inside, breathing deep and becoming overwhelmed with a sense of everything clicking into place. I'm home. The apartment is stuffy, the air is stale and a small layer of dust is visible on the furniture, but to my eyes, this place hasn't looked so beautiful since the day I bought it and realized it was mine.

I immediately grip Calliope's handlebars and close my eyes with a squeal of delight. I'm itching to take her out for a ride, but I know that will have to wait until tomorrow. I give her bell a quick ding and then run across the living room to the windows. I fling them open, savoring the cold gust of wind that flows in. I do a quick spin, soaking in the feeling of total comfort.

I charge into the bedroom next and stop dead in my tracks. I smile down at my bed before I leap forward and fling myself onto the mattress. God, I missed my bed! Italy was great but their mattresses are crap.

I reluctantly roll over and bounce onto the floor to open the bedroom windows. With the breeze on my face, I lean out to drink in my Midtown East view. I'm darn close to singing when my cell phone rings with an alert from the front desk. I tuck my head back inside and answer it.

The doorman tells me Cristina is here and I ask him to let her up. I hold the door open before she even arrives, hopping in excitement as I hear the elevator getting closer and closer.

She comes into view moments later and barrels into me, screeching and throwing her arms around my shoulders. We hug and yell for a considerable amount of time before letting go. My face hurts from cheesing so hard as she quickly walks into the apartment and I close the door.

"Kara, you look beautiful! Completely Italian!"

"Grazie," I say, jokingly tossing my new cream-colored pashmina over my shoulder. "You look great too! I've missed you so much!"

"I've missed *you*! How do you feel? Are you happy to be home?"

"It's a little strange," I admit. "Don't get me wrong, I'm overjoyed to be back, but it's still a little weird."

"I'm seriously so, so happy you're back. You can never leave me again! Promise you won't."

"I wasn't gone that long," I say, pulling her over to sit down on the couch.

"What are you talking about? Six months is a lifetime. I

latched onto Jason like a barnacle because I missed talking to you so much. He thinks I'm a psycho but that's what he signed up for."

"Poor guy."

"Don't worry about him! I know you were holding out on me with the details of your trip so I want to hear it all. What was it like? Did you meet anyone? Is it wrong that I secretly hoped you wouldn't make any new friends?"

"Um, no. Anytime you ever mention another friend I instantly die a little inside."

"That's oddly comforting," she says.

"I'm glad. But still, I'm sure you were fine without me. You're close with way more people than I am. I could easily be replaced."

Cristina nearly gasps. "What? Kara, you're my human diary. I have been going nuts these past six months without you to confide in. With the honeymoon and all the trying for a baby stuff...you're one of the only people I can talk to without a filter."

She means every word. She really does tell me everything. It makes me feel selfish and petty for keeping her at an emotional distance for the past few months, but I'm about to repay her in full.

"I missed talking to you, too. I actually put a character like you in the book I'm working on now."

"I can't believe that after a year of misery trying to finish your last novel you suddenly pounded out another. I thought you went to Italy to relax."

"Trust me, this latest manuscript is very much a first draft. Now I get to edit, edit and edit it again as I try not to slowly slip into insanity before I edit it twelve more times."

"Well, I'm sure it's wonderful. Your books are always amazing."

I smile at her encouragement and take a breath. "I'm glad

you think so because if you're up for it, I'd love for you to read this one and tell me what you think."

"Really?" she asks, seeming shocked. "You've never had me do that before."

"I know, but this one is different and your input means a lot to me. Specifically, you can tell me if you like the direction I went in for the ending."

Cristina's surprised expression morphs into a radiant smile. "Of course! This is so exciting! Should I keep notes as I go?"

"Notes are always appreciated but on top of your feedback, I also have one rule. Once you start reading it, you can't talk to me until you finish it all the way through."

"What? Why? What if I have a question about something?"

I shake my head. "That's the rule. Do you accept?"

She thinks about it for a few moments until she says, "Fine."

"Are you sure?"

"Yes, I'm sure. But just know that I'm going to fly through this thing in less than a day. I can finally call and see you again and I plan on being your attached-at-the-hip friend/minion for the foreseeable future."

I smile at the notion. "Same here."

I go on to tell her a bunch of my stories from Italy and she fills me in on what's been going on with her, but an hour later, I need to get ready for dinner at my mom's. As we get up from the couch, I head over to my carry-on bag beside the door and dig out my typed manuscript. I hand over the three hundred and fourteen pages with a nervous smile.

"Happy reading."

When I walk into the living room of my childhood home, I'm surprised when I don't find my mom or Jen waiting by the door. I use the unexpected moment of privacy to step farther inside and sit down in my dad's recliner for the first time in a long time, running my hands across the cool leather of the armrests.

"Italy was amazing, Dad," I say quietly. "But I'm sure you know that. I felt you there with me all the time."

In the past, my dad's absence in this world felt like a numbing ache I could never get accustomed to. An amputated limb I kept trying to use. But something changed after the grief-ridden moment of clarity I had at my dining room table in Italy. From then on, my dad was so obviously present that the feeling of missing him switched from emptiness to a calm sense of warmth—something to reach for instead of something to fear.

"Kara! Is that you?" I hear my mom call.

I push my back into the recliner, knowing this is as close as I can get to hugging my dad. I give myself one more second before I stand up and make my way into the kitchen. I'm about to walk in when Mom comes bursting out with Jen following close behind.

"Hey!" she yells, pulling me in for a big squeeze. "You're finally here!"

"I'm here!"

She lets me go with a happy sigh. "Six months really is too long to be away, Kara. If you go on a trip like that again, I think a couple of weeks is good enough."

"I couldn't agree more," I say with a smile. Jen makes her way to me next and my jaw almost hits the floor. She is now seven months pregnant and has a full-fledged, in your face baby belly.

"Jen! You're humongous!" My sister's intense glare tells me that perhaps I should have chosen a more delicate phrase. "But so beautiful," I amend. "Glowing. Ethereal."

"Yeah, you better say I'm freaking ethereal."

I move forward and give her a tight hug, my stomach bumping her tummy as Mom nudges us out of the doorway and into the dining room so she can begin carrying in the food. Jen takes a step back and pulls me to the side.

"Okay, now that you're in front of me, no more dancing around my questions. You need to tell me about you and Ryan right now. Commence."

"What was that?" I then ask, obnoxiously loud. "You said Denny *isn't* the father?"

Jen pinches my arm with savage strength and I yelp and jump away before she can get me again.

"Will you girls stop fighting?" My mom bustles past us, placing the salad on the table and picking a shopping bag up from the floor against the wall. "Kara, before we have dinner, I got these for you." She holds out the bag and I hesitantly take it, feeling a nervous twinge in my stomach. Old habits die hard.

"Thank you, but you really don't have to keep buying me clothes."

"Sure I do, I buy Jen clothes all the time."

"She does," my sister confirms. "I'd be rocking a muumuu right now if she didn't snag me all my cute maternity gear."

I chuckle as I slowly open the bag, and my eyes bulge as I pull out two of the nicest sweaters I have ever seen. One is heather gray and hangs open with no buttons, feeling so smooth that it has to be cashmere. The other is made with navy blue wool and looks so warm and cozy that I want to snuggle into it indefinitely.

"I love them!" I tell her, yanking off my current green cardigan and slipping into the navy blue dream. It fits perfectly over my white T-shirt and I can already tell it's going to be a premiere player in my weekly rotation. This is a day-to-night sweater that I will protect at all costs.

"You look wonderful," my mom says with a smile. "And

for some exciting news, I actually applied for a part-time job at Loft when I bought those last week. I was hired yesterday and I start my training at the beginning of next month."

"Really?" Jen asks excitedly. "Does that mean you get an employee discount?"

"It does. It will also mean that I'll have to cut back on my gym time, but maybe that's not the worst thing. And it'll be nice to have something else to focus on besides you two for a change."

Jen and I raise our brows, surprised and impressed. Hearty congratulatory hugs are given by us both and a couple minutes later, we're all sitting down at the table. I tell them the highlights of my trip, about my apartment and how I met Liam. I tell them that my publisher loves my latest historical romance and how I finished a draft of my next book. I'm convinced they're satisfied with my vivid stories until Jen decides to stir the pot—no doubt as revenge for me playing hard to get with my relationship status.

"So, Kara," she says as I take a bite of quinoa. "Tell us more about Liam. Did anything romantic go on during your trip?"

I pause, taking note of the impish look in her eyes as she tries to play the part of my innocent sister. I need to tread carefully.

"Liam is amazing and yes, technically, lots of romantic things happened during my trip."

My mom drops her fork. A massive smile spreads across her face as she recovers and picks it back up.

"Well," she says. "It sounds to me like you got everything you've always written about. You fell in love in Italy."

"Yeah, I guess I did." What my mom doesn't know is that I'm referring to a blond American and not a British redhead.

"And he has an accent?" she asks.

"A light one," I answer.

"And he's handsome?"

"Very handsome."

"And charming?"

"Almost too charming."

"He sounds incredible. When is he coming to visit? Or are you going to see him in London? I don't love the idea of you traveling again and long-distance relationships can be very tricky."

"To be honest, Mom, I'm not sure when I'm going to see Liam again."

"You mean you didn't arrange anything? How can you two be dating and not plan on seeing each other?"

Okay. She's really not going to like this part. I try to speak in my most calming tone. "Interesting story... Liam and I aren't dating."

By the look on my mom's face, you'd think I'd just run over her childhood pet. Maybe I should have been a little more forthright about the Liam situation.

"I'm sure he'll get here eventually, though," I offer. "He said he'd maybe try to visit in a few months once he figured out what he's going to do business-wise."

"But I thought... Who were you talking about falling in love with then?"

I look over at Jen with a guilty smile and shrug. She rolls her eyes in response.

"Jen?" my mom asks. "Do you know who she's talking about?"

My sister looks back at me and I wordlessly give her permission to tell Mom whatever she wants.

"I may have an idea of who she's referring to," she says cautiously.

If Jen thinks I'm sticking around for this conversation, she is sorely mistaken. I pile as many bites of roast chicken into my cowardly mouth as possible as I stand up from the table.

"All right, I would love to stay and chat but I really need to go. I have tons of unpacking and editing to do. Thanks for dinner, Mom. See you guys next week!"

I push my chair in and kiss my mom and Jen goodbye before scurrying out of the room. As I'm walking away, I pick up on Jen saying something about "that guy from college" before hearing Mom go off like a rocket.

I close the front door, thinking to myself that next week's dinner will certainly be eventful. I walk half a block when I finally feel ready to do what I have been thinking about doing for the past six months. My hand is clammy as I dig through my bag, searching for my phone and feeling an anxious pang when eventually I find it.

I'm going to do this. I'm not going to back out. I pull the phone out of my bag and find Beefcake's number in the contacts section. I close my eyes and refuse to think about the myriad of possibilities that can follow as I push down on the call button.

Hang up! Hang up! Hang up! He's probably over you. You took too long. Hang up! Hang up! Hang up!

"Hello?"

Hearing a woman's voice, I nearly drop the phone onto the concrete. I look at the screen to make sure I dialed the right number and see that I called Ryan's home phone and not his cell. My first question is, why does he even have a home phone? My second question is, why did he feel the need to program it into my contacts along with his cell number? And my third—much more pressing—question is, why is a woman answering?

"Hi," I say, pushing the phone back to my ear and trying not to sound horrified. "I'm sorry, is Ryan there?"

"He's out right now, can I take a message?" The voice is clearer this time and it must be her. Madison. He's back with her. Maybe he never ended things. Not even when he came to Rome.

"I…" I have no idea what to say. I can't let him know it's me. "I was just calling to see if he'd like to hear more about America's leading credit union."

The call almost immediately goes dead and I click the screen off, frozen in place.

Disappointment wells in my throat as I slip the phone into my peacoat pocket. I guess six months was too long to wait. Ryan and I are truly over. No more grand gestures, no happy epilogue with us on our wedding day. The truth sinks in and slithers through my body, slippery and cold and stinging everywhere it touches.

It's a long and bitter walk back to the train. I try to tell myself that it's better that I found out this way before I sent the journal. That with the truth comes freedom. Ryan has moved on and it's time I did, too.

I'd like to say that prospect takes some of the pain away, but it doesn't—so I won't.

24

Two days later, I'm cooking chicken cutlets and brown rice for dinner as I talk to Maggie on the phone.

"So have you heard anything yet?" she asks. After telling her the whole story at lunch yesterday, she knows exactly what was in the draft of the novel I gave to Cristina and is just as anxious to hear her opinion as I am.

"Not yet. To be honest, I never thought she would actually wait until she finished to call me."

"And just to double-check, the manuscript you gave her was what you wrote in the journal but typed out, right? Everything that happened with you and Ryan, college to present day?"

"Not present, present day. It ended with when I was leaving Italy."

"When you thought you guys would be getting back together?"

I give the rice another stir and hit the spoon on the side

of the small metal pot a touch harder than necessary. "Yes," I answer.

"That stinks."

"That it does."

"And you still won't even consider sending the journal back to him?"

"That's a hard no. That journal will either be donated to science upon my death or will stay locked in my desk for all eternity." Just then, my phone vibrates, alerting me to a text message. "One second." I lower the phone and look at the screen. It's from Cristina. I hit the view button and read the message twice before bringing the phone back to my ear.

"Who was it from?" Maggie asks.

"Cristina. It said, 'I sent you a present. You can return it if you don't like it, but I think it will fit you great.'"

"That sounds nice. Is she there? Did she drop something off?"

"I don't know." I turn off the stove and walk over to my door to look through the peephole. "She isn't outside." I then open the door to check if she left something in the hall. "Nothing's here."

I'm about to turn back into the apartment when I hear a strange noise coming from the stairwell beside the elevator. It sounds like a disgruntled combination of stomping, running and grunts.

"What are you doing?" Maggie asks. I don't answer as I listen to the sound more closely. It gets louder and louder, seeming to reach some kind of a crescendo. I move the phone a few inches away from my ear and grip the doorknob as I slowly back into the apartment.

"What the…"

"Kara? Are you okay?" Maggie is trying to get my attention but her voice seems so far away.

I remain glued in place as Duke erupts from the stairwell, throwing himself down into the hallway not ten feet away from me. Ryan appears next and time stands still. He and I look at each other for a long time.

I snap out of my stupor when I hear Maggie's screeching voice. "Kara! What's going on? Should I call the cops?"

I move the phone back to my ear. "Ryan is here."

She pauses. "Wow. Yeah, okay, call me later!" She hangs up before I can respond. Still in the doorway, I place my phone onto the table above my bike as Ryan walks forward at a leisurely pace.

"Welcome back, Sullivan."

Countless responses rush through my mind. And somehow, from all the things I can possibly say, I clear my throat and ask, "Why didn't you use the elevator?"

He continues moving towards me. I inhale and exhale an uneven breath.

"Duke and I dodged the doorman and the stairwell was closer than the elevator. I carried him most of the way, but he did the last two floors by himself."

I nod, still in shock and unable to get over it. "What are you doing here?" I eventually manage.

He reaches into the travel bag that's slung over his shoulder and pulls out the draft copy of my novel. "I got an overnight FedEx from Cristina yesterday."

Crap.

"I called you," I blurt out. "I called you when I got home and a woman answered."

"What? When?"

"Two days ago. It was your house line."

He thinks for a second until something seems to come together in his mind. "If you called the house then that was my sister who picked up. She's staying with me while her condo gets renovated."

"Oh." Yeah, that's my big comeback. "I thought it was…"

"No," Ryan says, knowing what I was thinking. "Madison and I broke up as soon as we left the wedding that night, partly at the wedding. We haven't spoken since." He pauses. "Except for one time when she called me to curse me out for a few minutes. Which was understandable."

"Completely," I agree, my hand still clutching the doorknob.

He keeps looking at me and I can see disappointment starting to spread across his face. "You thought I would have gone to Italy if I was still in a relationship?"

"I didn't know. After what happened…"

"Is that why you didn't send me the journal?"

I give a quick nod and Ryan's eyes fall to the ground. He stays that way for a few seconds until he looks at me again, vulnerable and scared—more vulnerable and scared than I've ever seen him.

"I know I said a lot in the letter I wrote with the journal. But I also know that after what I did, they were just words. What I want now, what I'm begging you to give me, is a chance to prove that I mean them." He takes the smallest step closer but I swear it shakes the floor.

"I really want to believe you."

"Then believe me," he says, almost whispering. "Forgive me."

I grip the doorknob tighter. My heart is pounding.

"I am so incredibly sorry, Kara. Sorrier than I could ever tell you. I messed up at such an intense level and I made it impossible for you to trust me. I see that now. So if you hate me—if you want nothing to do with me, I want you to know that I'll understand and I'll accept it. I hate *myself* for what I did. I know I hurt you but all I want from now on is to make you happy…for you to be happy with me."

It feels like the air has turned solid in my lungs with only the slightest gasps slipping through. My fingers fall away from the door one by one.

"I'll do whatever it takes to earn your trust back. We can just be friends. I'll move to New York on my own with Duke, and you and I can get to know each other again. I'll stick to any pace that's right for you because what's between us is worth fighting for and I'll fight to the end if that's what you want."

His gaze never falters. His right hand twitches a little and I somehow know he's stopping himself from reaching out to me.

"Is that what you want?" he asks. His eyes are honest and true. Duke shuffles around by our feet but neither of us looks anywhere else but at each other.

For a second, I see the college version of Ryan. A hoodie and jeans. A backpack and cap. He's standing across from the bookworm he thinks is so special, and even though we're not those people anymore, we can always remember that they led us here. We don't have to live up to their legacy. We can choose to build our own.

"Yes," I answer, my voice soft but entirely steady. "That's what I want."

An awestruck expression streaks Ryan's face, like he's about to laugh or maybe cry, but he settles for a hopeful smile instead. "Are you sure?" he asks.

"I'm sure. I can't promise how fast things are going to go. This is going to take time, but I want to fight for us, too. I know what we have is worth it. *You* are worth it."

Ryan swallows and his eyes tell me just how much my validation means to him. The air between us goes from thick and tense to crisp and calm. We can finally breathe, drifting through the moment like we're floating down a lazy river.

He's the first to break the spell when he holds up my manuscript.

"So, this was a quick read. I finished it in less than five hours. I only took one break and that was to take Duke for a walk. Surprisingly, I needed some air after all that." He takes a final step, now standing directly in front of me. "This feels a little more lighthearted than your other contemporaries."

"I figured I'd try my hand at rom-coms." Ryan chuckles and I can't believe that this is my new reality. My book-boyfriend is my real boyfriend. "And just so you know, this is just a first draft. I'm going to change the names and other aspects, obviously."

"I hope so. Every time you describe me in here you call me cute. The guys in your other books get virile and warrior-like and a bunch of other manly stuff." He moves in then, leaning closer and bracing his hands against the door frame around me. "And all I get is cute? Your other characters are going to laugh me off the shelf."

He's still so cocky. I want to kick him. And kiss him forever.

"This novel isn't even about you," I tell him in my haughtiest voice. "The fact that the male lead has the same name as you is a coincidence."

Ryan smiles and shakes his head. "I don't think that's true, Sullivan."

Oh, I've missed him. "It is," I say. "I would never write a book about you. I don't even like you."

"I don't think that's true either. In fact, I think you love me." He pushes off the door frame and steps back as he opens up the manuscript. I close my eyes and scrunch my face as he begins to read aloud.

"'Nothing could change how we felt—not the mistakes we made, the pain we put each other through or even our years apart.'"

"'When love is real you can feel it,'" I say instinctively, knowing most of the words in my manuscript by heart.

"We felt it when we were kids, and we feel it again now. Every second we're not together is a complete waste of time."

My eyes pop open. "Every second we're not—I didn't write that line."

"I know," Ryan says. "I did." He puts the manuscript back in his bag and takes my hand. "I've been useless without you, Sullivan. I don't even remember much of the last six months. And Duke has been impossible to live with. He's always looking at the door and I know he's hoping you'll walk in." He pauses for only a moment. "I think he's as in love with you as I am."

I spare Duke a quick but affectionate glance before I look back at Ryan. "Don't say that unless you really mean it."

Ryan grasps my hand tighter. "I do mean it. And you need to get used to hearing it because I'm going to be saying it to you a lot. I'm aiming for every day for the rest of our lives."

I have to bite the inside of my cheek to keep from smiling. "I'm going to ask you something now, and if there's going to be any chance of us moving forward, you need to be one hundred percent honest with me."

"Okay." He looks nervous and I enjoy it.

"Did you or did you not...name Duke after *The Devilish Duke*?"

A grin spreads across Ryan's face. His arms encircle my waist to pull me forward and there's a finality about it that feels completely right. "Of course I did," he says.

"I knew it." He never forgot the book that brought us together. Even after all those years.

I stretch up onto my toes to kiss him just as he leans down and scoops me up into his arms. I shriek in surprise and Duke instantly springs at our feet, his bellowing barks filling the hallway.

"What are you doing?" I ask through my laughter.

"Relax, Sullivan. I'm pulling off a trademark romance novel move."

I smile wider than I knew was possible and cover my eyes with one hand.

"Is it wrong for me to carry you over the threshold before we get married?"

"As if I'd marry you," I scoff, bringing my hand down and secretly beaming at the thought.

"Oh, you're marrying me, Sullivan. There's no way I'm letting you get away again."

I loop my arms around Ryan's neck and pull myself even closer. "Not ever?"

"Never," he says. And I believe him. I can see our future together so clearly. A wedding, a home, a family—they're all there. All we have to do is make them real.

I wonder if Ryan is thinking the same thing as he smiles back at me and steps inside the apartment. Unfortunately, Duke also storms in at the same moment, causing Ryan to pivot fast. He avoids stepping on Duke but winds up bumping my head against the wooden doorway.

Sure, it hurts. And I yell. But I'm also laughing as I touch my hand to my head.

So really, I wasn't lying when I told my mom that I fell in love in Italy. I did. And the man I love does have an accent and is handsome and charming. He just happened to be thousands of miles away at the time. Leave it to me to go all the way to Italy only to fall in love with someone who was waiting for me in North Carolina.

And as Ryan carries me deeper into the apartment, a bump forming on my head and Duke slobbering on the couch, I realize this moment is nothing like the last chapter of a romance novel. It's chaotic, a little weird, it's silly and it's ours. What I mean to say is—it's perfect.

25

Robert stepped down from his carriage and strode to the door of his London townhouse. Hollis, the eighty-year-old butler who had worked for the Weston family for the past five decades, was waiting for him when he arrived. Robert was surprised to find the ever cool and composed Hollis visibly sweating and out of breath as he stood exhausted in the entryway.

"Are you all right, Hollis?" he asked.

"Sir, there is a young gentleman and a lady waiting for you in the blue room. They've run us all very near to distraction." At that exact moment, a loud crash—the sound of breaking glass—sounded through the house. Hollis gasped and Robert feared the man would collapse on the spot. "That would be the tea, sir."

Determined to discover what was going on in his own home, Robert went directly into the blue room. He then stopped cold when he saw little George Destonbury standing above the broken tea set.

"I'm sorry, Robert. I thought I'd surprise everyone by pouring out the tea but the whole tray toppled over."

Robert's demeanor softened as he walked over to George, going down on one knee and bringing himself to his eye level. "Think nothing of it. Hollis will have all this cleaned up in no time." George instantly relaxed and Robert couldn't help but smile. "So, young man, when did you arrive in London?"

"Just this morning," George answered. "We've already ridden through the park and Charlotte promised to take me again tomorrow."

Robert felt his breathing halt at the mere mention of Charlotte. "And tell me, where is your sister at the moment?"

"She was just here but now she's waiting for you in the library."

Robert slowly stood up. "Thank you, George. Let me go find her and we'll be back straightaway. Hollis?"

The old butler hesitantly appeared in the doorway, looking quite worse for the wear.

"Have someone clean this mess up and call for fresh tea. And please keep an eye on Master George until his sister and I join him."

Robert swore he saw Hollis cross himself as he brushed past him to make his way down the hall. He reached the library in just a few determined strides and swung the door open.

At first, he saw nothing. It wasn't until he stepped behind the sofa in the center of the room that he found Charlotte lying on her stomach on the plush Italian carpet, looking completely at ease as she flipped through a book.

Charlotte looked up as Robert stood austerely before her. "You own a surprising amount of novels," she said. "I've always loved a good romance. Do you enjoy them as well?"

Robert ignored her question. "What are you doing here?"

"George wanted to see London."

"I'm aware of that, but what are you doing lounging about on a rug in my private home?"

She closed the book and moved her legs forward to sit upright. "You once said you fell in love with me when I rolled around on a library floor. I was hoping magic would strike twice."

"I don't have time for this," Robert said, turning and walking towards the door. "Tell George he may come to visit whenever he likes so long as you are not with him."

"Will you please wait? I want to apologize."

"What you want holds little importance to me anymore."

Charlotte promptly stood up. "Oh, really? Then why did you take it upon yourself to rearrange my entire life?"

Robert stopped walking. "You mean why did I bring your lunatic father to heel and free you from your ancient fiancé? I have no idea. I really shouldn't have wasted my time."

"Tell me how you managed it all." Robert didn't answer, leading Charlotte to cross the room and spin him around by the elbow. "I have the right to know."

"Fine," Robert said, pulling his arm free. "First I went to Lord Brinton. I reimbursed him the money he spent on your father's debts and threatened him within an inch of his life until he agreed to release you from your engagement. I then went to your father and swore to see him rot in debtor's prison if he didn't agree to what I wished. I paid off the full amount of what he owed and sent him to live in one of my family's estates in Ireland, where he will receive an annual allowance. I also informed him I would tear him limb from limb if he ever stepped foot in England again."

Charlotte took a strained breath as she absorbed Robert's revelations. "Just so you know, I had a plan of my own."

"I have no doubt you did." Robert tried to control his patience as he stepped around her to walk back deeper inside the library.

"I did," she insisted. "I was never going to go through with marrying Lord Brinton. I have friends in the country—distant relations of my mother. They would have kept George and me hidden. We may have even left England to live abroad."

"As I said, I assumed you did have a plan, Charlotte. Maybe I spent enough time with you to know that you would never bend to the will of any man."

"Then why did you—"

"I did what I did because I wanted to give you the world. I wanted to play some part in helping you live the life you deserved, even if you didn't want to spend that life with me."

Charlotte stood completely still for several moments until she spoke again.

"Considering you just told me you never wish to see me again, it seems like you went through a fair bit of trouble on my behalf."

"Your life is your own now. You need answer to no one. You have your freedom."

"Yes," Charlotte answered, taking a small step forward. "And now that I have my freedom, I want to use it to stay here—with you."

Robert's jaw tightened. He would not allow himself to hope. Not again. Not unless he was certain this was what Charlotte truly wanted. "Are you quite sure?" he asked, knowing full well that his heart would shatter to pieces if she left him for a second time.

"I'm sure that I love you. I'm very sure of that."

Robert remained silent at Charlotte's simple declaration. The air in the room seemed to spark with anticipation as she moved forward to leave no distance between them. Giving her ample time to move away, Robert gripped her waist as he leaned down and closer still, gently pressing his lips to hers. He had already begun to kiss her for a second time when another shattering crash echoed through the house.

Charlotte pulled back with a sigh. "I'm also sure that George and I will be the death of your butler if you still wish to marry me."

"Hollis is more resilient than you think. He will adore George in less than a week. You...maybe a few months. A year at the most."

"But you love me, don't you?"

Robert wrapped his arms fully around Charlotte then, basking in the knowledge that he never had to let go again. "More than anything," he said.

"Then why didn't you come back to Greenspeak after my father was sent away? It's been six months since I saw you last."

Robert grinned and kissed Charlotte once more, softer and more sweetly than either had ever experienced. "I just had to believe that I would see you again someday, and then all the waiting would be worth it."

Charlotte smiled up at Robert, silently promising to give him the life they had both always wished for. She would see to it that their home was forever a place filled with laughter and warmth and above all else, love.

Epilogue

Five Years Later

"It's your turn."

Agitated gurgling noises echo from the baby monitor and are growing louder by the second.

"No way," I answer. "Those two belong to you and you alone until midnight."

"I'll give you a million dollars if you go instead." Ryan's words are barely audible with his face pushed down into the pillow like it is.

I pull the covers more snugly around me and turn the other way. "You already owe me twelve million."

His hands slip around my waist, pulling me back until I'm flush against him. He breathes in deep along the side of my neck and I'm somehow able to smile through my exhausted haze.

"They like you better than me," he says.

I flip onto my back. "Yeah, right. Mia is a daddy's girl through and through."

"She smiles more for you, though."

"That's because I stare and sing and talk to her all day. She only smiles at me to throw me a bone and to keep me from fully descending into insanity."

"No, she loves you." Ryan twists away and grabs the baby monitor screen from off the nightstand. "Tim is still passed out like a champ, though. Maybe if we wish really hard, Mia will go back to sleep."

Ryan and I both close our eyes and ten seconds later, we have two ten-month-old babies crying at full blast.

I open my eyes and look over at my husband, fully defeated. "My wish didn't come true."

Ryan looks back at me with a drowsy but content smile. "Mine did." He rolls over and kisses me before dragging himself out of bed.

I rub my eyes with one hand as I pick up my phone with the other to check the time. It's only 9:46 p.m. but it feels like 4:00 in the morning. Parent sleep deprivation is so very real. I drop my phone back onto the nightstand with a groan.

Motherhood has, without a doubt, been the most earth-shatteringly wonderful thing that has ever happened to me, but it has also been the most physically and emotionally draining. When I found out I was pregnant, it was one of the happiest days of my life. When I found out that I was pregnant with twins, I almost fainted in terror.

Ryan has been beyond incredible. He was able to take four months off work for paternity leave when the babies were born and I honestly don't know what I would have done without him. When we first got home from the hospital and I was still sore from my C-section, he must have changed a hundred diapers with barely any help from me. He made sure that the fridge was stocked and my pump parts were clean, and minus the fact that he gets about three more hours of sleep a night than I do, I'd still give him a five-star dad review.

I hear his footsteps coming back down the hall and I already know what I'm about to see. I turn onto my side and smile as he enters our bedroom with both Tim and Mia in his arms.

"This," I say as I sit up, "goes against everything we read about in the baby sleep books."

"I know, but they told me they want you to tell them a story."

"Really now?" I hold out my arms to take Mia as Ryan sits down on the bed with Tim already back to sleep and nuzzling into his shoulder. With my daughter safely in my arms, I pull her bunched-up pink onesie away from her chin.

"And what story do you want to hear tonight, little lady?"

She reaches her chubby hands up towards me and I lean down so she can touch my cheeks. Yes, she's basically rubbing drool into my face but I'm grossly okay with it. I lay her down next to me on the bed as Ryan lays Tim beside her.

Now, I know I'm biased, but I do think my babies are the cutest things to have ever crawled this planet. They're both blonds but have my brown eyes. Mia is slightly chunkier than her brother but that's only because Tim is taller. I used to think they both looked just like Ryan, but I see more of me in them every day.

I lean over to give Tim a kiss and have to chuckle when I see his little cheek pulled back in a half smile. His name fits him so perfectly. My mom said Dad smiled in his sleep, too. Mia tugs on my hair a second later and I twist my head away, trying to untangle my ponytail from her crazy strong grip. I've lost more than enough hair post-babies, thank you very much.

Ryan rubs Tim's stomach and looks over at me. "How about I do the story tonight?"

"This should be interesting." I slide down the bed until I'm snuggled up next to Mia. I tickle her neck as Ryan lies down on his side next to Tim, propping himself up with one arm.

"Once upon a time, there was a strong and very handsome cowboy who met a princess when they went to college." Ryan winks at me and I roll my eyes as he goes on, "The cowboy fell in love with the princess at first sight. He was so excited to meet her that he sat right next to her and do you know what? The princess was reading a book that was very inappropriate for a princess to be reading."

"I don't think that's true," I coo to Mia. "I think the book the princess was reading was romantic and classy and the prince was probably illiterate."

"Excuse me, who's telling the story here?"

I make my eyes big for Mia and she giggles as Ryan continues, "Anyways, somehow, the cowboy got the princess to fall in love with him. But then, a terrible curse was cast upon them. The cowboy was banished and the princess forgot all about him."

"How terrible," I say. "But are you sure that's what happened? Maybe the cowboy was a bit of a narcissist at the time who deserved to be banished after neglecting the princess."

"No one knows for sure since the curse made everyone's memories fuzzy. All the cowboy and the princess could remember was that they loved each other very much."

"Oh, I see." I look down at Mia and her eyes are starting to flutter closed. The foolish hope that I may actually get a decent stretch of sleep tonight starts to bloom inside me. "And what happens next?" I ask quietly.

"The cowboy never forgot the princess. He always hoped he would find her again and then, one day, he went to a party at his friend's castle and guess what?"

"What?" I whisper. Tim is snoring and Mia's eyes are ninety percent shut. *Dear Lord, let this happen.*

"The cowboy found the princess. He pulled her into his arms and they immediately fell back in love and got married with zero issues whatsoever." I try not to laugh as Mia finally dozes off after her two-hour refusal. I hold up my hand and Ryan gives me a silent high-five above our now-sleeping children.

"That was a really good story," I tell him.

"I learned from the best."

He switches off the bedside lamp beside him as I shift onto my back, trying to get comfortable without waking the babies. "So how does it end?" I whisper into the quiet of our moonlit room.

Ryan pauses, tiredly smiling over at me and saying, "It doesn't."

I grin with a dreamy look in my eyes as he slips out of bed, gearing up to carry the twins back to their room. My gaze falls to Mia and Tim one last time before my eyes slowly close.

"I couldn't have written it better myself."

★ ★ ★ ★ ★